PENGUIN BOOKS

1562

DOCTOR AT LARGE

RICHARD GORDON

*The other books by Richard Gordon published
by Michael Joseph are*

DOCTOR IN THE HOUSE · DOCTOR AT SEA

THE CAPTAIN'S TABLE

DOCTOR IN LOVE · DOCTOR AND SON

DOCTOR IN CLOVER

*

DOCTOR IN THE HOUSE

DOCTOR AT SEA · DOCTOR AT LARGE

DOCTOR IN LOVE

*are published by Penguin Books in conjuction with
Michael Joseph on the occasion of the Twenty-Fifth
anniversary of Michael Joseph and will be the only
Richard Gordon novels to be available in paper-back
editions for four years.*

Doctor at Large

RICHARD GORDON

PENGUIN BOOKS

Penguin Books Ltd, Harmondsworth, Middlesex
AUSTRALIA: Penguin Books Pty Ltd, 762 Whitehorse Road,
Mitcham, Victoria

—

First published by Michael Joseph 1955
Published in Penguin Books 1961

Made and printed in Great Britain
by Hunt, Barnard & Co. Ltd.
Aylesbury

I

QUALIFYING as a doctor is an experience as exciting for a young man as first falling in love, and for a while produces much the same addling effects.

Before my own new diploma had uncurled from its cardboard wrapper I was prancing through the streets hoping every pretty girl in sight would be seized with a fit of fainting, and longing at each crossroads for a serious accident. I scattered prescriptions like snowflakes, and squandered my now precious opinion on relatives, friends, and even people not looking very well who happened to sit opposite me in railway trains. I frequently started conversations with, 'Speaking as a medical man – ' and an appeal for a doctor in a theatre would have brought me from my seat like a kangaroo.

After six years as a suppressed medical student this sudden importance was intoxicating, and was refreshed every morning with thick envelopes pouring through a letter-box which had previously breakfasted only on slim bills and orange packets from the football pools. The drug manufacturers pressed me with free samples, diaries the size of hymn-books, and sufficient blotters to soak up the Serpentine; shops in Wigmore Street offered to sell me clinical equipment from brass door-plates to X-ray machines; societies opposed to vivisection, smoking, meat-eating, blood sports, socialism, and birth control jostled on the breakfast table for my support; the bank that a week ago echoed my footsteps like a police court begged to advance me money, safeguard my valuables, and execute my will; even the British Medical Association officially recognized my existence by sending a free sixteen-page booklet on *Ethics and Members of the Medical Profession*, advising me henceforward to live a pure and moral life and not associate with unqualified midwives.

Unfortunately, both young doctors and young lovers soon descend from their rosy clouds on to the spiky realities of life. At the age of twenty-four I had to look for my first job, like a prospective office boy out of school. The quest was a serious one, for today even those students whose most thoughtful work in the lecture-room is carving their names on the benches are determined to become specialists. There seems no point in being anything else, when it is common knowledge in medical schools that general practitioners under the National Health Service are all seedy men signing forms in insanitary surgeries until they drop dead at forty through overwork.

Long before qualifying I had decided to become a surgeon. I had rather fancied myself cutting up the dogfish, frogs, and rabbits in the first-year zoology class, and thought the principle was probably the same further up the evolutionary tree; once I had passed my finals the only problem seemed to be finding the smoothest channel for pouring my surgical energies upon the public. My own hospital, St Swithin's, did not foster its sons beyond inviting them to the annual reunion dinner, at two guineas a head exclusive of wines; but I remembered that outside the medical school office hung a secretive notice in faded copper-plate behind speckled glass saying *Newly Qualified Men Should Consult the Secretary, Who Will Advise Them on Their Careers*. Few graduates obeyed the invitation, for the office was established in the students' eyes as a magistrate's court, which could give summary punishment for minor offences and refer promising cases to the more powerful majesty of the Dean next door. The secretary himself was a shrivelled old man with pince-nez on a thick black ribbon, who must have been the last person in London to wear elastic-sided boots, and he sat surrounded by piles of dusty official papers growing slowly from the floor like stalagmites. He suggested that I become a medical officer in the Regular Army. This advice was depressing, because I knew that he was an old-fashioned man who suggested the Army only to graduates he thought unfit to attend ordinary human beings.

Although I had won no distinctions, scholarships, or prizes at St Swithin's I boldly asked the secretary to enter me for one of the house surgeon's jobs, for these were well known among the students to be distributed in the same sporting spirit that enlivened the rest of the medical school. They were awarded by the hospital consultants sitting in committee, and represented their last chance of getting their own back on students they disliked. Youths who had sat on the front bench at lectures and asked intelligent questions to which they already knew the answers were turned down; so were earnest young men in open necks and sandals who passed round the *New Statesman* and held intense little meetings in corners of the common room on *The Conscience of the Doctor in a Capitalist Society*. Another advantage to an applicant like myself was the consultants' habit of always voting against the favourites of colleagues they disliked. A surgeon with the overwhelming personality of Sir Lancelot Spratt had condemned several dozen promising physicians to start their careers in provincial hospitals because the Professor of Medicine had once refused to let him

9

park his Rolls in the shade of the medical laboratory.

'I fear you are letting your recent qualification unbalance you somewhat,' the secretary told me. 'There are over eighty-three thousand practitioners on the British *Register*. So you have added less than one eighty-third thousandth to the medical strength of the country. If not the Army, how about the Colonial Service?'

But St Swithin's showed extravagant confidence in its educational ability, and the next afternoon I was appointed Junior Casualty House Surgeon to the Professor of Surgery.

'They won't allow you to go cutting up real live people for a bit,' said my landlady with satisfaction, while I was excitedly doing my packing. 'They used to let the learners do the poor people who couldn't afford to pay, but the Government's gone and stopped all that with the National Health Service.'

'I am perfectly entitled to go cutting up whoever I like now I'm qualified,' I told her with dignity. 'Naturally, one starts in a small way, like in everything else. Bumps, ganglions, and cysts, you know – you work your way up through varicose veins and hernias, but after your first appendix it's more or less plain sailing.'

She sniffed. 'I certainly wouldn't want you to go cutting up anyone belonging to *me*.'

'I must ask you to remember, please, that I happen to be a doctor now, not a medical student.'

'Well, there's twelve and six to pay, Doctor, for the breakages.'

The casualty job was admittedly one of the lowliest in the hospital, coming ahead in academic status only to an obscure appointment known as 'Skins and V.D'. It was performed in the casualty-room, which was really nothing more than a dressing-station in the battle between

London's drivers and pedestrians, and its clinical responsibilities could have been undertaken by any confident member of St John Ambulance Brigade. These thoughts did not occur to me as I crossed the hospital quadrangle the next day to start work. The subaltern joining his first regiment sees only his promotion to colonel, the new clerk plans his managerial reorganization, and even the freshly-ordained clergyman probably spares a thought for the suitability of his calves for gaiters. At the time, the end of my career was clearer to me than the beginning. I saw myself already rising through the profession to become a consultant surgeon at St Swithin's itself, collecting on the way honours, fellowships, and degrees like a magnet in a box of iron filings.

'I say!' someone called across the courtyard, as I strode in my new stiff white coat towards the casualty entrance. 'I say, old man! Half a jiff!'

I turned, and recognized the first obstacle in my professional path. It was Bingham, the other Junior Casualty House Surgeon. He was a pale youth with thick spectacles and bushy hair, who still looked seventeen and always had boils. As a student he was never a front-bench squatter, but he had once won the Dean's Prize in applied anatomy and thereafter always walked through the students' quarters with the *Lancet* sticking from his pocket like a flag and a couple of large books under his arm. Every lunch hour he carried these books to the library, where he ate his cheese sandwiches and removed from the reference volumes dust which he transferred during the afternoon to the instructive abdomens of patients in the wards. Every Saturday when the library closed he moved to the surgical pathology museum, where patients' organs were stored away in thick glass jars on shelves like left luggage, and carried his books round the galleries instead. Bingham seemed to absorb a good deal of knowledge from the armpit.

'I'm jolly pleased you got the other cas. job, old chap,' he said, grabbing my sleeve. 'I wondered who it'd go to. Could have been deuced tricky. Suppose they'd given it to some awful stinker. See what I mean? But we'll get along top-hole together, won't we?'

'Yes, we're pretty well bound to, I suppose.'

'I say,' he went on enthusiastically. 'This is a lark, isn't it?'

'What's a lark?'

'Being qualified and all that. I mean, now we can get on with things properly. I've got a couple of septic fingers, a lipoma, and four circs. lined up for minor ops. already.' He rubbed his hands, as if contemplating a good dinner. 'The Prof. stuck his nose in and said I was pretty quick off the mark. By the way, old chap, he asked why you weren't there.'

'But why should I have been there?' I asked in surprise. 'The job only starts today, surely?'

'Yes, but from midnight last night or something, old chap. Technical point. Didn't you know? The last H.S. has cleared off, anyway. I told the Prof. you were really quite a reliable sort of fellow, and even if you were a bit prone to nip off for long week-ends you'd be back in a few days. I said I'd willingly cope with the extra work in the meantime.'

I looked at Bingham coldly. 'And what, may I ask, did the Professor say to all that?'

'Nothing, old chap. He just sort of snorted and went off.'

'I see.'

This was a bad start. Before I could seriously begin my career I would have to win promotion to senior house surgeon and work in the wards themselves under the Professor of Surgery. The appointment would be made after we had finished three months' work in casualty – and only one of us could be chosen. The reject would be turned out in his medical infancy to wail on some other hospital's doorstep.

'I say, old chap,' Bingham continued as we walked along. 'You simply must nip up to the ward after supper and have a dekko at some wizard pancreatic cysts. There's a wonderful perf. up there too – pretty sick, you know, but I think he'll last till we've had a squint at him.' Bingham had the true surgeon's mentality, for it never occurred to him that interesting signs and symptoms were attached to human beings. 'There's a kid with a smashing ductus, too. Murmur as loud as a bus. Could hardly take my bally stethoscope away.'

'I thought casualty house surgeons weren't supposed to go into the wards?'

'No really, old chap, but I told the Prof. I was working for Fellowship already and he said I could nose round as much as I liked. I expect it'll be all right for you to come too, as long as you're with me.'

I began to hate Bingham before we first crossed the threshold of our common work-place.

The casualty-room at St Swithin's was not likely to fire in any young man the inspiration to be a second Louis Pasteur or Astley Cooper. It was a long, tiled, semi-basement place, lit by small windows high in the walls, smelling strongly of carbolic and always crowded, like a public lavatory at a busy crossroads. As St Swithin's had to find money to buy all the latest antibiotics and isotopes, it saw no point in spending it on a department where the therapeutic technique had hardly changed since its patients were brought on shutters from beneath the wheels of hansom cabs. Everything in casualty was old: there were old horsehair examination couches, sagging screens of old sacking, dull old instruments, battered old dressing drums, and steamy old sterilizers. Even the porter was past retiring age, and all the nurses seemed to be old ladies.

As we entered, the rows of old wooden benches were already filled with people – one-quarter men, and a quarter each women, children, and policemen. There were policemen everywhere, as thick as tom-cats in a fish market. They stood in the corners holding their helmets, they hid behind the screens with open notebooks, they drank pints of free tea solemnly round the sterilizer, they peered across stretchers and requested eternal 'particulars.' Policemen are inseparable from casualty surgery, and it was well known at St Swithin's that anyone falling over in the district and not getting up damn quickly was immediately seized by the police and enthusiastically borne into the casualty-room.

I sat down at an old desk in one end of the room, which held a large brass ink-pot and a pile of different coloured forms. My job was simple. I handed one of these forms to any patient who I felt was beyond my own professional ability and thankfully disposed of him for ever into some inner department of the hospital. As my only post-graduate guidance from St Swithin's was a leaflet on what to do in case of fire and another describing the most fruitful way of asking relatives for a post-mortem, I was at first worried about matching the correct form to the case. Fortunately, the old porter had long ago accepted the responsibility of running casualty himself, and tactfully brought me the right document to sign after selecting it with the infallible diagnostic instinct of a St Swithin's employee.

The casualty-room never emptied before evening, and for a week I was too busy even to notice Bingham. We met professionally only once a day, at the noon interlude in the clinical rough-and-tumble known as 'minor ops'. This was for surgery too lowly for the main operating theatres, and was performed by Bingham and myself in an undignified theatre made by a partitioned corner of the casualty-room, containing a galvanized-iron operating table, an Edwardian dental-chair decorated with gilt *fleurs de lys*, and a small anaesthetic apparatus on which some former house surgeon had written *Property of the Gas, Fight, and Choke Company*. Although we made our incisions with scalpels that would have been hurled to the floor in the main theatre, and probably had been, it was minor ops. that made the casualty job tolerable: as newly-qualified prospective surgeons, both of us had the same enthusiasm for the knife as the Committee of Public Safety for the guillotine.

I shortly became aware that Bingham always had far more cases waiting on the benches outside minor ops. than I did. As we took alternate patients coming through the casualty-door I envied his luck, until I discovered that he had the habit of stopping people he saw in the street with promising boils, warts, moles, or cysts, handing them his card, and telling them to come to the casualty-room of St Swithin's at midday and ask specifically for himself. This brought him a brisk practice of taxi drivers, railway porters, bus conductors, tea-shop waitresses, newsvendors, and roadmenders, and he not only removed the lump and others found by a more searching examination than was possible in public, but usually pulled out their ingrowing toe-nails and extracted their bad teeth as well.

This unsporting approach to surgery so annoyed me that one morning when Bingham was out of the casualty-room I felt justified in harvesting some of his crop myself. I was half-way through removing under local anaesthetic an interesting sebaceous cyst on the nose of an Underground ticket collector, when Bingham burst into the theatre.

'I say!' he started, his white coat flapping furiously. 'That cyst's bally well mine!'

I looked at him over my mask. 'Oh, is it?' I said in surprise. 'I thought you'd gone to lunch.'

'Lunch! Have you ever known me go to lunch during minor ops.? Of course I wasn't at lunch, you chump. I was having a dekko at a p.-m. – jolly interesting ruptured kidney – and having a chat about it with the Prof., if you must know.'

'Well, there's plenty more,' I said, picking up the cyst in a pair of forceps. 'I'll be finished in five minutes.'

'That isn't the bally point,' he went on crossly. 'The fact is, old chap, I particularly wanted to do that cyst. I've been looking forward to it all morning. And I might add it's pretty unethical to pinch another chap's patients, old chap.'

'It's also pretty unethical for a chap to go round the streets of London touting for custom.'

He blushed. For a few seconds he said nothing. 'I don't think I like your tone, old chap,' he muttered.

'And I don't ruddy well care if you don't.'

The patient, now alarmed that his medical advisers were about to come to blows over his body, reminded them of their obligations with a noise through the sterile towels like the neigh of a dying horse.

'I'll report you to the Prof.,' Bingham hissed, and swept out.

He revenged himself immediately by directing all the 'old chronics' to my desk. These patients were a human sludge in the machinery of St Swithin's, of which it could never rid itself. They appeared regularly with notes as large as the score of a symphony, on which the words 'Rep. Mist.' were scrawled in the writing of twenty successive house surgeons. These abbreviations entitled them to another bottle of medicine, the original purpose of which was generally forgotten and the original prescriber probably dead.

The old chronics that morning seemed unending as they shifted slowly up the benches towards me. By two o'clock there were still a dozen left; I hadn't had my lunch, and I was in a bad temper. Then I noticed a patient queue-jumping.

He was a shifty-looking, elderly man dressed in a shabby black coat and striped trousers. He had sneaked down the room and sat himself on the edge of the foremost bench. He held the finger of one hand in a blood-stained handkerchief, and he still wore his black Homburg hat. I knew his type well : we often saw head clerks and managers from surrounding offices who carried their self-importance on to the equalizing benches of the casualty-room, and we were encouraged by the Professor to stop it.

'One minute, missus,' I told a fat woman with some obscure but ancient condition of the feet. 'Now look here, daddy,' I began sharply, crossing to the interloper. 'What's the meaning of this?'

He looked up at me in alarm.

'Yes, I saw you,' I went on sternly. 'Thought you were being clever, didn't you? Sneaking up the side like that. You ought to be ashamed of yourself. You won't bleed to death with that little cut, and there's plenty of people in the room more seriously injured than you. Where's your treatment card, anyway?'

'Card? I – I'm very sorry, but – what card?'

'Can't you read, daddy?' I asked in despair. 'There's a notice the size of Marble Arch inside the door. It says all patients must ask the clerk for a treatment card. So hop off and get one.'

'I'm sorry, I didn't think –'

'Run along, daddy,' I said waving him away. I returned to the lady's feet, feeling in a better temper already. Medical pomposity is an invigorating draught to a young doctor.

Within a few minutes the man had returned with his card. Now he started hovering round the back of my chair. For a while I pretended to ignore him, then I turned round and demanded angrily, 'What the devil's the matter with you now, daddy?' Why can't you go to the end of the queue like everyone else?'

'Yes, but you see, I *am* in rather a hurry –'

'So is everybody else. So am I, if it comes to that. Now get back to the last bench.'

'Perhaps I should explain –'

'I'm not in the slightest interested. If you don't jump to it I'll get you shifted by one of the policemen.'

His mouth opened in horror. I congratulated myself – I had judged my man shrewdly. A fellow of his type would be frightened by such an indignity.

'Really, I must say, Doctor, it's a most –'

'Now stop arguing. You can't chuck your weight around as usual in here. And for God's sake, daddy, *take your blasted hat off!*'

'What on earth's going on here?'

I spun round, and found the Professor looking down at me. I had hardly spoken to him before, because he was far too occupied with the higher problems of academic surgery to worry about the poultices and finger-stalls of the casualty-room. He was a chilly, scientific man with a gravelly voice and a long nose and chin like Mr Punch. He had only once been known to laugh, the day Sir Lancelot Spratt arrived at the hospital in a brand-new plum-coloured Rolls and was rammed by an ambulance in the courtyard in front of all his students.

'This patient, sir – ' I began.

'Are you in some sort of trouble, Charles?' the Professor asked.

'Yes, I am. This young man here has been behaving extremely rudely.'

The Professor looked at me as if I were one of the rats in his laboratory developing an interesting disease.

'Perhaps I had better introduce my friend, Mr Justice Hopcroft,' he said slowly. 'He unfortunately happened to cut his hand while we were lunching at my club. I have been collecting some instruments to suture it.'

I stared at him in silence. I felt the casualty-room was revolving round me at high speed.

'What did you say your name was? It's slipped my mind since making the appointment.'

'Gordon, sir,' I croaked.

'Gordon, eh?' The Professor grunted and nodded his head several times, shaking it well into his memory.

'What name?' demanded Mr Justice Hopcroft, staring hard into my face.

I repeated it.

He grunted too. 'Gordon. Yes, Gordon. I'll remember that.'

As they disappeared into minor ops. it not only seemed likely that I wouldn't retain my job, but that my first brush with the law would land me in Dartmoor for life.

2

FOR the next few weeks I read with equal anxiety the opinions that the Professor expressed in his case-notes on my diagnoses and those that Mr Justice Hopcroft expressed in court on the characters of his convicted criminals. Bingham now smirked every time he spoke to me, and had become intolerable. He was a bad case of the seasonal disease that struck the medical school known as 'Diplomatosis', which was characterized by delusions of grandeur and loss of memory for recent events. He had thrown away his ignominious short student's jacket, and appeared everywhere in a long white coat which he reluctantly removed only for meals; his stethoscope, which he had never carried secretly, now sprouted from his head as proudly as the horns of a rutting deer; he hurried round the hospital with jerky, urgent strides, which implied that consultations of the gravest aspect waited round every corner; he addressed patients, relatives, and junior probationers like a Victorian practitioner breaking bad news; and the responsibilities of qualification left him too preoccupied to recognize the faces of fellow-students who had been less fortunate with the examiners.

I thought Bingham's most irritating performance was in the lift. As well as the wide lifts for stretchers, St Swithin's provided for the staff a small creaking cage that usually had a worn notice on the gate saying OUT OF ORDER, which was traditionally forbidden the students. Bingham now used this lift even to descend between adjoining floors; he was particularly careful to summon it when walking along the corridor with a crowd of students, and would wait for them to arrive breathless upstairs. 'Jolly convenient, the old lift,' he said to me one morning. 'Can't understand how we used to manage without it.'

I was not left much time to brood on him, for either the drivers and pedestrians of London were becoming more careless or I was becoming less efficient: the patients in the casualty-room never thinned until supper-time, and I often had to go without my lunch as well.

'I say, old chap,' be began late one evening, as the benches were at last clearing. 'How about buzzing up to the ward and having a quiz round some cases? There's an absolutely top-hole pyelonephrosis and a retroperitoneal abscess side by side – bet you half a dollar you can't spot which is which.'

'No thanks,' I said. 'As a matter of fact, I'm fed up at looking at suffering humanity for a bit. I'm going out for a pint.'

'Forgive me for saying so, old man, but it's hardly the way to get through the Fellowship, is it?'

'I don't care a monkey's damn for the bloody Fellowship at the moment. My feet hurt, I've got a headache, I want my supper, and I'm thirsty.'

'Yes, cas. is a bit of a bind. I'll be glad to get out of it next month and start proper surgery in the wards.'

I looked him in the eye. 'I will remind you that the post of senior house surgeon will go to only one of us.'

He smirked 'Of course, old man. I was sort of forgetting for a minute. Best man win, and all that, eh?'

'Exactly, Bingham.'

Another fortnight went by, and I began to hope that the Hopcroft affair might be forgotten by a busy man carrying the responsibilities of a surgical Chair. Then one afternoon the Professor appeared in casualty. He stood before my desk, looking at me with the same stare of scientific interest and holding in his hand a patient's treatment card.

'Did you write this?' he asked.

I looked at it. It was directed to the Surgical Registrar, a genial young specialist with whom I had played rugger and drunk beer, and who disliked Bingham almost as much as he did the Fellowship examiners. The card asked for his opinion on a suspected orthopaedic case, but in the stress of casualty I had scribbled only three words:

Please X-ray. Fracture?

Now I remembered with alarm that the Registrar had the afternoon off to visit the Royal Society of Medicine, and the Professor was taking over his work.

'Yes, sir,' I admitted.

'Have,' he snapped. 'Isn't.'

He turned on his heel and disappeared.

Bingham said eagerly a few days later, 'The Prof. was talking about you this morning, old man.'

'Oh, yes?'

'I'd nipped into the theatre to have a dekko at him doing an adrenalectomy, and he asked if I knew what school you went to. I told him I couldn't say off-hand. Then he made a most surprising remark, old chap – he thought it was probably one of those progressive ones, where the kids learn all about self-expression and bash the teachers over the head with rulers but are never taught to read or write. I suppose you didn't really go to a place like that, did you?'

'As a matter of fact I did. We never learnt to read, write, do arithmetic, play cricket, or swap marbles, but at least we were brought up not to go around kissing the backsides of people we wanted to get jobs from.'

Bingham stiffened. 'I might say that's an extremely offensive remark, old chap.'

'I might say that I meant it to be. Old chap.'

My ambition to be a surgeon now burned low. But it was not extinguished until the week before my casualty job was to end.

Bingham and I lived on the top floor of the Resident Medical Staff Quarters at St Swithin's, a tall, gloomy building containing a couple of dozen bleak bed-sitters and a dining-room enlivened by a battered piano and a picture of Sir William Osler gazing at us chidingly down his sad moustaches. On the table was a collecting-box in which anyone talking shop at supper had to drop half a crown; this was labelled FUND FOR THE BLIND, and underneath in smaller letters *And What a Blind!* Every six months, when half the house surgeons left, this box was broached. As the Professor's retiring house surgeon had also passed his Fellowship, found a new job, and become engaged on the same day, he asked me to take his night duty for him. I was delighted, because it showed I was capable of accepting higher surgical responsibilities. Also, it made Bingham furious.

There was usually a trickle of emergency cases entering St Swithin's during the night, but that evening I was disappointed to find that the admission-room inside the gate was quiet. About midnight I went to sleep, leaving Hamilton Bailey's *Emergency Surgery* beside my bed and my trousers hopefully receptive on the chair. I dreamed that I was in casualty, operating with a soup spoon on Bingham's double hernias without an anaesthetic, and I woke with a start to the porter's knock.

'What is it?' In a second I was scrambling out of bed, switching on the light, and jumping into my shoes. 'What's the time?'

23

' 'Arf past three. Case of intermittent abdominal pain. Getting worse over last three days. Mostly subumbilical.'

'Really? Does the patient look very ill?'

'Nah. Came in a taxi.'

I immediately felt sorry: it looked as though I would not have the chance of assisting at an emergency operation. The porter stood picking his teeth while I pulled a sweater over my pyjamas. 'Gall-stone colic I reckon it is,' he said.

I made my way downstairs, through the cold, empty, black halls of the out-patients' department. It was a bitter night outside, with sleet falling heavily and freezing immediately on the pavement. There was no one in sight except a porter sweeping in the distance in the thin light of a lonely bulb. I suddenly felt that I was the only doctor in the world.

I found the patient sitting under a blanket on an examination couch. He was a thin, neat-looking man in a blue suit and a white collar, with a small moustache, carefully-brushed hair, and horn-rimmed spectacles. He looked worried, but unfortunately not like an immediate candidate for the operating table.

'Well now, what's the matter?' I began, as briskly as possible.

'I'm extremely sorry to have troubled you, Doctor. Extremely sorry indeed.' He spoke quietly, with a faint Cockney accent. 'I have took you away from your no doubt well-earned repose. I apologize, Doctor, and ask your forgiveness for that which I have done.'

'That's quite all right. It's what I'm here for.'

'I said to myself as I came in, "The doctor is now, no doubt, reclining in the arms of Morpheus. He is sleeping the sleep of – " '

'What's the matter with you, please?' I interrupted.

He suddenly clutched his abdomen with both hands and groaned.

'Abdominal pain?' I said, flicking the pages of my surgical text-book through my mind. 'Colicky, no doubt? Any relation to food?'

He relaxed, looked round, and whispered, 'Are we alone, Doctor?'

'Alone? I assure you, professional confidences will not be divulged.'

'You're the Professor's house surgeon, ain't you, Doctor?' I nodded. 'Well, Doctor, it's like this here. The Professor operated on me six months ago – partial gastrectomy, up in Faith Ward. All was well, Doctor, until three days ago. Then I began to have pains.' He groaned as another spasm caught him. 'Something shocking, Doctor. Tonight, after a bite of supper, I coughed and found something hard in my throat.' He glanced over his shoulder again and whispered, 'It was a nut, Doctor.'

'You mean you'd been eating nuts?'

'No, no, Doctor. I mean a metal nut. Then five minutes later I produced a screw. And after that two more nuts and a bit of spring. I've been bringing up bits of old iron all night, Doctor. So I thought I'd better come along here.'

'But dash it, man! That's almost impossible. Are you sure?'

'Look, Doctor,' he said proudly. From his pocket he pulled a screwed-up piece of the *Evening News*, which held several bright nuts and bolts and a small coiled spring. We looked at them solemnly. Our eyes lifted and met. I licked my lips.

'They *could* have come from a surgical retractor,' I murmured.

He nodded. 'That's what I thought, Doctor,' he went on in a low voice. 'I know, see. Used to be in the R.A.M.C. Come to think of it, after my operation I heard a sort of rumour something might be missing.'

'Let me have a look at your stomach,' I said.

There was a gastrectomy scar, about six months old.

'Umm,' I said. I scratched my head. I looked up and down the room. There was no one in sight. Even Bingham would have been welcome.

'This might be serious,' I suggested.

'That's why I came in, Doctor,' he continued calmly. 'Mind, I'm not one of them people that makes trouble with law courts and that. But if anything happened . . . Well, I've got a lot of relatives, Doctor.'

'Quite,' I covered him with the blanket and began to walk round the couch slowly. The hospital rules were clear: all serious cases at night were to be referred immediately to a consultant. And if the Professor had somehow managed to leave a spring-loaded retractor inside an abdomen, he certainly would want to know of it before anyone else.

'I think we'll hang on for a bit,' I said. 'By eight o'clock I can get your notes from the registry and organize proper X-rays –'

He grabbed his stomach violently. 'Something else, Doctor,' he cried. 'Coming up!'

The Professor had a Wimbledon number, and after ringing a long time the telephone was answered by a cross female voice.

'Yes?'

'Could I speak to the Professor, please?'

'Who's there?'

'St Swithin's.'

26

'Oh dear, oh dear! Don't you ever leave the poor man in peace? Ar-thur!'

When the Professor reached the telephone, which seemed to be several minutes' walk from his bed, I began, 'I'm terribly sorry to bother you, sir. This is the house surgeon – '

'Rogers?'

'Er – no, not Rogers, sir. Gordon.'

I heard him draw his breath. 'Where's Rogers?'

'He's out for the night, sir.' I felt this was truthful, as I had seen him carried to bed. I steadfastly gave the Professor a brief clinical history of the case.

'It's perfectly possible, I suppose,' he admitted. I could tell that he was worried. 'I can't remember the case offhand, but six months ago I certainly had a new theatre sister. . . . You're sure it's bits of a retractor?'

'Oh, definitely, sir.'

There was a pause.

'Very well,' he decided grudgingly. 'I'll drive in. The Lord only knows how I'll manage it this weather. Admit him to Faith, and get the theatre ready for an emergency laparotomy.'

'Yes, sir.'

'And – er, Gordon.'

'Sir?'

'It was quite right of you to phone me.'

'Thank you, sir!' I said in delight.

But he had already rung off.

I spent the next half hour organizing the operation. I woke the theatre sister and her staff, brought the night sisters and porters from their suppers, and ordered the night nurses on Faith Ward to prepare a bed with hot-water bottles and electric blankets. Then I went back to the patient, who was now lying quietly on the couch.

'Don't worry, old man,' I said heartily, slapping him on the shoulder. 'Everything's under control.' I glanced at my watch. 'The Professor will be here any moment, and he'll fix you up in no time.'

'Thank you, Doctor,' he said, with a sigh of gratitude. He took my hand touchingly. 'I'm real pleased with the way you've looked after me, Doctor.'

'Oh, it's nothing. Just part of the service.'

'No, honest I am, Doctor. Real pleased. Mind you, I've got a soft spot for doctors. Especially young doctors trying to get on in the world like you.'

'That's very kind of you.'

'As a matter of fact, Doctor,' he said more cheerfully, 'I'd like to meet you again when all this is over. Socially, you know.'

'Perhaps we will,' I said with an indulgent smile. 'Who knows?'

'I'd like you to come and stay with me for a week-end. I've got quite a nice little place in the country. Down by the river. It's an old castle I picked up cheap. There's a bit of shooting and fishing if you care for it. Private golf links, of course. So bring your clubs along, Doctor, if you play.'

'I don't think I quite – '

'Tell you what I'll do. I'll send the Rolls for you on the Friday afternoon. The chauffeur can pick you up here. You can't miss it, it's solid gold all the way through, even the piston-rings. Just looking at me now, Doctor,' he said proudly, 'you wouldn't think I owned the Bank of England, would you '

*

I met Bingham in the lift.

'Hello, old chap.' He grinned. 'Sorry you didn't get the senior H.S. job and all that.'

'Yes, I'm sorry, too.'

'You had hard cheese rather, old chap, didn't you? About that loony, I mean. You ought to have had him X-rayed before calling the Prof. Or asked "patient's occupation" as your first question. I'd have done.'

'I suppose I ought.'

'Now you're going to look for a job in the provinces, aren't you? There's some jolly good hospitals outside London, so they tell me. Not up to St Swithin's standards, of course, but you might do pretty well in time. Do you want me to say good-bye to the Prof. for you? I don't suppose you'll want to see him again, will you – after that.'

'It happens I've just been to him. For my testimonial.'

'Any time I can be of help to you, old chap, just let me know.'

'Thanks.'

We reached the ground floor, and I got out.

'I'm going to the basement,' Bingham explained. 'Going to have a dekko at some slides in the lab. Now I'm senior H.S. I thought I'd better run over my path. and bact.' I slammed the gates. 'Don't expect I'll see you before you go, old chap. Got to give a talk to the new cas. H.S. – they don't seem to know a thing, you know, these chaps who've just qualified. Toodle pip!'

He pressed the button. The lift moved six inches and stopped. Bingham pressed all the other buttons in turn. Nothing happened. He rattled the gate. It wouldn't open.

'I say, old chap,' he called after me anxiously, 'I'm stuck in the lift.'

'So I see, Bingham.'

'Absolutely bally well stuck.' He gave a nervous laugh

and rattled the lattice again. Several nurses, porters, and patients had gathered round to watch. Passengers were often stuck in the St Swithin's lift, which provided a regular diversion to the otherwise monotonous aspect of the corridors.

'I say, old chap.' His voice wavered. 'Get me out, will you?'

'But I don't think I know how.' Some of the nurses began to titter. 'Do you mean I ought to send for the fire brigade, or something?'

'No, dash it, old man. This is beyond a joke.' He rattled the gate loudly, terrified that his dignity was slipping away from him. 'Be a sport, old chap,' he implored. 'Get some help. You can't leave a pal like this, can you?'

'Oh, all right,' I said testily. I supposed even Bingham had human rights. 'Wait a minute.'

'Thanks, old chap. I knew you'd do the decent.'

As I strolled away as slowly as possible to fetch a porter, I noticed a loaded food trolley moving down the corridor with the patients' lunch. An idea struck me. When I returned to the lift I was pleased to see the crowd had doubled and Bingham was rattling the bars again.

'Ah, there you are, old chap!' he said with relief. 'You've been pretty nippy, I must – here! What's the idea?'

I slowly peeled half a bunch of bananas and poked them one after another through the bars. This simple pantomime delighted the audience, which had now been joined by a party of convalescents from the children's wards and blocked the corridor. Bingham himself became mildly maniacal.

'I won't forget this!' he spat at me. 'I won't bally well forget it! You wait and see!'

I left him still in the lift and walked straight out of the hospital, for the first time in my qualified career feeling reasonably contented.

On the bus I opened the Professor's testimonial. It was short:

To Whom It May Concern

Dr Gordon has been my Casualty House Surgeon for the past three months, in which time he has performed his duties entirely to his satisfaction.

3

I BEGAN to open the *British Medical Journal* as the Chinese open their newspapers, from the back: the last twenty pages are filled with advertisements for jobs, and I suddenly found myself less concerned over the progress of medical science as a whole than the next source of my own bread and butter.

There were plenty of hospitals advertising for house surgeons in the provinces, so I bought a book of stamps and wrote a dozen elegantly-phrased applications. As I would receive free third-class tickets to attend the interviews I felt that at least I would see something of the country at the National Health Service's expense.

I soon found that I was not a success at interviews. First of all, the waiting-rooms upset me. Before an oral examination, a group of students enjoy the deep, sad comradeship of a bunch of prisoners awaiting the firing squad, but when a job is being decided the atmosphere in the ante-room is more like a lifeboat with the food and water running low. Although none of the candidates could have wanted work more urgently than myself, I always reached the empty chair at the foot of the committee table with subconscious feelings of guilt. This made me always say the wrong things, find difficulty in knowing what to do with my hands, fiddle with my tie, break pencils in two, and tear the sheet of pink blotting-paper into little bits.

I went through several interviews, though now they are as indistinguishable in my mind as different visits to the dentist's. They were all held in hospital boardrooms, containing a fireplace crammed with coal, three portraits of men in frock-coats suffering from obesity and hypertension, the hospital reports since 1840 bound in red leather, a bust of Hippocrates in the corner, and black panels of donations recording in gold leaf how ennobled local manufacturers cast their bread upon waters with reliable tides. In the middle of the room was a mahogany table that looked strong enough to support a tank, round which sat a dozen of the most intimidating people I had seen in my life.

It was important to decide on entering the room which of the committee were doctors and which were lay governors, in order to tune the pitch of each reply correctly – there was no point in giving a clinical examination answer to a wholesale draper in his best suit. At one of my earlier interviews I was asked solemnly by a man in a clerical collar. 'What would you do, Doctor, if you were operating alone at midnight and suddenly produced an unstoppable haemorrhage?'

Feeling sure of myself, I replied, 'Pray to God for guidance, sir.'

A small man on my right stirred. 'Don't you think, young fellow,' he said quietly, 'you might ring up a consultant surgeon before calling on the advice of an unqualified practitioner?'

I didn't get the job.

Some of the committees wanted to know if I played cricket, others if I played the piano; some if I were married, or if I were moral; one chairman asked my politics, another the names of my clubs. Whatever answers I gave never seemed to be the right ones: there was always a sharp silence, a slight 'Oh!' from somewhere, and the chairman was thanking me very much and saying they would let me know in due course. My saddest discovery of all was that an education at St Swithin's did not automatically waft you to the head of the profession on the sweeping bows of your colleages. We had been brought up to assume the same relationship to the graduates of other hospitals as Sherlock Holmes to Watson, and it was a shock to find someone who had never heard of the place.

'What's your hospital, lad?' demanded one florid, fat surgeon, who held the degree of a northern medical school never mentioned in our wards.

'St Swithin's, sir.'

'Ee, lad, you'll live it down,' he said, and everyone roared with laughter.

This was too much, even at an interview. 'I might say, sir,' I declared indignantly, 'that I am extremely proud of the fact. At least, they say you can always tell a St Swithin's man.'

'Aye, lad, and you can't tell him anything.'

I didn't get that job either.

After a disheartening month of cold train journeys I began to feel worried. I no longer faced the problem of finding a befitting start to my surgical career, but of keeping myself alive and fed. I had four pounds ten in the bank, one suit, a bag of golf clubs, a roll of minor surgical instruments, and a small plaster bust of Lord Lister. I lived in a furnished room in Muswell Hill, the weather was wet and icy, all my shoes needed repairing, I always seemed hungry, and my depressing circumstances made me want to drink twice as much as usual. My microscope had been sacrificed long ago, and my skeleton lay in a pawnbroker's near St Swithin's, whose cellars must have resembled the catacombs after a plague year.

The only objects of value left were my text-books. I

looked at them, packing my landlady's cheap bookcase with their plump smooth backs and rich gold lettering, like a hungry tramp eyeing a flock of geese. For a week I resisted temptation. Then I decided that there were two or three volumes on subjects like public health and biochemistry that a rising surgeon could do without. Later I unashamedly took the lot, one after the other, to the second-hand medical bookshop in Gower Street, saying at every meal a grace to its provider. Whitby and Britton's *Disorders of the Blood* gave only bacon and eggs and coffee in a teashop; but Price's *Text-book of the Practice of Medicine* was much more nutritious, and ran to tomato soup, steak and chips, a pint of beer, and apple tart. I saved up Gray's *Anatomy* for my birthday, and when I at last carried *The Encyclopaedia of Surgical Practice* downstairs I booked a table at Scott's.

Soon I had nothing left but a few *Students' Aid* handbooks, *What to do in Cases of Poisoning*, and *A Table of Food Values*, which together would hardly have risen to tea and sandwiches. I therefore set out to my next interview, at a large hospital in Northumberland, determined to win the job. I stood in the waiting-room staring out of the window, trying to forget the other candidates; I marched into the committee room, clasped my hands under the table, and answered all the questions like an efficient policeman in court. This time I had the whole length of the table to myself with the committee in a line opposite, which somehow increased my confidence. I felt I was doing well, particularly when the tall surgeon in the corner who had been asking most of the questions nodded after investigating my career at St Swithin's, and said, 'That seems all very satisfactory. And you really mean to go in for surgery, do you?'

'Most certainly, sir,' I answered promptly. 'However

much personal hardship it means at first, that's always been my ambition.'

'Excellent. That's the spirit I like to see in my house surgeons. Don't you agree, gentlemen?'

A heartening volley of grunts came across the table.

'Very well,' the surgeon said. 'Now Dr Bryce-Derry, our Chairman, will ask you a few routine questions.'

The Chairman, who sat immediately opposite me, was a pleasant-looking, youngish man in a tweed suit, a check shirt, and a homespun tie.

'Now, Dr Gordon,' he started with a smile. 'You're certain you really want to work in our hospital?'

'Yes, sir.'

His smile vanished. His lips tightened.

'You have been qualified a little over three months, I believe?'

'Yes, sir.'

He paused. He glared at me.

'You are a member of the Medical Defence Union, I take it?' he went on slowly.

'Oh, definitely, sir.'

I felt bewildered. There was suddenly an odd atmosphere in the room. All the committee members were either looking at the ceiling or staring hard on to their squares of blotting-paper. Nobody spoke.

'And of the B.M.A.?' the Chairman continued, now scowling.

'Y-yes, sir.'

This sudden malevolence was impossible to explain. I felt awkward and nervous, and wanted fresh air. I pulled out my handkerchief to wipe my forehead, and pushed back my chair. Then I saw opposite me under the table the edge of a tweed skirt, thick fish-net stockings, and a pair of sensible brogues.

36

'I – I'm terribly sorry, my dear sir – I mean madam –
I – I – Oh, God!' I jumped up and ran for the door.
I didn't get that job, either.

*

In the train to London I pulled the latest medical journal from my overcoat pocket and sadly turned again to
the advertisements, which were conveniently arranged
alphabetically under specialities from Anaesthetics to
Venereology. It seemed time to try my luck at a different
branch of medicine. Bacteriology meant regular hours
and no talkative patients, but there was always the risk
of catching something like smallpox or plague. Tuberculosis offered work in pleasant country surroundings
with plenty of fresh butter and eggs, but the drowsy
routine of a sanatorium often drugs the doctors as well
as the patients. Orthopaedics needed the instincts of a
carpenter, and pathology the instincts of Burke and
Hare. Radiology sent you to work in unhealthy, dark,
dripping grottoes underground, and paediatrics meant
children being sick over your trousers.

I looked gloomily through the window at the English
industrial landscape thirstily soaking up an afternoon's
rain, and tried to review my years at St Swithin's to find
another subject for which I had shown some aptitude.
But my education was represented in my memory only
by a series of smells – there was the acrid smell of the
first-year chemistry class, the soft smell of Canada balsam used for mounting zoology slides, the mixed stink of
phenol and formaldehyde in the anatomy room, the rich
aromatic breath of the biochemistry laboratory, the
smell of floor-polish in the wards and ether in the
operating theatre, and the smell in the post-mortem
room like a badly-kept butcher's shop. I sighed, and

37

reluctantly turned back the pages: there was nothing left but general practice.

Under *Practices (Executive Councils)* was printed *For vacancies (except those in Scotland) apply on Form EC16A, obtainable from the Executive Council.* . . . The first breath of bureaucracy! It had such a depressing effect that I turned to the less formal advertisements tucked among prospectuses for private lunatic asylums and offers of used cars and second-hand R.A.M.C. uniforms in the back. One on the cover itself struck me:

EMINENTLY SUITABLE FOR RECENTLY QUALIFIED PRACTITIONER

1. Medical Officer in luxury liner on world cruise. America, South Seas, West Indies, Australia, Japan, India. Leaving almost immediately. All found and salary £2,000 per annum (in U.S. dollars).

2. Personal Medical Officer required by South African millionaire travelling widely Africa, America, Asia. Salary by arrangement, but money no object for suitable man. Apply at once.

3. General Practice. Suitable partner required for quiet practice in Wye Valley. Free sixteenth-century house, fully modernized, free fuel and food, free car and chauffeur, three months' holiday a year.

Many Other Similar Posts

Apply to
WILSON, WILLOWICK AND WELLBELOVE|D
Medical Agency

The address was not far from St Swithin's.

The next morning was foggy, my rent fell due, and I was developing a cold, but even from Muswell Hill the agency shone brightly with hope. I made for it directly after breakfast. I had never seen the office, but I found it at the top of a bare, sagging staircase between a hospital for chronic diseases and a pub.

On the door was a notice saying WALK IN. Inside was a small room lined with varnished planks, containing two plain wooden benches facing each other and fixed to the wall, like seats in a French railway compartment. Opposite was a door with a cracked, frosted-glass panel saying PRINCIPAL; there was a window curtained with London grime, and on the floor the small, upturned face of a circular electric fire gave a wan greeting. Sitting on one bench was a pale, thoughtful man about my age reading *The Journal of Neurology, Neurosurgery, and Psychiatry*, and on the other an old, untidy, dirty-looking fellow with an insanitary moustache and a crumpled trilby was staring at the floor and muttering.

I sat next to the young man. None of us spoke. I waited until both of them had entered and left the inner room, then I went in myself.

The office was smaller than the waiting-room, and contained a high, narrow desk at which a benevolent-looking old man with gold-rimmed glasses and side-whiskers was sitting on a stool. He was wearing a wing collar, a cravat, and an old frock-coat. A light in a pale green shade hung from the ceiling to the level of his nose.

'Mr Wilson, Mr Willowick, or Mr Wellbeloved?' I asked cheerfully. The sensation of applying for a job as a customer rather than a supplicant was unreasonably stimulating.

'Alas, Doctor, I am neither,' He smiled good-heartedly. He put down his pen and clasped his arthritic fingers. 'And what can I do for you?'

'I came about your advertisement. I'd like the million-aire one if it's still going, but if not I'll take the cruise liner instead. I can pack up and go any time. I'm perfectly free.'

'Alas, again, Doctor,' he said, still smiling kindly, 'but those vacancies are already filled.'

'But the advert. only came out yesterday!'

'The rush was very great. . . . However, I have many equally attractive posts to offer. You wish to go abroad, Doctor?'

'I wouldn't mind. As long as it's sunny.'

'Then I have just the very place. The Acropolos Oil Company – a Greek concern, but most respectable – require a doctor in Iraq. Most interesting. The first tour of duty is five years. I have the contract here – '

'I don't think I want so much sunshine as that.'

'Are you a man of faith, Doctor? You look it, to my eyes. A medical missionary is needed in Siam. The remuneration is admittedly not high, but – ' he sighed – 'one gains one's reward in Heaven.'

'I should prefer to gain my reward here.' I was beginning to feel disappointed. 'I suppose you haven't any ordinary practices? I'm working for my F.R.C.S., you know, and taking up surgery and all that. I thought I'd better get a bit of G.P. experience first.'

'Of course, Doctor.' He picked up another bundle of papers. 'I thought that you wished to leave the country for some reason or another. . . . Of course we have many practices. I wouldn't like to say how many bright young men like yourself I've set on their way. It's a sort of hobby, really. This' – he indicated the office – 'is not my true habitat. Oh, dear me, no! You'd be surprised if you knew what it was. I have many interests. But once' – he became sad – 'the life of one I hold very dear to me was saved by the skill of a young doctor. Now it is my only pleasure in life, helping such young men along their difficult path.'

He looked as if he were about to burst into tears, and I was beginning to feel it was my lucky day. 'Some might call me eccentric, but –' He smiled faintly, and dabbed beneath his spectacles with a handkerchief. 'Forgive an old man's ramblings. I am always touched at the sight of a doctor at the threshold of his career.'

He became more business-like and continued, 'Here's just the thing for you. Semi-rural in the Midlands – the Dukeries, you know. *Locum tenens.* I know the doctor personally. A most excellent gentleman and a fine clinician, a fine clinician. You will learn a great deal from him. And the remuneration, Doctor! All found and ten guineas a week. Not to be sneezed at, eh?'

I hesitated.

'It'll be gone by lunch-time, I guarantee.'

'Semi-rural, you said?'

'More than semi.'

'All right. I'll take it.'

'You're very wise, I think. Now I expect you'd like some money?' He chuckled. 'Forgive me, Doctor, forgive me! An old man's privilege. I know with young doctors things are often a little – strained. You'll need your books. And some equipment. Eh?' He drew an old leather wallet from his pocket, took out a packet of white notes, and laid them on the desk. 'A hundred pounds would perhaps be of use to you '

'But – but you mean as a gift?' I said in amazement. 'It's ridiculous! I couldn't take it.'

'Well, let us call it a loan, then? Yes, a loan. I understand your embarrassment perfectly, Doctor – '

'I haven't a scrap of security – '

'That doesn't worry me in the least. Not in the least. Just to make you feel it's no more than a business transaction perhaps you'll sign here – '

41

I signed.

'There's a little interest, to make it less personal,' he admitted. 'Fifteen per cent per annum, payable quarterly. Now perhaps you'll favour me with a signature on this too, Doctor – '

'What is it?'

'Just the usual form about the practice. I take a small commission to pay for overheads. So expensive these days.' He blotted both my signatures. 'That'll be thirty-three and a third per cent of your salary for the first year. After twelve months you won't have to pay me a cent. Not a cent. Good morning, Doctor. Here's the address of your practice. Go as soon as you can, won't you? The train service is very good. Don't lose touch with me, now. That would never do. Send me a postcard. Good-bye, Doctor. Good-bye. Next, please.'

4

I DESCENDED the stairs feeling as though I had nodded to a friend at an auction and found myself the purchaser of a large suite of Chippendale furniture. At the bottom I bumped absently into someone coming through the door.

'Sorry,' I mumbled.

A violent blow on the back sent me staggering.

'Richard, you old bastard.'

'Grimsdyke!'

We shook hands delightedly. Although we were close companions in medical school, I hadn't seen him since the afternoon he failed his finals.

'What the devil are you doing in this den of thieves?' he demanded at once.

'Looking for work.'

'God help you! Is Father Bloodsucker up aloft?'

I looked puzzled.

'Old Pycraft – the vile criminal in a frock-coat and brass glasses.'

I nodded.

'Damn! Sure it wasn't old Berry? Tall thin character, bald as a pillar-box?'

'No, it's Pycraft all right.'

He frowned. 'I thought it was Berry's day. He's almost human, sometimes. But Pycraft – Oh, hell! We must go and have a drink.'

'In case there's any danger of this developing into an

all-day session,' I said as we stepped out, 'I must warn you that I've just been given a job to go to.'

'What, by those people? Then you'll need a drink. Come on, they're open.'

The lights of the pub next door sent a warm yellow welcome through the fog. The bar was old-fashioned and cheerful, with a sprightly young fire leaping in the grate and the landlord screened away behind an arrangement of mahogany and frosted glass that afforded a cosiness contemptible to modern pub architects.

After several minutes' conversational back-slapping, Grimsdyke ordered the drinks and asked through the barrier. 'Have you the morning paper – *Times* or *Telegraph*? Thanks.'

He searched for the City page and read closely through it, moving his lips.

'Forgive me, Richard,' he said, glancing up. 'I was all right at the close of yesterday's business, but I'm a bit worried about Cunard and Vickers. However, they're holding their own. Pretty satisfactory all round, I'd say. My brokers are the smartest chaps in the City, but I like to keep an eye on my investments. Ah, the beer!' He folded the paper and poked it back, 'To the happier days of our youth!'

'And our future prosperity!'

After the first draught I lowered my glass and looked at him in puzzlement. As a student he had more money than the rest of his companions together, and had presented a smart and fashionable contrast to the remainder of the medical school. Now he was wearing a torn mackintosh over a baggy Donegal tweed suit, and a frayed yellow-and-green check waistcoat with brass buttons. His shoes were worn, his collar curled, his cuffs were grubby; one of his gayest bow-ties flew from his

44

neck in jaunty defiance of the rest of his outfit. There was a moment of embarrassment as he noticed my look, then he put down his drink and announced, 'I'm qualified.'

'Qualified? Congratulations, my dear fellow! But – but how? There hasn't been an exam. since the one you failed.'

He laughed. 'Not in London, certainly. But I take a broad view of the whole subject of examinations. I am now entitled to put after my name the proud letters "P.C.A.M." I am a Preceptor of the College of Apothecaries of Mayo. Ever heard of it?'

'I can't say I have.'

'You're far from the only one. You know I never saw eye to eye with the examiners here. I take an intellectual view of medicine, old lad, and let's face it – medicine isn't an intellectual subject. Any fool with a good memory and a sharp ear for squeaks and rumbles can become a doctor.'

'True,' I admitted sadly.

'I heard about the Mayo College from a bloke I met in a pub in Fleet Street. Apparently this useful institution is still allowed to award diplomas that put you on the *British Medical Register*, and no one's tumbled to it. It's like not paying any income tax in Jersey, and all that. I booked a ticket to Mayo and arrived a couple of days later. It was early in the morning, so I walked up and down the street looking for this College, but all I could find was a door with a bloody great brass knocker on it, which I knocked. Inside was an old hag scrubbing the floor. "Have you come to be made a doctor?" she said. "I have," I told her. "Upstairs," she said, and went on scrubbing.

'Upstairs was a sitting-room with a nice fire and a

young fellow sitting reading the *Irish Independent* over his breakfast. When I acquainted him with the nature of my business he said he'd be delighted to accommodate me, and if I'd come back after the week-end I could have the examination. I told him that was ridiculous – I had many pressing engagements in London on Monday morning. He said he was sorry, but he was off playing golf in the country and there was nothing he could do about it. Eventually he said, "Well, the examination consists only of a *viva voce*, and seeing that there's only one candidate we can just as well hold it in the taxi. Hand me my golf clubs, Mr Grimsdyke, and we'll be off."

'In the back of the cab he started. "Now tell me something about urea?" I asked, "You mean that chemical substance, or are you referring to my lug-hole?" He said, "Well, we won't go into it further. How would you treat an old woman of eighty who went crazy one Sunday afternoon and fell down and broke both legs?" I thought a good bit, and said, "I would bring about the unfortunate creature's timely demise with the soothing juices of the poppy." He agreed, "I think that's about right. I'm anti-clerical myself." He asked me a few more questions walking down the platform, then took his clubs and said I'd passed and the examination fee was fifty guineas. It happened I had fifty-odd quid on me, so he stuffed them in his mackintosh pocket and wrote out the receipt on a bit of newspaper. As the train left he yelled out of the window that my diploma would follow, and sure enough it did. Damn great thing with a seal on like the Magna Carta. I hear the Government's got wind of the place now, and they're going to shut it down. Shall we have the other half? Your turn.'

When I had ordered the drinks, Grimsdyke continued,

'That was the beginning of my troubles. You remember my grandmother's bequest – a thousand a year during my training to be a doctor? That stopped on the nail, of course. In short, my financial affairs were unprepared for the sudden disaster of my passing, as I had already got through the next three or four years' allowance on tick. A certain amount of retrenchment was necessary. Visits to the pop-shop. The car's gone, and so have the golf clubs. Even some of the suiting. Hence the appearance of having dropped off a hay-cart. Damn unpleasant.'

'But why on earth,' I demanded, 'did you ever bloody well qualify at all? You could have gone on failing and stayed a medical student the rest of your life. At a thousand a year, that's what I'd have done.'

'Pride, old lad,' he explained, looking into his glass sadly. 'Do you know why I failed my finals in London? I was doing damn well in the clinical. It was one of those days when golf-balls look the size of footballs and the greens as big as Piccadilly Circus – you know. The physical signs were sprouting out of my patient like broccoli. I found he'd got an effusion at his left base, and I spotted he was fibrillating. I even heard his diastolic murmur, a thing I'd never been able to accomplish all my years in the medical school. Gave me quite a start. I trotted all this out to the examiner, feeling pretty pleased with myself. He kept nodding and saying, "Quite so, Exactly. Excellent", and I saw myself bowing out in a lofty sort of way to the applause of the assembled company. Then he asked, "Anything else?" And I said, "Impossible, sir!" And do you know,' said Grimsdyke savagely, banging his glass on the bar, 'the bloody patient had a glass eye. And the old fornicator failed me.'

47

'That really is hard luck,' I said sympathetically.

'Particularly as I'd been out the night before with Nicky Nosworth from Guys, who's had a glass eye for years. In fact, he showed me the bloodshot one he's got for the morning after, and the one he upsets everyone with when he gets bottled, with crossed Union Jacks instead of a pupil.'

We drank in silence for a few moments, contemplating this tragedy.

'All you fellows had got through,' Grimsdyke continued. 'So I thought, "To hell with the cash! I can damn well be a doctor too!" and look where it's got me.'

'There's always your investments.'

'Ah, yes,' he sighed. 'My investments.'

'Have you got a job?'

'I'm a sort of chronic *locum tenens*. Life really got difficult when I fell into the hands of the crooks next door. You must have been pretty hard put to it, ending up with those financial fiends?'

'I was. The cash was running pretty low. I had to get work somewhere, and I was lured by their advertisements.'

He nodded. 'How much is the job paying?'

'Ten guineas a week.'

'You ought to have stuck out for sixteen, at least. I suppose you've never been in practice before?'

I shook my head.

'Then watch out. It's not the doctors who are the trouble – it's their wives. Remember that, old lad, if nothing else. By the way, can you lend me some money? My investments take practically every penny these days.'

'Of course! My small resources are at your disposal.'

'I suppose Wilson, Willowick, and Wellbeloved pressed a hundred quid on you? A tenner will do me. Here's my

48

card, though I hope you won't have to remind me. I may be poor, but I'm still honest. Thanks, old lad. Do you want any tips for the market? No? Then your very good health.'

*

Before going to my practice I had two essential purchases to make.

I went to a ready-made tailor's in Oxford Street and gingerly walked through the chromium halls looking at the dummies, which demonstrated that the suits fitted all right if you were in the grip of *rigor mortis*. I was sneaking towards the door when a salesman sprang at me from a thicket of Shaftesbury Avenue tweed, and within a minute was helping me off with my clothes in a cubicle.

'I want something for – er, business. Pretty dark and dignified, you know.'

'But you don't want to look like an undertaker's clerk, sir, do you?'

'No, I certainly don't want to look like an undertaker's clerk.'

'How about this, sir?' he said, briskly producing a suit with the air of a *maître d'hôtel* offering something exceptionally choice from the kitchen. It was a blue tweed, with a pronounced herring-bone, a mauve check overlay, and a faint red stripe. 'Wears like tin plate, sir. Just feel. Lovely bit of cloth. Magnificent quality. You won't be seeing anything like this again, sir.'

The suit certainly looked good value; but the pink lights and rosy mirrors in the shop would have sold out a stock of sackcloth and ashes.

'The sleeves are a bit long,' I said dubiously.

'They'll work up in no time, sir. Never fear.'

'All right, I'll take it.'

'I'm sure you'll be very satisfied, sir,' he said, immediately wrapping it up. He winked. 'You'll be cutting quite a dash with this at the Palais on Saturday nights, eh, sir?'

My next necessity was a car. A G.P. without a car is as useless as a postman without legs, but I had less than seventy pounds left with which to buy one. I looked wistfully in the manufacturers' showrooms in Piccadilly, where brand-new cars were displayed as carefully as the cigarette-cases in the jewellers next door, but even the second-hand ones in Euston Road garages were beyond my means. I finally arrived at a bomb-site in Camden Town where a line of cars with prices whitewashed on their windscreens stood under a banner saying HONEST PERCY PICK.

'Lovely job, this one,' said Percy Pick, kicking a tyre affectionately. He managed his business without moving his hands from his pockets, his hat from his head, or his cigarette from his mouth. 'Good for another fifty thou., easy.'

'The price is a bit steep for me, I'm afraid.'

He snorted. 'Garn! Don't expect me to give it away, do yer? I'll come down to a 'undred.'

I shook my head.

'How about this?' He slapped a bonnet in a row of cars waiting pathetically to be bought like puppies in a dog's home. 'Only one owner.'

'He must have died a very old man.'

'How about a mo'bike if you're so broke?'

'How much is that one over there?' In the corner of the site was a large, black, heavy, hearse-like car which looked as immobile as a chicken-coop. Percy Pick seemed surprised to see it.

'You can have it for fifty,' he said quickly.

'Does it go?'

'Go? Of course it goes. All my cars go.'

'Very well,' I said. 'Let's see.'

The next morning I set off to my practice, wearing my new suit and driving my new car, reflecting that I had already learnt much of the sordid world outside the over-protective walls of St Swithin's.

5

THE journey north was exciting, for neither the car –
which I had christened 'Haemorrhagic Hilda' – nor I
had been on the road for some time. Hilda was originally an expensive limousine, but now she was constructed of so many spare parts that I thought of her
fondly as the bastard of some noble line. Her vertical
windscreen, which opened horizontally across the
middle, was colourful with rainbows and bright with
stars; there was worm in the dashboard, where all the
dials pointed to zero except the engine temperature,
which was stuck at boiling; her furnishings had been
replaced by a former owner, and now consisted of a pair
of bucket seats from an old baby Austin perched on a
fruit-box in front, and an ordinary small domestic horsehair sofa in the back. Behind the sofa were pieces of
sacking, some old gnawed bones, a yo-yo, and scraps
of newspaper prophesying the fall of Ramsay Mac-
Donald's government. The front windows would not
open, and the back windows would not shut. Birds had
nested under the roof, and mice under the floorboards.

The mechanical part of Haemorrhagic Hilda aroused
my clinician's interest rather than my alarm. The engine
produced more rales, sibili, and rhonchi than a ward of
asthmatics, and the steering gear, which had a wheel fit
for a London bus, was afflicted with a severe type of
locomotor ataxia. The only pleasant surprise was the horn.
This was a long silver trumpet creeping from the windscreen to coil comfortably over the bonnet and front

mudguard, which in squeezing the rubber bulb sounded like feeding-time in the seal pool. Hilda's other surprisingly good point was her brakes, which I shortly had a chance of demonstrating.

Outside Stony Stratford a police car waved me to the roadside.

'You the owner of this vehicle?' the policeman demanded, taking my licence.

'And proud of it,' I said cheerfully.

'I suppose you know there are regulations concerning the roadworthiness of motor vehicles?' he said in the tone used by Customs officers asking you to open the other suitcase. 'Is the vehicle equipped with an efficient braking system?'

'Brakes? Absolutely wonderful, officer. She can pull up on a postage stamp.'

'I am going to test the truth of your statement. Proceed along the highway at a reasonable speed. I will follow, and when I blow my horn apply your brakes.'

'Right-ho,' I said bravely.

I swung the engine, wondering what was going to happen: if the police decided to hound Hilda off the road, I would not only arrive late but lose the greater part of my working capital as well.

After I had travelled a few hundred yards my thoughts were interrupted by the urgent blast of a horn behind me. As I drove the brake-pedal into the floorboards I realized that it was not the policeman but a Bentley sweeping past our procession at eighty. There was a crash behind, and my windscreen fell on to the bonnet. As Haemorrhagic Hilda had been built in the same spirit as the Pyramids, she suffered only another dent in the rear mudguard; but the police car lay with its wheels turned out like flat feet, bleeding oil and water on to the roadway.

'You'll hear more about this,' the policeman kept muttering, as I dressed the small cut on his nose. I gave him a lift to the next telephone box, and continued my journey in an unreasonably cheerful frame of mind.

I began to move down the psychological slope towards depression as I entered the district where I was to work. It was a small English industrial town, which like many others stood as a monument to its own Victorian prosperity. There were long solid rows of grimy houses, factories walled like prisons, and chapels looking like pubs or pubs looking like chapels on every corner. There was a Town Hall ringed by stout old gentlemen petrified as they rose to address the Board, the station was a smoky shrine to the Railway Age, the football ground was a mausoleum of past champions, and the streets had not yet echoed the death rattle of their trams. Only the main thoroughfare had been changed, and consisted of cinemas, multiple chemists, tailors, and cheap chain-stores, looking exactly like anywhere else in the country.

Shortly it began to rain, though from the soggy ground and the depressed aspect of the pedestrians it appeared to have been raining there continuously for several years. I became gloomier as I searched for my address on the other side of the town, and finally drove into a long road of gently dilapidating Victorian villas behind caged gardens of small trees shivering in their seasonal nakedness. On the last door-post I spotted a brass plate.

The front door was opened by a cheerful-looking young blonde in overalls, holding a broom.

'Is Dr Hockett in?' I asked, politely raising my hat. 'I'm Dr Gordon.'

'Well, fancy that, now! I said to the Doctor this

54

morning, I said, "I'm sure he ain't coming!" ' She grinned. 'Silly, ain't I?'

'I was delayed on the road. I had to give medical attention in an accident.'

'The Doctor ain't in yet, but give us your bags, and I'll show you up to your room.'

As she climbed the dark stairs with my two suitcases, the maid called over her shoulder, 'You ain't 'arf young.'

'Well, I'm – I'm not exactly in the cradle, you know,' I said, wondering whether to feel flattered.

'Garn! I bet you ain't any older than what I am. The Doctor's had some real old fogeys, I can tell you. Old Dr Christmas was the last one – Cripes! He must have been ninety. Real old dodderer. Then there was Dr O'Higgins and Dr O'Rourke and Dr O'Toole – grandpas, they were. And before them there was Dr Solomons and Dr Azzis and Dr Wu – '

I was alarmed. 'There's been quite a number of assistants here?'

' 'Undreds and 'undreds of 'em.'

'Oh.'

'Here's your room,' she said brightly, opening a door at the top of the last flight of stairs. It was a bedroom the size of a cell, and furnished as sparsely. She dropped the cases and flicked briefly at the enamel washbasin with her duster. 'Bit chilly this weather, but it's comfy enough in summer.'

'Home from home, I assure you,' I murmured, looking round.

'You can get a nice fug up if you keep the window shut. Dr Wu, now – he used to burn incense and things. You won't be doing that, will you?'

'Not very much.'

'The light's switched off at the main at eleven, you pays your own laundry, it's extra if you've got a wireless, and you can have a bath on Saturday mornings,' she went on cheerfully. 'That's the Doctor's orders. He likes to keep an eye on the housekeeping.'

'I should ruddy well think he does!' This seemed too much to tolerate, even as a junior *locum*. 'Far be it for me to judge a man in advance,' I told her, 'but I must say he seems a bit of a mean old devil.'

'He can be a bit stingy sometimes, that's straight. Likes to look after the pennies.'

I sat down on a bed as unresilient as a park bench, and contemplated the discouraging start to my career as a general practitioner. The blonde continued to grin at me from the doorway, and I wondered if she was waiting for a tip; but as I felt in my pocket she went on, 'I must say, it is nice to see someone from London Town again. How's the old place getting along?'

'About the same I suppose. I thought you weren't a local girl,' I added.

'Not me! I ain't one of them provincials. 'Ow did you guess?'

I hesitated. 'You have a sort of sophisticated air about you.'

'Go on with you! I suppose you don't know the old "Bag o' Nails" in Ludgate Circus, do you? I used to be behind the bar there for a bit.'

'What, old Harry Bennett's pub? I know it very well. Often went there with a lot of chaps from Bart's.'

Her face took a tender look. 'Dear old Harry Bennett! After all these years! Funny you should know it, ain't it? We'll have a good old pijaw about it as soon as you're settled in. It'll be just as good as a holiday for me.'

56

'Have you been out here long?'

'Near on four years. I've got an old mum, you know –' A door slammed. 'The Doctor!' she gasped. 'Cheery-bye,' she whispered. 'I'll say you'll be down in a minute.'

I found Dr Hockett in the gloomy living-room, where the table was laid for high tea. He was standing in a green tweed overcoat in front of the gas fire, which was unlit. He was a tall, stooping man of about fifty, with a thin lined face and a thick grey moustache. His hands were clasped behind him and his gaze was fixed on his toes; his only movement as I entered was turning his eyes sharply up and glaring at me beneath his eyebrows, which hung across his face like a tuft of steel wool.

'Good afternoon, sir,' I said politely.

'Good afternoon, Doctor. I had expected you a little earlier.' He spoke in a soft monotone, as though saying his prayers. Taking one hand from behind his back he shook mine flaccidly and replaced it. 'Remarkably warm for the time of year, isn't it?'

'Well, it strikes a little chilly up here after London.'

'No, I don't think it does,' he went on. 'I always wear wool next to the skin, Doctor. That is much more hygienic than filling the house with the fumes of combustible gases. If that is your car outside, you will have to leave it in the open overnight. There is only room in the garage for mine, and as it is no more than a few years old I don't intend to expose the coachwork. I often do my nearer visits on bicycle – it is much more healthy to take exercise in the open air. You might like to follow my example, though as you're paying your own petrol bills it's entirely up to you. We could make an arrangement by which you had part use of the bicycle, and I would make the appropriate deduction from your salary.'

As I said nothing he continued muttering, 'You've not been in general practice before, I believe? No, I thought not. The work here is hard, but the experience will be sufficient reward in itself.'

The door opened, and the blonde maid entered with a tray containing a large brown enamel teapot, a loaf of bread, a packet of margarine, and a small tin of sardines, half-empty.

'It is much healthier for the alimentary tract not to be overloaded with a heavy meal at night,' Dr Hockett continued, still looking at his feet. 'I never take further food after this hour, but if you wish to buy yourself some biscuits or suchlike for later consumption, of course I have no objection. Shall we sit down?'

He took off his overcoat and sat at the head of the table. Seeing a third place, and suddenly remembering Grimsdyke's warning, I broke the silence by asking, 'Are you married, sir?'

He gave me another glance under his eyebrows.

'I didn't quite catch your remark, Doctor,' he muttered. 'I thought you said, "Are you married?"' As the blonde took the third chair he went on, 'Pour the doctor his tea first, my dear. Possibly he likes it weaker than we do. Will you take a sardine, Doctor? I see there are one and one-third each. What, nothing at all? Perhaps after the excitement of your journey you are not very hungry? Well, it is best in the circumstances not to overwork the metabolism.'

6

THE shock of finding the Cockney blonde was Hockett's wife did not lead to my losing much nourishment. Nothing followed the bread and sardines, Hockett maintaining that margarine was biochemically the superior of butter, and weak tea had a low caffeine content which prevented eventual nervous, alimentary, and moral degeneration. The wife, whose name I gathered was Jasmine, said little because she ate steadily through a pile of bread and margarine; but while Hockett was carefully mopping up the sardine oil with his bread I was horrified to see her wink at me.

As we rose from the table Hockett was struck by an afterthought. 'You *didn't* take sugar, did you, Doctor?' he muttered.

'It's all right, I can do without it at a pinch.'

'I'm so glad, Doctor. Extremely unhealthy, sugar. Pure carbohydrate. Surplus carbohydrate in the diet leads to obesity, and then what? We all know that obesity is a cause of arteriosclerosis, arteriosclerosis causes heart failure, and heart failure is fatal. Taking sugar in the tea is suicidal, Doctor.'

'I want the fire on,' Jasmine declared.

'Do you, my dear? But it's extremely warm. I find it warm enough, anyway. So does Dr Gordon. You feel warm, don't you, Doctor? A remarkably mild winter we're having.'

'I'm frozen to the marrow, I am,' Jasmine said. She clutched herself and shivered dramatically.

'Very well, my dear,' he said with an air of solemn generosity, as though reading her his will. 'You shall have the fire. Doctor, do you happen to have a match on you?'

This conversation had taken place in the dark, as the daylight had been fading swiftly during the meal and neither of them had thought of turning on the light.

'Very restful, the twilight,' Hockett continued, stumbling over the furniture as he groped for the switch through the blackness. 'Extremely valuable for restoring the sensitivity of the retina. We suffer from far too much light.'

He lit the fire, carefully turned it half down, sat in a chair beside it, and began reading the *Daily Express* steadily from the headlines to the printer's name at the foot of the last sheet.

'You may smoke, if you wish, Doctor,' he said, looking up. 'We ourselves do not – '

'Liable to give fatal disease of the lung, you mean?'

'Exactly. If you wish for something to read, there are some books on the table behind you. They were left in the waiting-room by patients, but I expect they are perfectly readable.'

I started on *Pears' Cyclopaedia*. When I became tired of reading this, I stared for a while at a stuffed duck in a glass case opposite. Once I had seen enough of the duck, I took another dip into *Pears*. Jasmine sat between us knitting, and every time I looked at her she winked. Thus the evening passed.

At nine o'clock Jasmine yawned and said, 'I'm off to get a bit of kip.'

'Very wise of you, my dear. Early to bed and early to rise is a perfectly sound motto physiologically.'

'Good night one and all,' she said cheerfully, gathering her knitting. 'Sleep tight, Dr Gordon.'

As soon as she had left the room Dr Hockett turned the fire out.

'Sweltering in here, Doctor, isn't it? Now that my wife has retired we can have a talk on professional matters. I don't like to discuss such things in front of her. First of all, your duties. You will see the National Health patients twice a day at the surgery in Football Ground Road, and take all the night calls. I see the rest and the private patients, such as they are, in my consulting-room here. I don't go out at night.' He gave me another look under his eyebrows. 'I don't like leaving Jasmine alone. She is still very young.'

'Quite understandable.'

There was a pause.

'A very attractive woman, Jasmine,' he added.

'Most attractive, sir,' I agreed politely. As he continued to stare at me in silence, I shifted in my chair and added, 'I mean, in a sort of utterly platonic way, and all that, you know.'

After gazing at me for several more seconds he suddenly produced a key on a string from his waistcoat pocket. 'This is the duplicate key of the drug cupboard in my surgery next door. There are only two keys in the house. Please see that the cupboard is always locked. I do not think it wise for Jasmine to have access to it.' He handed me the key and went on, 'Jasmine is in many ways somewhat childish. As we are to work closely together, Doctor, I think it best for me to confide in you now. It may come as a shock to you to hear that Jasmine was my daily maid before becoming my wife.'

'No! Really?'

'I had practised abroad for many years. Out East. I

61

never married. Marriage somehow seemed always beyond my means. However, when I settled here – I nevertheless love Jasmine very deeply, Doctor,' he continued, staring hard. 'I would not like to see anyone harm a hair of her head.'

'That's the spirit,' I said brightly. I was now feeling badly in need of a drink. 'After all, you're her husband and all that, aren't you?'

'Yes, Doctor,' he murmured. 'I *am* her husband.'

He then rose, switched out the light, and suggested we went to bed.

*

Breakfast the next morning was tea and porridge. Dr Hockett didn't believe in overloading the gastric absorption so early in the day.

The meal was begun in silence, because Hockett was attending to his morning mail. The general practitioner's daily postbag is filled with advertisements from the pharmaceutical firms and boxes of free samples, which are passed by most of their recipients directly into the waste-paper basket. But Hockett carefully opened each one, smoothing the envelopes for future use and reading the shiny pages of advertisements from the coloured slogans at the top to the formulae in small type at the bottom.

'Surely, sir, you don't believe in all that rubbish?' I asked. I felt I had been bullied long enough in the house, and I had slept sufficiently badly to have the courage of a bad temper. 'At St Swithin's we were taught to chuck advertisements away unopened.'

'On the contrary, Doctor, I find I derive a great deal of medical information from them. One of the difficulties of a general practitioner is keeping up with the latest work. And all the medical journals are so infernally expensive.'

'But look at the muck they send in free samples! No G.P. in his right mind would prescribe it. This, for instance –' I picked up a large bottle of green liquid labelled DR FARRER'S FAMOUS FEMALE FERTILITY FOOD.

'Careful, Doctor! Don't drop it. As a matter of fact I keep all the samples. I have several hundred in the cupboard in my consulting-room. My private patients seem glad enough of them.'

'You charge for them, I suppose, sir?' I asked coldly.

'Naturally,' he replied without hesitation. 'Patients do not appreciate what they do not pay for. That is surely recognized as one of the evils of the National Health Service? Now I really think you should be getting along, Doctor – your surgery is well over a mile away, and it is bad for the practice to arrive late.'

I drove Haemorrhagic Hilda through the rain towards Football Ground Road, trying to suppress my feelings. If I were to be a G.P. I was going to be a damn good one, despite Hockett, Jasmine, a bed as uncomfortable as the rack in the Tower, and the effects of incipient frostbite and starvation. This determination wavered when I saw the surgery itself: it was a shop-front with the glass painted bright green and DR HOCKETT'S SURGERY written across it in red, like the window of a four-ale bar.

There was already a queue of patients on the pavement as I unlocked the door. Inside I found a single room filled with parish-hall chairs, with a partitioned cubby-hole for the doctor in the corner. This cubby-hole was largely filled with filing cabinets, though there was an old examination couch, a small stained desk, a basin, a Bunsen burner, and an oil stove, which I immediately lit. I washed my hands, took out my fountain-pen, put my head round the cubby-hole door, and said, 'First patient, please.'

A fat mother accompanied by a fat adolescent school-girl rose from the first line of chairs, and advanced on me with the expression of purposeful dislike used by women when demanding to see the manager.

'*Adiposa familians*,' I said brightly, as they entered.

'What's that?' the mother asked sharply.

'A Latin expression. Medical terminology. You wouldn't understand it.' I waved them towards the two chairs jammed beside the desk, placed my finger-tips together, and began, 'Now, what's the trouble?'

'Where's the doctor?' the mother asked.

'I am the doctor.'

'No, the real doctor.'

'I assure you I am a perfectly real doctor,' I said calmly. 'Surely you don't want me to produce my diploma?'

'You're Hockett's new boy, are you?'

'I am Dr Hockett's most recent assistant, certainly.' She assessed me for some seconds.

'Well, I can't say I like the idea much of you meddling with our Eva' she declared. Eva was meanwhile staring at me malevolently, saying nothing, and picking her nose.

'Either you want me as your daughter's medical attendant or you don't,' I said emphatically. 'If you don't, you can take your National Health card elsewhere. I assure you I shall have no regrets about it whatever.'

'It's the chest,' she said, nodding towards the girl.

'What's wrong with the chest?'

'Cough, cough, cough all night long she does. Why, I never get a wink of sleep, I don't sometimes,' she added indignantly.

'And how long have you had this cough, Eva?' I asked, with my best professional smile.

64.

She made no reply.

'Very well,' I said, picking up my stethoscope. 'I'd better start by examining her, I suppose. Off with your things, now.'

'What, you mean take all her clothes off her chest?' the mother asked in horror.

'I mean take all her clothes off her chest. Otherwise I shall not be able to make a diagnosis, we won't be able to start treatment, Eva will get worse, and you won't get any sleep.'

Eva said nothing as her mother peeled away several layers of cardigans, blouses, and vests. At last her chest was exposed. I laid my stethoscope over the heart, winked at her pleasantly, and said with a smile, 'Big breaths.'

A look of interest at last illuminated the child's face. She glanced at me and grinned. 'Yeth,' she said proudly, 'and I'm only thixteen.'

*

The morning passed quickly. The patients came steadily to my cubby-hole, though every time I began to think of lunch and peeped outside there seemed to be as many waiting as ever. I was relieved to find that my work was reduced through most of them not needing a full diagnosis and treatment, but only a 'Sustificate, Doctor'. I signed several dozen of these, certifying that people were in a state to stop work, start work, go to the seaside, stay away from court, have a baby, draw their pension, drink free milk, and live apart from their relatives. I gained confidence with every signature, and was beginning to feel I had a flair for general practice when I came against the case of the cheerful old lady.

'Hallo, Doctor,' she began. 'And how are you this fine morning?'

'I'm extremely well,' I said, delighted to have a pleasant patient. 'I hope we'll find that you are too.'

'I'm not so dusty. Especially considering. Do you know how old I am, Doctor?'

'Not a day over fifty, I'll be bound.'

'Go on with you, Doctor!' She looked coy. 'I'm seventy next birthday, that's a fact.'

'You certainly don't look it,' I told her briskly, feeling it was time to start the professional part of the interview. 'And what's the trouble?'

'Trouble?' She looked startled, as if I had asked her whether she wanted lean or streaky. 'There ain't no trouble, Doctor.'

'Then why – forgive me if I ought to know – have you come to the doctor's?'

'To get another bottle of me medicine, of course.'

'Ah, I see.' I put my finger-tips together again. 'And what sort of medicine is this?'

'The red medicine, Doctor. *You* know.'

'I mean, what do you take it for?'

'The wind,' she answered at once.

'You suffer from the – er, wind?'

'Oh, no, Doctor!' She was now humouring the teasing of a precocious child. 'Haven't had the wind for years, I haven't.'

'And how long have you had the medicine?'

'Oh – let me see – I first 'ad it the year we went to the Isle of Wight – no, it couldn't be that year, because our Ernie was alive then. It must have been the year after. Except it couldn't have been, because we had our Geoff with us, and he's been under the sod a good fifteen – '

'Quite,' I interrupted. I saw before me as clearly as the eyesight chart hanging from the wall the Ministry

66

of Health circular on extravagant prescribing. 'Well, I'm afraid you can't have any more medicine. You're as sound as a bell, really, and you don't need it. Take a walk in the park every day instead. Good morning to you.'

At first she didn't believe me. Then she said in a sad faint childish voice, 'But I must 'ave me medicine, Doctor.'

'You really don't need it.'

'But I always 'ave me medicine, Doctor – always. Three times a day regular after meals – ' Then she suddenly burst into tears.

'Now please control yourself,' I said anxiously. I began to wish I had taken the Hospital Secretary's advice and chosen the Army. 'It's nothing to do with me. It's simply a Ministry regulation. If it was up to me you could have a dozen bottles of medicine a day. But we doctors have to cut it down.'

'I want me medicine!' she cried.

'Dash it! Do you wish to unbalance the Budget and ruin the country? Please be reasonable.'

Suddenly her grief became anger. Beating the desk with her umbrella she shouted, 'I want me medicine! I know me rights! I've paid me National 'Ealth like everyone else!'

'I will not stand for this,' I said, wondering if there was anything in the Hippocratic Oath against losing your temper. 'Kindly leave the surgery.'

'You thief! You robber! That's what you are! Taking all them shillings every week from poor folk like me what can't afford it! I know what 'appens to them insurance stamps! I know! Lining the pockets of the doctors, that's what! I want me medicine!'

She left the cubby-hole, but repeated her demand to

the patients who had been listening intently outside, inciting them to riot. I held my head in my hands. For five years at St Swithin's I had probably ruined my health through overwork and deprived my parents of the last comforts of their declining years – for this. It would have been easier to face if I had eaten a nourishing breakfast.

'Sit down,' I said dully, hearing another patient enter. 'Name, age, and occupation?'

'Wilkins. Twenty-one. Trades union organizer.' A youth in a tight blue suit sat down, still wearing his hat. 'But I ain't a patient. At least, not at the minute.' He spoke softly and slowly, as though demanding my money and valuables in an alley on a dark night. 'You've upset my mother you 'ave.'

'If that lady outside is your mother, I'd be obliged if you'd kindly take her home.'

'Under the Regulations for the Conduct and Control of the National Health Service,' he continued, staring at the ceiling, 'a patient what receives inefficient service from a doctor can state a case before the local Executive Council, who, if they shall decide the facts proved, shall deduct an appropriate fine from the doctor's remuneration.'

I lost my temper.

'Get out!'

'Take it easy, Doc., take it easy,' he continued in the same tone. 'I'm not saying nothing against you – I'm only quoting regulations, see? It just happens that I know 'em.'

'And I suppose you go round making a damn good thing out of it?'

Picking his front teeth with a matchstick, he continued, 'I'd be careful what I was saying, if I was you.

Doc. There's a law of libel in the land, don't forget. As a matter of fact, I've had five cases against doctors. Won every one. All fined. I'm worth near a thousand quid a year to the Executive Council, I'd say.'

'Now look here, Mr Watkins – '

'Wilkins.'

'I don't care who the bloody hell you are or what you intend to do, but if you don't get out of here at once I'll kick your ruddy coccyx so hard – '

'Violence won't get you nowhere,' he said imperturbably. 'I could lay a complaint before the General Medical Council in that case. That you was guilty of infamous conduct in a professional respect.' He rose. 'Don't forget the name, Doc., Wilkins. You'll be hearing more from me.'

7

WHEN I got home Jasmine was laying the table for our midday dinner.

'Hello,' she said brightly. 'You look like you're a bear with a sore head, and no mistake.'

'At the moment I'd make a pack of bears with sore heads look like a basket of puppies. Where's Dr Hockett, Jasmine?'

'The Doctor ain't in yet. He had to go out to the Vicar.' She laughed. 'That's the first time what you've called me Jasmine.'

I threw myself into a chair and picked up my *Pears Cyclopaedia*. After a while she went on, 'Didn't 'arf give you a start, didn't it? Yesterday at tea.' She giggled. 'Didn't know I was married to the Doctor, did you?'

'If you must drag the incident up again, Mrs Hockett, I will tell you that I didn't. And it did give me a start. Quite put me off my sardine.'

She laid out the last of the plates. 'I'm not blaming you,' she said amiably. 'Fancy me being the wife of a doctor! Phew! I can't get over it yet, sometimes.' As I said nothing, she came nearer my chair. 'Of course, he only married me to save the wages. Or mostly, I suppose. He's a mean old devil, like you said. Still, I acted for the best.'

'My dear Mrs Hockett – '

'Call me Jasmine, ducks.'

'I really cannot give opinions on your strictly domestic affairs. I have had an exhausting – in fact, excruciating – morning, and quite enough trouble for today, thank you.'

'Do us a favour, duckie,' she said.

'No.'

'Yes, go on. Be a sport.' She came near enough to stand over me. 'The Doctor's given you the key of the drug cupboard, ain't he?'

'No.'

'Yes he has – he always gives it to the assistant.'

'And what of it?'

'Be a gent and give us the lend of it a minute.'

'I certainly will not.' I turned to my *Cyclopaedia* again with finality.

'Oh, go on! I'll give it back. Dr Azziz let me have it.'

'Well, Dr Gordon won't.'

'Fetch us a bit of nembutal from the cupboard, then. I love nembutal.' She rubbed her stomach and rolled her eyes. 'Lovely grub, it is. Sends you to sleep and makes you forget what a bloody old miser the Doctor is.'

'That hardly seems the way for a woman to talk about her husband.'

Suddenly she made a grab for my waistcoat pocket. 'Come on! Give it over!'

'For God's sake, woman – !'

'Ooo! Let go! You're hurting!' she cried pleasurably.

'Damnation! Can't you control yourself?'

We struggled over the chair and fell on to the floor. Jasmine was a sturdy girl and obviously experienced in parlour fighting. I had managed to push her from above me with difficulty, when Dr Hockett came in.

I scrambled up. My collar had flown from its stud, my face was red, I was sweating and breathless. Hockett stood in his overcoat in the doorway with his hands behind him, staring at me in the usual way.

71

'We – er – I had lost something on the floor,' I explained.

He nodded.

'Jasmine – Mrs Hockett, that is – was helping me find it.'

There was a long silence, while Jasmine smoothed down her clothes.

'Time for dinner,' Hockett said quietly. 'My dear, it is surely not necessary to have the fire on at this hour of the morning? It is really remarkably warm for the time of year.'

None of us spoke during the meal, which was sausage and mash. When Jasmine had cleared away the dishes and left, Hockett said in his usual voice, 'Surprising the numbers of doctors who have sinned, isn't it?'

'Sinned?' I looked at him uncomfortably. 'You mean – er, sexually?'

'I mean who have committed murder.'

'Oh, yes?' I said faintly. 'I suppose it is.'

'There was Crippen – Palmer the Poisoner – Neil Cream in London. And many more. Do you remember the Ruxton case? He cut them up in the bath.'

'I suppose it's – sort of tempting to have all the stuff around. To go murdering people with.'

'Exactly.'

'Ah, well!' I said. I stood up, clutching the table for support. 'I must be getting along.'

'Many murderers are never detected, Doctor,' Hockett observed.

I ran to my room and wedged the bed behind the door.

*

The evening nevertheless passed the same way as the

one before. Dr Hockett sat beside the faint-hearted fire and read the *Express;* Jasmine knitted, and winked every time she caught my eye; I looked at the duck and read my *Cyclopaedia.*

We went to bed at ten, parting as amiably as any trio which has shared for supper the same cod fillet. I heard Dr Hockett turn the electricity off at the main. I felt for my torch beside me, and went to sleep.

The telephone rang at one-thirty. As it was my job to take all night calls I automatically climbed out of bed, crept downstairs, and answered it.

'Fifteen Canal Place,' a man's voice said immediately. 'And hurry up.' The line went dead.

I pulled on my clothes, started up Haemorrhagic Hilda, looked for Canal Place on my new map, and bounced over the deserted tram-lines into the night. After losing myself three or four times I found the address at the far end of a long, narrow, twisting street too cramped for Hilda to pass. I walked the rest of the way, and as it was raining again I knocked on the door with my new suit soaked through to the pyjamas underneath.

'You've taken your time, I must say,' said the man who opened the door.

I shone my torch in his face. 'Wilkins!'

'The very same.'

'If this is some sort of joke – ' I began angrily.

'Joke? I don't play jokes, Doc. Some people say I ain't got a sense of humour. It's mother.'

'What's wrong with her?'

'She's dying.'

'She is, is she? Well, we'll see.'

I found Mrs Wilkins in bed upstairs, suffering from the wind.

73

'She wants to go into 'ospital,' Mr Wilkins announced in a threatening voice.

'No doubt she does. So do half the population of the country. She needs a large glass of hot water, that's all.'

'She wants to go into 'ospital,' Mr Wilkins insisted.

'Good night,' I snapped, picking up my stethoscope.

''Ere!' He grabbed my lapel. 'You 'eard what I said – she ought to be in 'ospital.'

Mrs Wilkins belched loudly. 'I'm dying!' she cried.

'Now look here. I don't want to threaten you with bodily violence twice in a day, Mr Wilkins, but if you don't take your hands off me this instant – '

He stared at me, tight-lipped. 'All right. Have it your own way. I'm going to the Executive Council in the morning.'

'Go to the bloody Town Council tonight, if you want to.'

'And I'm going to the General Medical Council, too. You mark my words,' he shouted after me as I made for the street. 'Infamous conduct – professional respect!'

The words followed me as I ran through the rain, while his mother recovered sufficiently to stick her head out of the window and swear in a way that would certainly have been inadvisable for a dying woman.

By the time I left the car outside Dr Hockett's house I was trembling with indignation. This was really too much. I had been treated worse than a man come to fix the drains. Already composing an outraged letter to the B.M.A., I opened the front door and flashed my torch along the hall. I found Jasmine standing at the bottom of the stairs in her nightie.

'Good God!'

She giggled. 'Hello, duckie. The Doctor's out. He had to go to the Vicar.'

'Get back to bed at once!'

'Go on! You sound like my old dad.' She came towards me. 'I'll go to bed,' she whispered, 'if you come too.'

I dropped the torch in fright. 'Have you gone insane, woman? Are you crazy? What do you think I am? He'll be back in a second.'

'No he won't, ducks. He's only just gone.' She grabbed me in the darkness. 'Come on! Now's our chance – don't you want a bit of fun?' Then she started kissing me, in the spirit of a boxer limbering up on the punching bag.

I managed to push her away and said desperately, 'Let me go! Let me go! Haven't I got enough to worry about as it is? Damn it – if you'll only leave me alone and go back to bed I'll – I'll give you some nembutal.'

She hesitated. 'You really will?'

'Yes, I really will,' I wiped my face with my handkerchief. 'In fact,' I went on breathlessly, 'I wish I could give you the whole ruddy bottle. But only if you'll go to bed at once and stay there like a good girl. Thus preventing both of us being cut up in the bath by tomorrow morning.'

She thought for a moment, weighing up the alternative delights of me and nembutal.

'O.K.,' she decided. 'It's a deal.'

'Run along then. I'll get it from the surgery and bring it up.'

As she disappeared upstairs I opened the drug cupboard and nervously flashed my torch inside. It was filled with several hundred small bottles of samples, which rattled like Haemorrhagic Hilda going downhill as they began to tumble on to the floor all round me. I grabbed the nembutal bottle, pushed the others back, locked the cupboard, and made for the stairs.

On the landing I hesitated. Jasmine had gone back to her room. Her door was shut. Was I in honour bound to keep my side of the bargain? Perhaps I could sneak back to bed and barricade the door. She might come after me, but Hockett would be back before she could make much more trouble. . . . I heard a creak inside the room: she was impatiently getting out of bed. Her bare footsteps crossed the floor. I grabbed the door-handle and pulled.

' 'Ere!' she called. 'What's the big idea?'

'The idea is that you stay inside, my good woman.'

'Oh, is it – '

Together we pulled at the handle, one on each side of the door. As I had the nembutal bottle in one hand, I had a struggle to keep it closed. I didn't hear the front door shut, and as Hockett had returned to the house silently on his bicycle the first I knew of it was finding myself standing in the light of his torch.

'Lord Almighty!' I cried. Immediately it struck me how the situation would appear to him. 'It's all right, I said urgently. 'Your wife couldn't sleep. I was just going to fix her up with some of this.'

I waved the bottle in my hand. Then I saw it wasn't nembutal, but Dr Farrer's Famous Female Fertility Foods.

8

'BACK so soon, Doctor?' asked Mr Pycraft.

'Yes. Dr Hockett and I had a difference of opinion about a difficult case.'

'You did, did you, Doctor?' Pycraft looked different from our last interview. He seemed twenty years younger, his sugary benevolence had hardened like the icing on a cheap wedding-cake, his side-whiskers had receded, his spectacles had enlarged, his clothes were cleaner, and his hands were cured of their arthritis. 'Well, now. Surely you won't let a little thing like that come between you and your career? We have gone to great trouble providing you with a start, in a magnificent practice – '

'Magnificent practice! The only thing magnificent about it is old Hockett's minginess. Why don't you give it to one of your medical missionaries? It would suit a chap who could live on a handful of rice a week and take the temptations of women in his stride.'

'I hardly find it a cause for levity, Doctor.'

'If you'd been working there for thirty-six hours like I have, you'd find it even less. I want another practice please, and damn quick.'

'But, Doctor – ' He picked up a steel pen and slowly tapped his cheek with it. 'I'm afraid we have no more on our books just at the moment. It's a bad time for inexperienced young men like yourself. Your only course is to return to Dr Hockett immediately, apologize, and continue your career.'

I banged his desk. 'I'd rather work tearing up the bloody road!'

'As you well might, Doctor,' he said calmly, 'Under the agreement you signed with Wilson, Willowick, and Wellbeloved – which I have in the safe there – you agreed to pay us thirty-three and one-third per cent of your salary monthly for twelve months, or the equivalent amount should you through any reason leave your post beforehand. That comes to fourteen pounds *per mensem*, which incidentally is payable in advance. We should like the first instalment now, Doctor, and if the rest is not forthcoming I assure you we shall have no hesitation in taking out a summons. Then there is the interest on the loan, of course. The publicity, Doctor – most undesirable, don't you agree? Especially at the very beginning of a career. The General Medical Council take an extremely grave view – '

'Oh, go to hell!' I said. I strode from the office, slammed the door, and clattered down the stairs.

I stood in the street for a minute, breathing hard and wondering what the recent floods of adrenalin were doing to my arteries. Then I dived into the pub for a drink.

Over a pint, I assessed my position in the medical profession. I had a diploma, a car, a new suit shrunk in the service of Mrs Wilkins, no spare cash, a debt of a hundred pounds, and the legal obligation to pay one hundred and sixty-eight pounds in the next twelve months to Wilson, Willowick, and Wellbeloved. I wanted a job and money – and unless I was prepared to make Haemorrhagic Hilda my home I wanted them at once. I was gloomily turning over these problems when I thought of Grimsdyke: although I gravely doubted that he could pay back my ten pounds, it would be

78

pleasant to look at someone who owed money to me.

The address on his card was in Ladbroke Grove, and I drew up Haemorrhagic Hilda a little later that morning before a row of tall frowsy houses by the gasworks. Grimsdyke's apartments were in the basement. I rang a bell beside a blistered brown door under the area stairs, which after several minutes was gingerly opened.

'Yes?' said a woman's voice.

'I'd like to see Dr Grimsdyke, please.'

'He's gone away.'

'I'm a particular friend of his. Tell him it's Dr Gordon, and I've just had a row with Wilson, Willowick, and Wellbeloved.'

'Just a minute.'

She shut the door, and returned a few seconds later to let me in. I saw that she was about nineteen, dressed in a dirty pink satin housecoat, and wore a rather vacant look. Inside the door was a small hall full of rubbish, and beyond that a large room with a window just below the ceiling. This contained a bed, a gas-stove, a washstand, and a table covered with dirty plates and empty Guinness bottles. Grimsdyke was in his pyjamas, with his hair dangling over his face.

'I thought you'd gone up north, old lad,' he said in surprise.

'So I had. Now I'm back again.'

'Forgive this squalor – ' He waved a hand round the room. 'Fact is, I took these rooms – there's a lot more at the back – to oblige some friends, rather messy people –'

'I wondered if you could let me have my ten quid back?'

Grimsdyke sat on the edge of the bed suddenly. 'Surely you can't have spent the other ninety? In two days?

That's certainly some going! You must have had a hell of a good time.'

'I bought a car.'

'What, that ruddy great thing that's blocking out the daylight? I thought the coal had arrived. A bit on the posh side, isn't it?'

'I felt a big car would be a good investment – to impress the patients.'

He nodded. 'It's the only way the blasted public chooses its doctors. Did I tell you about a pal of mine called Rushleigh? Good scout, he qualified right at the end of the war, when you couldn't get cars for love, money, or blackmail. Unless you were a doctor, of course. So he filled in the forms, and got a nice new little family bus for about three hundred quid. He'd happened to pal up with a Free French bloke who'd been in the orthopaedic wards, and when this fellow went home with a couple of bone grafts Rushleigh got an invitation to stay at his place down at Nice, buckshee. So he set off in his car, but he'd only got as far as Rouen when it conked out. You know what cars were like after the war. He went to a French garage, where they mumbled a bit about spare parts and so forth, and told him it would take at least a month to get anything to patch it up. However, the British being considered good chaps in France at the time, they sportingly offered to lend him a very old aristocratic English car they had in the back, which hadn't been used for seven years and then only for funerals.

'Rushleigh proceeded towards the sunny south, feeling he was driving a greenhouse. But he got there all right, and a month later showed up at Rouen. This put the garage in a bit of a fix, because there were apparently no spare parts anywhere. So they suggested to Rushleigh they did a straight swap. They could fix up his little family bus some time or other, and such vehicles sold like *gâteaux chauds*. Hot cakes, old lad.'

I sat down on the bed myself and asked, 'Did he agree?'

'You bet he did. He'd quite taken to the old hearse. One of the garage bloke's brothers was in the Customs and Rushleigh wasn't averse to a spot of fiddling, so off he went. When he was safely back in England he thought he'd send the thing up to the makers in Derbyshire somewhere and have her done up. A few days later he got a letter from the managing director asking him to come at once and enclosing first-class ticket with cheque for incidental expenses and loss of valuable time. Rushleigh went up there preparing to be led away by the police, but instead he was given a ruddy great lunch and asked what he'd sell the old conservatory for. Apparently this firm had a museum of all its old crocks, and the one he'd picked up in Rouen was the only model of its type ever made, for some millionaire or other in Cannes in 1927. Fortified by the directors' brandy, Rushleigh said he didn't see the point of selling, because where would he get another car to continue his life-saving work? "My dear sir," said the managing director, "if you prefer, we should be delighted to give you one of our brand-new Golden Sprites instead." Rushleigh now drives round his practice in one of these, and the old devil's worth an easy five thousand a year.'

'How about my tenner?' I said.

'Would you like a cup of tea? Virginia will make some.'

Virginia was standing with one foot on the table painting her toe-nails.

'No, thanks. I've just had a pint of beer.'

'Is it as late as that? I must be getting a move on. I've

a good many appointments in the City. So if you'll excuse me – '

'At the moment I face bankruptcy, disgrace, and starvation,' I said. 'If you've got any of that ten quid left, I'd regard it as an act of charity if you'd let me have it. I owe Lord knows how much to that agency – '

'I can't exactly give you the cash, old lad, because I haven't got it. The market's been very sluggish of late. But I will tell you what I'll do – Would you like a job?'

'As long as it isn't like the one I got from Wilson and Willowick.'

'This is *bona fide* and real McCoy. Have you heard of Dr Erasmus Potter-Phipps?'

I shook my head.

'He's about the most posh G.P. in England – high class stuff, you know, none of this bob on the bottle and sawdust on the waiting-room floor.'

'Where's he hang out?'

'Park Lane, of course.'

'What's his wife like?'

'He isn't married.'

I felt encouraged for the first time since driving out of range of Dr Hockett in the middle of the night. 'The only fishy thing that strikes me is – I mean, I've the highest regard for your friendship and integrity, but why haven't you grabbed it yourself?'

'Long-term planning. I'll tell you in confidence – don't breathe it to a soul, particularly anyone in the district – I'm leaving for the country. Big opening. I shall settle down scratching pigs with walking-sticks – '

'Is Miss Virginia coming too?' She had taken no more notice of me and was leaning on the table among the plates plucking her eyebrows.

82

'No. She's psychologically unsuited for the country. I've found that out – I've been psychoanalysing her for the last few weeks. That's why she's here. You can't psychoanalyse anyone competently if you're not with them day and night. Jung and Adler, and all that. She's got a jolly interesting little ego.'

'I'm sure she has.'

Grimsdyke got up and felt in his jacket pocket. 'Here's the address. Give me half an hour and I'll speak to him on the blower first.

'But how about references? A G.P. like that wouldn't take an assistant out of the blue.'

'Leave it to me,' he said confidently. 'It's all part of the Grimsdyke service.'

9

DR POTTER-PHIPPS practised in Park Lane from the first floor of a large modern block of flats, though the only indication of this was a small silver plate with his name on the door, as discreet as the single hat in a Bond Street milliner's window. Downstairs I was saluted by the doorman, bowed to by the porter, and grinned at by the lift boy; upstairs, the door was opened by a butler. Dr Potter-Phipps himself, who sat in a consulting-room like a film-producer's office, was a slim, good-looking, fair-haired, middle-aged man wearing a grey suit with narrow trousers, a red carnation in his button-hole, a fawn waistcoat, a white stiff collar, and an Old Etonian tie.

'A frightful tragedy, dear boy,' he said languidly, offering me a gold cigarette-case. 'My partner's perforated his duodenal ulcer, poor fellow. Operated on by old Sir James last night. He'll be away a good three months. It's so terribly difficult to get a suitable man to replace him. This is a rather special practice, you understand.' He held his cigarette with his finger-tips and waved it airily. 'We have rather special patients. To some people the National Health Service did not come quite as the crowning gift of parliamentary democracy. They still like manners with their medicine.'

'I'd certainly be pleased to meet some of them, sir,' I said feelingly.

'Of course, you've been out of the country a good time,' he went on. 'You must have found that Himalayan expedition quite fascinating. Grimsdyke told me about it when he rang up. I met him at the races last week-end, and rather hoped he could help us when this disaster occurred. A remarkable young man.'

'Oh, remarkable.'

'I must be getting old, dear boy, but I find most young doctors today are terribly dull. And they *will* treat their patients like guinea-pigs. It must be the result of this frightful slave-driving in medical schools these days. When I was at St George's, medicine was still acquired slowly, like any other gentlemanly accomplishment. But someone with the Alpine temperament like yourself would be eminently suitable. Did you meet old Charrington in the Himalayas?'

'Charrington? No, I don't think I did.'

'Really?' He looked surprised. 'But he's always shinning up mountains and things.'

'Big place, of course, the Himalayas.'

'Oh, of course.'

I had decided to stand up, draw a deep breath, make a confession, and go directly to the agency to throw myself at the mercy of Mr Pycraft. Then Dr Potter went on – 'Consider yourself engaged.'

'What – just like that?'

'Just like that, dear boy. I'm rather conceited that I can judge my fellow men.' He sighed. 'I wish I could do the same with horses. So much more profitable. By the way, if you want any salary ask the secretary next door. In my family,' he continued pleasantly, 'we never discuss money. It's thought rather vulgar. And forgive me – but perhaps you've something a little more formal to wear?'

I looked down at my new suit.

'I suppose you picked it up in Tibet or somewhere?'

he suggested charitably. 'Here's the name of my tailor. Ask him to make you something quickly and charge it to the practice. It's a chastening thought, but good clothes are more important to the G.P. than a good stethoscope. You needn't worry about a car – we run three Rolls –'

'Three?'

'We have an extra one for the electrocardiograph. Do you know how to use it?'

'Oh, yes, sir,' I said eagerly, glad at last to be able to tell the truth. 'At St Swithin's they taught on the heart most thoroughly.'

'I'm glad. Terribly glad. I'm a little hazy about all those beastly dials and wires and things myself, but I must say once you've connected them up to the patient and pulled a few switches it makes them feel very much better. We got it second-hand from a doctor who went abroad, and I thought it worth using. I take it to almost every case. After all, even in neuralgia and appendicitis it's useful to know what the heart's up to, isn't it? And *two* cars arriving at the patient's door makes so much difference. When can you start? Tomorrow?'

That afternoon I again found myself in a tailor's but this time it was a dark, dusty, devout little shop in Savile Row, where the assistants moved with a funereal tread, everyone spoke in whispers, and the customers were measured in cubicles of dark carved wood like choir-stalls.

'What sort of suit did you have in mind, sir?' asked the old man who was pulling a tape-measure shakily round my middle.

'What's the well-dressed doctor about town wearing these days?'

'You can't go wrong with the black jacket and striped trousers, sir,' he said solemnly. 'A lot of the younger gentlemen in the medical profession are favouring ordinary lounge suits these days, sir. One surgical gentleman I couldn't care to mention even goes so far as' – he dropped his eyes – 'tweed, sir.'

'Very well. Black jacket and striped trousers it is.'

'I *am* glad, sir,' he said. 'I really am. Just like old times, sir.'

I took a bed-sitting-room in Bayswater, and arrived for work in Park Lane the next morning. As I was still wearing my Oxford Street suit even Dr Potter-Phipps' good manners did not prevent a pained look crossing his face when I appeared, as though I were suffering from some exuberant skin disease. 'Perhaps, dear boy,' he suggested, 'you should stay in the background for a while. Get to know the practice. Would you like to wear a white coat? So easy to get one's clothes messy doing clinical tests with strange apparatus.'

For a week I spent my time in the small laboratory converted from a bathroom, performing medical-student pathology at five guineas a go. Then my black jacket and striped trousers arrived, and I was allowed to try my hand at Park Lane medicine. I started at the top: my first patient was a Duke.

During the morning Potter-Phipps hurried into the laboratory, where I was preparing blood samples. For the first time I saw him looking worried.

'A terrible thing has happened, dear boy,' he announced. I prepared to hear that someone had dropped dead in the waiting-room. 'It's my morning to visit old Skye and Lewis, and now this damn film actress has gone and got laryngitis. Which one shall I go to?'

He paced the floor, trying to solve this grave therapeutic problem.

'Couldn't one wait?' I asked.

'Dear boy,' he said patiently. 'In this sort of practice no one waits.'

After some minutes he decided, 'I'll take the actress. The newspapers will be there by now. Yes, definitely the actress. I can bring the electrocardiograph, too – it's important to see that the heart will stand the strain in such a nervous creature. You do the Duke. And pray, dear boy' – he laid a hand on my sleeve – 'remember constantly that for all practical purposes, you and I, at any rate, are not living in an egalitarian society.'

'I shall not fail you, sir,' I said stoutly.

'Good fellow!' He made for the door.

'What's wrong with the Duke?' I called after him.

'Just give him his usual treatment,' he replied over his shoulder, and disappeared.

I drove to the Duke of Skye and Lewis in our number two Rolls, feeling as if I were again going to an examination. One outstanding problem worried me: what *was* the Duke's usual treatment? Apart from the electrocardiograph, our practice did not own much medical equipment, and I had with me only a stethoscope, a throat torch, a gadget for measuring the gap in sparking plugs, a short plastic ruler advertising a cough mixture, a silver-plated presentation bottle-opener, and a small brush for cleaning my lighter, with which to effect my ministrations.

The car stopped outside a door in Eaton Square. As I got out I said to the chauffeur, 'You must have taken Dr Potter-Phipps here a good few times. I don't suppose you know what the blue-blooded old boy's usual treatment is, do you?'

He shrugged his shoulders. 'Sorry, Doctor. There was a duke what lived round the corner, I remember, and he had varicose veins. There was another with prostate trouble up the road – but come to think of it, he was an earl.'

The door was opened by a young maid.

'The doctor,' I said, suddenly feeling that I was delivering the groceries.

'This way.' I followed her, tugging at the edge of my new jacket for support. Could I conceivably ask this girl what the usual treatment was? Then it struck me that I should have to start referring to my patient in a more regular manner. This was my second difficulty in the case. Although I had secretly bought the silver-covered book invaluable to young Englishmen wanting to get on – *Titles and Forms of Address: A Guide to Their Correct Use* – I had found the paragraphs more difficult to memorize than my anatomy and physiology. I summoned the pages urgently to mind, but in the perverted way that I could always remember in examinations the full structural formula of anhydrohydroxyprogesterone and forget all the signs of pneumonia, I now recalled only that the wives of the younger sons of earls share their husbands' titles and honorific initials never appear on visiting-cards.

'His Grace will see you in a minute,' said the maid.

His Grace! That was it. But did I call him 'Your Grace?' Or was that only for the Archbishop of Canterbury and York?

The Duke of Skye and Lewis was a fat red-faced man with a large moustache, lying on his bed in a yellow silk dressing-gown.

'Morning, Doctor,' he said amiably. 'I had a call to say Potter-Phipps couldn't come. Pity. Busy this time of the year, I shouldn't wonder?'

'Yes, er, your – your – sir.'

'Have a seat. You're not rushed for a minute, are you?

89

Potter-Phipps said you knew everything about my case, but I like to have a chat with my doctor. I don't like being pulled about by someone I don't know. It's almost indecent. Doctoring's a man-to-man business, whatever you cook up these days in test-tubes. Do you play golf?'

We argued about mashie shots for ten minutes, then the Duke said with a sigh of resignation, 'Well, Doctor, I suppose it's time for you to give me the usual treatment?'

'Of course. The usual treatment.' I stood up and rubbed my hands slowly together. 'And how,' I asked craftily, 'is the usual complaint?'

'About the same.'

'I see.'

I nodded sagely. There was a pause.

'Let's get on with it, Doctor,' the Duke continued, settling himself on the bed, a brave man about to face an ordeal. 'The sooner it's started, the sooner it's finished.'

What the devil could it be? Manipulation of the vertebrae? Syphonage of the sinuses? Something internal with irrigation? Hypnosis?

'Come along, Doctor.' The Duke was becoming impatient. 'Potter-Phipps does it in a jiffy, with his bare hands.'

I blurted out, now desperate, 'Perhaps you will forgive me for asking, sir – '

'Oh, the new ones? They're in the box on the chimneypiece.'

I shot a glance hopefully towards the fireplace, but met only an unhelpful ormolu clock and some statuettes. 'Of course, sir, new ones – '

'They need new ones this time, and no mistake,' the Duke went on, waggling his feet. Suddenly I saw – I had been summoned to change his corn-plasters.

At the end of the operation the Duke said, 'I suppose you'll be expecting the same sort of outrageous fee as old Potter-Phipps?'

'I really couldn't say,' I told him, smiling with relief. 'I never discuss the money side of it.'

'Neither do I,' he agreed. 'In my family it's thought rather vulgar.'

DR POTTER-PHIPPS ran his practice as efficiently as a motor-car factory. Every morning at eight, three men in green overalls arrived with vacuum cleaners; at eight-fifteen a man dressed as a postilion called with the day's supply of clean towels; at eight-twenty a page-boy brought the waiting-room papers and magazines; at eight-thirty a girl looking like Lady Macbeth with pernicious anaemia came from a West End florist's to change the flowers; at eight-forty a fat man in a frock-coat and bowler entered with Dr Potter-Phipps' freshly-pressed suits; at eight-fifty the chauffeurs, the butler, the secretary, and the nurse appeared, and at nine sharp we were open for business.

The nurse was needed only to show patients from the waiting-room to the consulting-room, and was dressed in a white uniform so crisp and sparkling that she always appeared to have been just unwrapped from cellophane. She was also one of the prettiest girls I had ever met, which had spurred me to start a cosy conversation of hospital reminiscences during my first morning's work.

'I haven't actually been a nurse in *hospital*, darling,' she told me. 'Of course, I looked after my poor sister when she was poorly, but I'm not what you'd call an *invalid's* nurse. Razzy's such a sweet, he gave me the job because he said I looked the part. I played a nurse once, in *Men in White*. Did you see it?'

I said no.

'After all, darling, it's not as if anyone we saw here was *ill*. We just don't have those sort of patients, do we, darling?'

She was right: most of our practice consisted of old gentlemen wondering if they could take out more life insurance, young gentlemen wondering if they'd caught unfortunate diseases, and young women wondering if they were pregnant. Anyone seriously ill was immediately sent north of Oxford Street to the consultants who kept in most successfully with Razzy. It was St Swithin's casualty-room again, first class; but even Dr Hockett's practice would have been bearable with three Rolls-Royces.

Everyone seemed to like Razzy, and I soon became as fond of him as the rest of his employees. He was a shrewd clinician who had the supreme medical gift of always knowing whether a patient was really ill or not; he was an equally shrewd business man, whose polite patter about money always made people give him more and accept less. The only faintly shady part of the practice was our electrocardiograph, an instrument for taking electrical records of the heart, which represented the conflict between Razzy the doctor and Razzy the financier: he knew that as a diagnostic aid it was almost useless, but he hated not seeing a return on his capital. It was an old model, as untidy as an experimental television set, but every time he set out on a professional visit the electrocardiograph followed in its Rolls. The only occasion I saw Razzy looking worried after the case of the Duke's corn plasters was the morning he returned from an urgent call to a newspaper owner, who had suffered a stroke in the bathroom.

'A near thing, dear boy,' he told me, as he came

through the door shaking his head. 'A damn near thing.'

'What, did you pull him through?'

'Oh, no, the old boy's dead. But I only got the electro-cardiograph there in the nick of time.'

Our most constant, and most profitable, patients in the practice were several dozen neurotic women, all of whom were in love with Razzy. He had long, soothing telephone conversations with them frequently during the day, and they often appeared dramatically at the front door in the evening, dressed up like an advertisement for Cartier's.

'Yes, of course, they're in love with me, dear boy,' he stated one day. 'Speaking quite objectively, it's the only thing that keeps most of them from suicide. What else would you expect me to do?'

'But surely, Razzy,' I protested, 'don't you sometimes find it rather awkward?'

'Not in the least, dear boy. I don't have to be in love with *them*.'

My spell in Razzy's practice was delightful; I soon forgot Dr Hockett, Jasmine, and the Wilkins family, and even managed to shift Wilson, Willowick, and Well-beloved from the front of my mind. Although I was never allowed to treat the aristocracy again, he let me try my hand at a few actors and an M.P. or two, until I had worked my way so deeply into the practice that a reminder of my impermanence came as a shock.

'I'm seeing my partner tomorrow,' Razzy said one Saturday morning, when I had been with him over two months. 'He's coming along famously. Absolutely famously. We'll have him back in another few weeks.'

'I'm glad,' I lied.

'And I expect you're simply itching to get back to the Himalayas again, aren't you, dear boy?'

'Well, not itching exactly – '

'I'm so pleased you came to help us out. You've done terribly well, you know. All my old dears think the world of you. The wife of that Coal Board fellow told me yesterday you were a pet.'

'I'll certainly be sorry to leave. I've even thought of having a go at a practice somewhere round here myself.'

For a second Razzy's eyes narrowed. 'I wouldn't advise it, dear boy. I really wouldn't. It's quite a dog's life really. The struggle to get started – terrible! And the competition. Most frightful. You'd be far better off in the Himalayas.'

There were no patients waiting, so we stood for a while looking silently out of the window. It was a brilliant spring day, the buds on the trees in Hyde Park were straining like hatching chicks, the passers-by were stepping along jauntily without their overcoats, and even the Park Lane traffic smelt warmly exciting.

'Spring, dear boy' said Razzy with a contented sigh, as if hearing that a millionaire had fallen a couple of floors down our lift-shaft. He stayed watching the people hurrying away for their week-ends. 'Do you know, dear boy, I haven't had an afternoon off since I met that fellow Grimsdyke at the races? That's the sort of practice we're in. Always on tap. It's what they pay for I suppose.' After a pause he added, 'I know it's your free afternoon, but I wondered if you'd care to do a little fort-holding?'

'More than delighted, Razzy. Honestly.'

'Bless you, dear boy. Then I'm off to Sunningdale. I'll dine out and turn up about midnight in case there are any messages. Everyone will be out of town on a week-end like this, anyway.'

After lunch he changed into flannels, rang up a well-known film actress and persuaded her to keep him company, picked up his clubs, and set off for the links in the number one Rolls. Alone in the flat, I slipped off my shoes and sprawled on the soft curtained couch used for examining patients in the consulting-room. Beside me I arranged a pile of the *New Yorker* and *Life*, *Recent Advances in Surgery*, a reprint of *The Citadel*, a box of chocolates I'd found in the secretary's desk, and the bottle of *Cordon Bleu* brandy kept in the medicine cupboard. I hoped that Razzy had an enjoyable day off, but I saw no reason for working on a Saturday afternoon myself in discomfort.

Before he had been away half an hour the door-bell rang. I jumped up, pulled on my shoes, swiftly pushed my comforts under the couch, and opened the door. On the mat was a tall, amiable-looking man with a droopy white moustache, who wore a tweed suit and carried a heavy dispatch-case embossed with the Royal cypher in gold.

'Good afternoon,' he said pleasantly. 'I have an appointment with Dr Potter-Phipps.'

I looked puzzled.

'My private secretary arranged it earlier in the week. I'm afraid Saturday afternoon is my only free time at present. I hope it is not unduly inconvenient for the doctor?'

'I'm terribly sorry, but there's been a mistake,' I said, letting him in. 'Dr Potter-Phipps is away at the moment. I'm his assistant. Just a minute, and I'll look at the book.'

'Thank you. My name is Beecham. It seemed simpler to call here than to ask him to visit me.' He smiled. 'And no doubt more economical.'

'But I'm afraid the appointment was made for *next* Saturday.'

'Oh, dear! How infuriating. This is not the first time such a mistake has occurred. And next Saturday I shall be in Edinburgh.' He assessed me. 'Perhaps I could have a consultation with you instead, Doctor? I did rather want to be off to the country this lovely afternoon.'

'I should be very pleased,' I told him, with a brief bow. 'Kindly come into the consulting-room.'

'You will be wanting my medical history first, no doubt,' he went on, as he sat down. 'I have it specially tabulated in my mind. Age, sixty-one. Married. Occupation, cabinet minister. Usual childhood complaints. I'm not going too fast?'

'Did you say "cabinet minister?" ' That was flying high, even for us.

'I am the Minister of Inland Development,' he added modestly, as though referring to a favourable golf handicap. I suddenly remembered seeing his photograph in the papers a week ago, snipping a tape and giving the country another bridge. He seemed a pleasant old boy, but as I had never even seen a cabinet minister before I wondered how to address him. I decided to play for safety, and treat him roughly like a duke.

'Of course, sir,' I said. 'I'm – I'm terribly sorry not to have recognized you at once. Please forgive me. Now perhaps you'd be so kind as to allow me to ask you a few questions?'

He folded his arms. 'Of course, Doctor. Do exactly what you wish. I place myself entirely in your hands. As I was saying to the Minister of Health yesterday, what on earth's the use of seeing a doctor if you don't follow his advice, disregarding entirely your own opinion of the complaint? He said your own opinion of the doctor was possibly more important.' My patient smiled. 'Of course, he was only joking. He has quite a wit.'

'Oh, quite. Now what's the trouble, sir?'

As the Minister seemed to be suffering from pains connected with the spinal column, I pointed to the examination couch and told him to take his clothes off.

'*All* my clothes, Doctor?'

'Yes, please. I want a good look at you.'

'Anything you say, of course.'

I had just drawn the curtains round him as he started unbuttoning his waistcoat, when the bell rang again.

'Just a minute,' I said.

On the doormat I found an attractive, tall, dark woman with a mink cape slipping off her shoulders, who clutched at her throat and cried, 'Oh, God! Oh, God! I'm going to die!'

All I could think of saying was, 'Here I say, steady on!' She pushed past me, threw herself on the waiting-room couch, and burst into tears.

I quickly shut off the Minister of Inland Development in the consulting-room.

'If I can possibly help you, dear lady,' I said anxiously, 'I certainly will. But if you could perhaps control yourself a little – '

'Razzy!' she cried. 'Razzy, darling! Where is he?'

'Dr Erasmus Potter-Phipps happens to have taken the afternoon off. He's playing golf.'

'He's with another woman,' she sobbed. 'Janet said he'd asked that bitch Helen.'

'Well, dash it, only golf,' I murmured. I began to feel I was not showing the mastery of the situation expected from the medical attendant. During my two months in Park Lane I had learned more about handling difficult people than in five years at St Swithin's, where most o↓

98

the patients treated the doctors with the same frightened respect they gave the police; but the dynamic women in Dr Potter-Phipps' unilateral love-life were beyond me.

The girl moaned, covered her face with her hands, and cried, 'What shall I do? What shall I do? I want to die, that's all. To die – to die –'

As I was deciding what to try next, she suddenly looked up as if she had never seen me before.

'Who are you?' she asked.

'I'm Dr Potter-Phipps' assistant,' I said politely. 'Can I help you?'

'*No one* can help me!' Her face was pale, her eye-shadow was streaked down her cheeks, her hat was awry with emotion. Suddenly she threw aside her arms and began to scream.

My visitor had at least no disease of the respiratory system. There was nothing of the wronged woman's sobs about her: when she screamed, she took a deep breath, braced her larynx, and let fly like the knocking-off whistle in a shipyard.

'Please, please!' I shouted. 'Can't you compose yourself?'

She immediately drew another breath and started again, now pummelling her forehead with her fists, and hammering her heels on the floor.

By now I was less worried about her clinical condition – she was obviously well filled with the life force – than about my reputation. The most solemn piece of clinical advice we had received in St Swithin's was never to treat a female patient unless a nurse was present; and any minute now the door would probably be broken down by the porters, the police, or the fire brigade, all thirsting to play St George.

'Damnation!' I cried. 'Stop it!'

She settled herself in a higher key, and continued. Here was a major clinical problem: the gynaecological instruction at St Swithin's was excellent, but had included no advice on the way to treat hysterical women single-handed. Fortunately, I remembered from reading novels that the traditional remedy was a sharp slap across the face, and overcoming the inhibitions of an English public school education I crouched down and caught her a smart smack on the left cheekbone. Instead of this quelling her, she immediately countered with a powerful left uppercut which knocked me off my balance, and started picking up all the movable pieces of furniture in the waiting-room and throwing them at me.

I managed to struggle to my feet from a pile of broken china and glass, torn magazines, and telephone directories, just in time to prevent her concussing me with the standard-lamp.

'What the devil do you think you're up to?' I demanded angrily. I gripped her arms. 'Are you trying to kill me or something?'

'You struck a woman!' Through her redistribution of energy she had thankfully stopped screaming. 'You cad!'

'Of course I did! For your own good, you idiotic female. Why, you're as hysterical as a cat stuck in a chimney-pot!'

She looked at me closely, narrowing her eyes. 'I hate you!' she hissed. Then she fell into my arms and collapsed into humble tears.

After some minutes of patting her on the back and murmuring consolation I said, 'Don't you think you ought to go home and lie down? If you like I'll give you a prescription for a sedative. Have a good sleep – you'll feel ever so much better.'

She blew her nose miserably. 'I'll stay here until Razzy comes back.'

'But Dr Potter-Phipps may be away all night. I mean, he might have to go to a case somewhere after his golf,' I said quickly. 'I'd go home now if I were you.'

Still clutching me, she asked pathetically, 'Take me home. Please take me. I couldn't face it. Not alone.'

'Really, that's asking rather a lot, you know.'

'Please! It's not far.'

I hesitated. 'Oh, all right, then.' I had to get rid of her somehow. 'If you promise to behave yourself on the way.'

She nodded her head. 'I promise,' she said, like a penitent schoolgirl.

I left the flat, and helped her down the stairs to the street. I called a taxi and we got in together.

'Who is there to look after you?' I asked.

She shook her head.

'Haven't you any relatives or friends you could get hold of?'

'I hate them all.'

I turned and stared at the beautiful blue and gold afternoon outside and wished I had been Dr Potter-Phipps' caddie.

The girl lived at the far end of Curzon Street, and we drove along in silence. Suddenly she announced more cheerfully. 'You know, I've been a bloody fool.'

I swung round, and found her carefully doing her make-up.

'I must say you've been acting a little oddly, even for this part of the world.'

She smiled for the first time. 'I *am* a silly thing, aren't I? Fancy getting all worked up like that. I suppose I did have rather a lot to drink at lunch time. That always sends me off the rails a bit. Didn't you think I was crazy?'

'It did cross my mind to send for the strong-arm squad, I admit.'

'I'm so glad you didn't. And such a heavenly day, too!' She closed her compact with a snap. 'Here we are. Won't you come in for a minute and have a drink? I should think you need one.'

'I really don't think I should – '

'Come on! I'll ring the exchange and have your calls put through to my number. Razzy often does.'

I wavered. Being alone with female patients was bad enough; going to their flats afterwards for drinks would certainly raise every eyebrow on the General Medical Council. Still, it was spring. . . .

'Just a quick one, then,' I said.

'My name's Kitty,' she told me, opening the door. 'I've only got a very tiny flat, but make yourself at home. Razzy does.'

The flat would have taken my Bayswater room a dozen times, and was furnished with an amiable extravagance that must have taken Razzy's fancy. Kitty immediately threw open the window, took a deep breath, and trilled, 'Spring, spring, spring! Isn't it lovely? Don't you adore the spring? With the primroses and the cowslips and the bluebells and things? I swore I'd have a window-box this year. What'll you have to drink, darling '

'I've started on brandy this afternoon already, I'm afraid. So I suppose I'd better go on, if you've got any.'

'Sure, my pet. Brandy it is. The place is stiff with it.'

She brought from the cupboard two tumblers, and a bottle with a plain label bearing only a crown and the date 1904.

'Here, steady on,' I called, as she half-filled both glasses. 'I'm sure that stuff's supposed to be drunk by the thimbleful.'

'Here's to life,' she said, taking a large drink. 'That's better!' Then she sat on the sofa beside me. 'Tell me about yourself.'

'There's not much to tell.' I licked my lips, savouring the brandy. 'I'm Dr Potter-Phipps's temporary assistant, that's all.'

'You're very young to be a doctor.'

'As a matter of fact – and it must prove something, because I wouldn't tell it to everybody – I haven't been a doctor very long.'

'I could tell you hadn't much practical experience the moment I fell into your arms in your flat.'

'Oh, dear! And I thought I was being such a commanding figure.'

She laughed.

'By the way,' I said modestly. 'I'm sorry I clocked you one.'

'And I'm sorry I clocked you one, too, Doctor darling.'

We both laughed and had some more brandy. After a while, everything seemed to become very cosy.

'It must be wonderful being a doctor,' she said dreamily. 'Curing people who are stricken.'

'There isn't all that much curing in it. And fortunately most of the people arriving on our doormat aren't very stricken.'

'But it's lovely to have someone to sympathize with you and hold your hand and tell you you're wonderful. even if you're not really ill. That's where Razzy's so marvellous. Have you noticed his eyes?' She threw back her head. 'Hypnotic! Cruelly hypnotic.'

'I'm afraid I can't reach those heights, but I can

certainly sympathize with you and –' I held her hand –
'tell you you're wonderful.'

'You're sweet,' she said, getting up. 'I'm going to
change.'

I helped myself to another half-tumbler of her brandy,
which had the effect of producing a pleasant conscious
detachment from the world, like addiction to morphia.
I recognized cheerfully that I was getting myself into a
dangerous situation. My conduct was certainly becoming
infamous in a professional respect, for Kitty's entering
our waiting-room and smashing the furniture on my
head had placed us henceforward in a professional relationship. What should I do about it? I felt in my wallet
for the B.M.A. booklet on *Ethics*, and turning over the
pages found a great deal of sound advice on the size of
doctor's door-plates, fee-splitting, and association with
the clergy, but nothing on the tantalizing frontier between professional and social obligations where I was
now dancing. A faint, fresh breeze rustled the curtains
and a bird started singing on the window-ledge. And
what the hell! I thought. It's spring. I put the book
away and drank some more brandy.

Kitty came back wearing a négligé.

'How's it going?' she asked cheerfully.

'I'm responding to treatment. Have some more of
your brandy. Liquor should be quaffed, not sipped.'

'Here's to life, Doctor darling.'

'Here's to you, patient pet.'

We drank with linked arms. With a sigh, she stretched
herself on the sofa. She held out her arms and smiled.

'Doctor darling,' she murmured invitingly.

I licked my lips. There was a terrible risk making
love to a patient. . . . But, damn it! Alone with a beautiful woman. Wasn't it worth it? Was I a man or a

mouse? Anyway, I couldn't possibly disappoint her. . . .

'Come to me,' she breathed.

How lovely she looked! But how much more lovely she would look lying there without any clothes on at all. . . .

I jumped up. 'Get me a taxi!' I shouted. 'Quick!' And what, I wondered, would I now say to the Minister of Inland Development.

II

WHEN I dashed into the flat I found a note neatly pinned to the examination couch:

Dear Doctor

I fear that some dire emergency has called you away. I fully realize the trials of a doctor's life, and that some poor soul is in a worse state than me. However, lying on your couch seems to have relieved the discomfort, and as I am so anxious to get away this afternoon I will go round the corner to an osteopath recommended by the Minister of Works. With thanks for your attention.

Yrs,
George Beecham

I had lost Razzy a patient, but my personal honour, and probably my professional life, were saved by the politician. I hoped he would become Prime Minister, and since that afternoon I have always read his speeches in the newspapers.

I did not tell Razzy the full story until the day that I was leaving the practice.

'Really?' he said mildly. 'Poor Kitty! I wonder what on earth you did to her psychology, bolting like that. I really must go round and see her soon.'

'And another thing,' I said gazing at the carpet, 'there aren't any Himalayas. As far as I'm concerned, I mean. I wasn't going to let on about it, but – well, you've been so good to me, Razzy, I hadn't the heart not to confess I've worked here under false pretences.'

'But I'm glad, dear boy. Terribly glad. Frightfully

uncomfortable it must be, in all that snow and ice. So what other plans have you?'

'I thought I'd stay on in London for a bit and work for my Fellowship. Thanks to you, I've got a few quid in the bank to pay the rent, and I might be able to make a little by standing-in for doctors at week-ends. You see', I told him solemnly, 'I'm still determined to become a surgeon.'

'And good luck to you, dear boy,' he added indulgently, as though I were a schoolboy saying I wanted to be an engine-driver. 'I've always found surgery fascinating. Completely fascinating. Let me know if there's ever anything I can do for you. Would you like a bonus? The secretary will fix it up – you know I loathe discussing money.'

We shook hands, and I stepped from out of the glossy picture of fashionable medicine for ever.

I now had saved enough to pay off my hundred-pound debt to Wilson, Willowick, and Wellbeloved, and to maintain a modest medical-student standard of living until the Primary Fellowship examination of the Royal College of Surgeons in six weeks' time. I kept my room in Bayswater, took copies of Gray's *Anatomy* and Starling's *Physiology* from Lewis's medical lending library, borrowed a box of bones from a friend at St Swithin's, and continued my surgical career.

The Fellowship, like all British post-graduate examinations, is run on the Grand National principle, except that the highest fence is placed immediately in front of the tapes. Before you can enter for the Final exam you have first to pass the Primary in anatomy and physiology, subjects which are learnt in the second year of medical school and forgotten in the fourth. I had now to reopen the pages I had sweated over on coffee-drenched nights five years ago, unpleasantly aware that such traditional *aides-memoire* for the student as:

> The lingual nerve
> Took a swerve
> Around the Hyoglossus –
> 'Well I'm mucked!'
> Said Wharton's duct,
> 'The blighter's double-crossed us!'

were inadequate for the Fellowship examiners, who wanted to know the exact seventy-four relations of the lingual nerve and what it did in the monkey, dog, and rabbit as well.

I worked at my books fairly happily, for three months in Razzy's practice had given me the feeling of being a man of the world who could deal with dukes, manage cabinet ministers, and chum along with beautiful women, and could therefore confidently approach such prosaic individuals as the Fellowship examiners. This was my first mistake.

My second mistake was arriving for the examination in my black jacket and striped trousers. I had learnt in my first year as a medical student that the correct wear for facing examiners was a well-pressed, neatly-darned, threadbare old suit, which invited them to take a kindly attitude of superiority; appearing in a Savile Row outfit was like arriving at the Bankruptcy Court in a Rolls. But this did not occur to me as I made my way through the crowd of candidates in Queen Square.

Before the war the Fellowship was a private affair, in which a few dozen young men were treated to an afternoon's intellectual chat with the examiners and the proceedings were said to be interrupted for tea. Since the

National Health Service the examination has been run on mass-production lines, but the traditional politeness of the examiners is steadfastly maintained. They politely made no comment on my Harley Street appearance, beyond smiling a little more heartily than usual in greeting; they brushed aside my ignorance of the precise location of the middle meningeal artery as unimportant among friends; they accepted my inability to identify the pathological specimens in glass jars as understandable between surgical gentlemen. The last examiner politely handed me a pickled brain and said, 'That sir, was removed post-mortem from a man of seventy. What do you find of interest in it?'

After a while I admitted, 'I see only the usual senile changes, sir.'

'They are not unusual, these changes, you mean, sir?'

'Oh, no, sir! After all, the patient *was* senile.'

'Alas,' he said gently. 'And I shall be seventy-six myself next birthday. Thank you, sir, for reminding me that I am rapidly getting past it all. Good day to you, sir.'

Politely, they thanked me; politely they bowed me out; just as politely they failed me.

Because I had been over-confident this depressed me more deeply than ploughing any of my student examinations. Once more I began opening my *British Medical Journal* from the back, but I was so dispirited that all I could bring myself to read in the rest of the pages was the obituaries. These are prepared on the first-, second-, or third-class funeral principle, overworked G.P.s succumbing in early life getting small print at the end, consultants larger type well-spaced out, and leaders of the profession whom everyone has thought dead long ago appearing with a photograph taken when they were twenty-four. All that could be said about the majority of dead doctors seemed to be that they were kind to their patients, popular with their colleagues, and liked walking in Ireland; at the most they had a disease named after them. I began to get deeply miserable about the futility of my profession, and wondered if I should have gone into the Church instead.

I found a part-time job helping a doctor in Brixton, and decided that if I gave up smoking I could afford to work for the next Primary Fellowship examination three months later. After a week I began to suspect he was doing abortions on the side, and I thought I'd better leave. My money was running out again, and I saw my Muswell Hill days returning: it was a moment of gathering depression. Then late one evening I had a telephone call from Grimsdyke.

'Where the devil have you got to, old lad?' he said crossly, as I leant on the coin-box in the hall and heard every door on the landing creak ajar. 'I've been trying to get you all over the place. Have you become a ruddy hermit, or something?'

'I've been working for my Primary.'

'Bit of a perversion this lovely weather, isn't it? I take it that now you've left Park Lane you're not in paid employment? Good. Then perhaps you could help me out. I've got an uncle who practises in the depths of the country – you know, simple rural G.P., beloved by all, full of homespun philosophy and never washes his hands – whose partner's off for his month's holiday. When I qualified I said I'd help him out, but unfortunately I have a pressing professional engagement elsewhere. Would you fill the breach?'

'I thought you *were* a country G.P.'

'On a different sort of level. Can't explain now. How about it?'

I hesitated. I wondered if it was wholly fair to judge Grimsdyke's relations by himself.

'Say you will, old lad,' he pressed. 'You can take your books and whistle through the work. It's a peaceful as a museum down there, but there's a nice pub next door and a pretty little bit in the post office if you feel like relaxation as well.'

'Tell me – is this uncle of yours married?'

Grimsdyke laughed. 'A widower. One daughter, permanently settled in Australia. How about it?'

I glanced round the dirty, stuffy hall of my lodgings, with the greasy green-baize board that would grow a crop of bills by next Friday morning.

'Well –'

'That's the spirit! I'll send you directions and a map. Can you start on Monday? The old boy's name is Farquharson. He's a funny old stick, but he thinks absolutely the world of me.'

After my first disastrous foray into general practice the prospect of playing the country G.P. for a month was alarming; also, I was a true Londoner who always felt uneasy beyond the friendly grin of the L.P.T.B. bus stops, or in the company of cows, sheep, cart-horses, goats, pigs, and other animals unknown in Leicester Square. But my confidence increased the next Monday afternoon as I drove Haemorrhagic Hilda deeper into the countryside, which wore a look of ripe and gentle peacefulness rarely captured outside brewers' advertisements. The village itself lay far from the main road, at the end of a winding lane in which a herd of cows, responding to the cow-attracting substance with which all cars are seemingly secretly coated by them anufacturers, licked Hilda over at their leisure. My new home consisted of a few houses, a couple of shops, the church, the vicarage, and the Four Horsehoes. In the middle was a triangular green on which a horse stared at me in offended surprise; across the green was Dr Farquharson's house, shaggy with creeper, its brass plate shining like a new penny in the sun, its front garden brilliant with flowers among which bees and wasps buzzed as contentedly as the people lunching off expenses in the Savoy Grill.

As Dr Farquharson was still on his rounds I was shown into the empty consulting-room by his housekeeper. This was a small, dark apartment tucked into the back of the house, containing a dirty sink, an old-fashioned sterilizer heated with a spirit lamp like a coffee machine, and an examination couch covered with white American cloth that looked as uninviting to lie upon naked as a fishmonger's slab. In one corner was a bookcase untidily filled with medical text-books, mostly by Scottish authors and all out of date; in another stood a dusty pile of old copies of the *B.M.J.* and *Lancet.* I shook my head sadly. Looking round, I could see no haemoglobinometer, no erythrocyte-sedimentation-rate apparatus, no sphygmomanometer, no microscope, no ophthalmoscope, no centrifuge, no auroscope, no patella hammer, no spatulae, no speculae, no proteinometer, no pipettes. . . . It seemed to me impossible for anyone to practise medicine in the room at all.

Dr Farquharson turned out to be a tall, bony Scot with thick white hair, gold-rimmed spectacles, and big nobbly hands. He was dressed in a pair of patched tweed trousers, a black alpaca jacket, a striped shirt, a wing collar, and a spotted bow tie.

'Afternoon, Gordon,' he said dryly, as though we had

parted just an hour ago. 'So you've come to help out an old fogy in the depths of the country, have you? How's that rascal of a nephew of mine?'

'He seems very well, sir.'

'How the Good Lord ever let him qualify I don't know. He hasn't half a brain in his head, and the rest of his cerebral space is filled up with a mixture of laziness and lubricity. Let's have a cup of tea.'

Tea was served under a mulberry tree in the garden by the housekeeper, whom Farquharson introduced as 'Mrs Bloxage, who's painstakingly kept my feet dry and my socks darned since my poor wife succumbed to *phthisis desperata* eighteen years ago.' We had raspberries and cream, tomato and cress sandwiches, brown bread and honey, buttered toast and home-made strawberry jam, scones and shortbread, and three kinds of cake. 'One of the few advantages for an out-of-date old man like me practising medicine in the back of beyond,' Farquharson continued, helping himself to more cream, 'is that the patients still bring you a little something out of the goodness of their hearts. They're simple souls, and haven't tumbled to it that the doctor's now a Civil Servant, like the Sanitary Engineer. What do you think of these raspberries?'

'Delicious, sir.'

'Aren't they? Old Mrs Crockett's varicose ulcer produces them year after year.'

When he had finished eating, Farquharson lit his pipe, pressed down the burning tobacco with a metal tongue spatula from his top pocket, and went on, 'The work's pretty easy round here, I suppose. There's hardly enough for two, especially this time of the year. But I'm glad enough to have someone to yarn to – I'm a bit of an old bore, you know. I was out in West Africa a good deal of my life. I settled down here because I totted up the ages on the gravestones across the way, and averaged out that this village has the lowest death rate in the country. I find plenty to interest myself in the natural history of the countryside – which includes the inhabitants. And in a couple of years the Government's going to chuck me out as too old and incompetent for anything except sitting on my backside and drawing my pension. God knows what I'll do then. But I'm rusty all right. Can't understand half the words in the *Lancet* these days.' He slapped me on the knee. 'You can put me right on all that, my lad. I suppose you know about these drugs they're bringing out like editions of the evening papers? You must give me a lecture on 'em some time. I'm just an old fogy of a country G.P.' He pulled a large gold watch from his pocket. 'I'm off to see a couple of patients before surgery. Settle in, and I'll see you for supper.'

Supper was cold salmon (the squire's gall-stones), cream cheese (the postmistress's backache), and to celebrate my arrival a glass of port (the vicar's hernia). Farquharson chatted entertainingly enough about West Africa, neatly comparing his native and his present patients, but I realized that he was as out of place in modern medicine as a jar of leeches. There were clearly several points on which I should be putting him right.

Within a week I discovered that medicine in the country is wholly different from medicine practised anywhere else. In the first place, most of the patient suffer from diseases totally unknown to medical science. At St Swithin's I examined my patients confident that their condition could be found somewhere between the green morocco covers of French's *Index of Diagnosis;* but in the country I puzzled over the significance of symptoms like horseshoes pressing on the head, larks in the stomach, and ferrets running up and down the spine at night. Even Dr Farquharson's former diagnoses were obscured by the patient's helpfully remembering the name, it taking me some time to recognize, for instance, that the woman complaining her child had been attacked by the infant tiger meant that he was suffering from impetigo.

Secondly, the visit of the medical attendant in most households provided less relief for the sufferer than entertainment for the rest of the family. The cry of 'Coo! it's the Doctor!' brought children running from their corners as powerfully as the smell of baking cakes. Arriving in the sickroom, I found it difficult to place the finger-tips together and demand with dignity, 'And how about the bowels?' when half a dozen small boys and girls were staring at me as though I were the hanging scene in a Punch-and-Judy show. When I insisted on having them shooed away they continued the enjoyment by taking turns to peer round the door, and my careful assessment of the pitch of a percussion note was often ruined by the awestruck whisper passing down the corridor, 'He's punching poor mummy all over the chest.'

In houses where there were no children, the patients reflected the more leisurely life of the country by using their attack of gastritis or summer flu to give the doctor a résumé of their life story and their opinions on their relatives. A brisk 'Good morning! And what can I do for you?' as I approached the bedside generally brought a contemplative folding of hands across the abdomen, a faraway look, a deep sigh, and the reply, 'Well, Doctor, in the 1914–18 war I was standing in a trench at Vimy . . .' or, 'I haven't been the same, Doctor, since that night me 'usband joined the Buffaloes. . . .'

When I mentioned these discoveries to Farquharson

after supper one evening, he said, 'Oh, folk need to unburden themselves a bit. They don't like boring their friends, and their relatives won't listen to 'em any more. They're scared of the parson, so the doctor's the only one left they can pour their hearts out to.' He began to scrape out the bowl of his pipe with a scapel he kept on the mantelpiece. 'I've got old-fashioned ideas, but that seems to me part of the doctor's job. That's something they never took into account when they got up this Health Service. Bloody silly, isn't it? Ask any G.P., and he'll tell you half his job is sympathizing with people, and that's ten times as difficult as treating 'em. Did you use the thermometer?'

'I couldn't – there's only one in the surgery, and it's broken.'

'It's broken all right. If I can't tell when a patient's feverish, I'm not much of a doctor. But shove it under their tongue, lad, and you've shut 'em up as long as you like. Or you can stick your stethoscope in your ears – it's not much good for anything else round here, because half of 'em think they'll drop dead if they take their vests off. Or you can take their pulse and scowl at 'em while you wonder what the devil's the matter. *That* shuts 'em up good and proper. You don't even need a watch. I couldn't afford a watch when I qualified, so I used to stare at my cupped hand instead, and nobody found out for eighteen months.

'As for the audience, always give 'em something to do. The public loves to see the vomit coming up or the baby coming down, but they love it even better playing the nurse. Get them to boil water – pots of it. When there aren't any saucepans left you can always start them tearing up the best sheets for bandages.' He lit his pipe, and went on reflectively, 'Never start off by asking a patient,

"What are you complaining of?" They'll say, "I'll have you know I'm not the complaining type, not like some I could mention", and start some rigmarole about their sister-in-law who's been living with them since Christmas. Don't try "What's wrong with you?" because they like scoring one over the doctor and they'll reply, "I thought that was what you were here to find out." That starts the consultation on the wrong foot. And never ask, "What brought you here?" because ten to one they'll tell you the tram or the ambulance. Always listen to a patient's story, however long it is and however much you want your dinner. Usually they've come about something quite different, and they're too embarrassed or too scared to bring it out. And always give 'em a bottle of medicine, even if you and the whole Pharmaceutical Society know it's useless – even a straw's a comfort to a drowning man. Never tell them they're an "interesting case". Patients have got enough sense to know the only interesting cases are the ones we don't know anything about.

'You can diagnose half your patients as soon as you step through their front door, with a bit of practice. Brass gongs on the wall and tiger skins on the floor mean high blood-pressure. Box of chocolates on the piano and a pekinese on the mat – that's obesity. Bills on the dresser and cigarette ash on the parlour carpet look like a duodenal ulcer upstairs. I've found aspidistras and antimacassars generally go with constipation. It's common sense. If you keep your eyes open you won't need the curate's legs sticking from under the bed to spot a case of female frustration. And never be squeamish asking about insanity in the relatives. I always start off, "How many in the asylum?" and you'd be surprised at the answers I get, even in the best families. But I'm rambling,' he said apologetically. 'You talk for a change. Seen any good cases today?'

'There was an unusual psychiatric one. A farmer came in complaining that he experienced a strong sexual sensation every time he blew his nose.'

Farquharson stared at his burning tobacco. 'Well, now, that is interesting. What did you say?'

'Nothing much. I'm not well up in psychiatry. What would you have done?'

'I should have told him' said Farquharson without hesitation, 'that some people get all the luck.'

For the first time it occurred to me that Dr Farquharson knew much more medicine than I did.

12

DURING my month in the practice I gained six pounds in weight, took on a deep sunburn, and learned more practical physic from Farquharson than I had gained from the whole staff of St Swithin's. The remaining gaps in my education were completed by the village constable, who was the fattest policeman outside pantomime, and seemed to have the single duty of supervising the nightly closing of the Four Horseshoes from the inside. After a pint or two he would unbutton his tunic and solemnly recount the medico-legal history of the countryside. 'It was but a year ago, as I recall,' he would begin with the air of a surgeon discussing a grave case with a colleague, 'that we had an indecency down at Smith's farm.' He frowned as he took some more beer. 'I can't remember off-hand whether it was a *gross* indecency, or just an ordinary one. But you'd be surprised what goes on round 'ere, Doctor. Why, we gets at least an indecent exposure once a week.' He continued to describe some of his recent cases in the odd anatomical terms used only by the police force. 'Mind you, it's hard work, Doctor,' he added proudly. 'You've got to be sure of your facts. It was only at the last Assizes there was an 'ell of a row because we had a case concerning a mare, and the barrister got hold of the idea it was one with a gold chain round his neck what we meant.'

A few days before I was due to leave, Grimsdyke paid a visit.

It was clear at once that he had enjoyed a change of

fortune. He roared up in a bright sports car, he wore a new tweed coat and a clean waistcoat, his shoes shone, his face was plumper and better shaved, his hair was tidy, and he had a brand-new monocle with a fine sparkle to it. He carried a pair of yellow gloves, and a bulldog puppy leapt at his heels. He looked like the young squire after a good day at the races.

Although Farquharson began by asking him how the devil he had got qualified and when was he going to start a decent job of work, Grimsdyke still seemed to imagine himself the favourite nephew. Only when his uncle's conversation had been reduced to a string of grunts he suggested the pair of us went out to the Four Horseshoes.

'The market seems to be doing well of late,' I observed, as we entered the bar.

'The market? Oh, yes, yes, of course. It's bouyant. By the way, I believe there's a few bob I owe you. Care for it now? Don't mind taking fivers, do you, it's all I've got? Cigarette – I suppose you like these black Russian things? Now let's have a drink. What can I get you?'

'A pint of bitter.'

'Beer? Nonsense! We'll have champagne! This is an occasion – the beginning of a great medical partnership. You know, Banting and Best, Florey and Fleming, Orth and Pettenkofer, and all that. I'll explain in a minute. Landlord! Your best vintage!'

The effect was lessened by the landlord of the Four Horseshoes having only a beer licence, so we had some Special Christmas Brew instead.

'Now what is all this,' I began firmly, wondering what trouble Grimsdyke was concocting for me and determined to stay clear of it.

'Have you had a go at the Primary yet?' he interrupted.

'Yes. The examiners were very undiscerning.'

'If you must wear a hair-shirt,' he said chidingly, 'you deserve to be tickled. Didn't you find out where they printed the examination papers? Some of these printer chaps'll do anything for a few quid.'

'I thought I'd better fail honestly, at least.'

'Quite right. I've been a great believer in professional honesty myself since old Moronic Maurice told me how he got through his surgical finals. At about the eighth shot, I might add. You know, those cases they got up for the exam – all the old chronics, the harvest of every out-patients department in London. Maurice spent a couple of months nosing around the teaching hospitals until he was pretty confident he'd seen all the old familiar faces. Of course, he sneaked a bloody good look at their notes to see what was wrong. He went into the exam room knowing he'd already examined and diagnosed every case in the place, which he said gave him a wonderful feeling of confidence.'

'There's nothing very honest about that.'

'But wait a minute. The examiner grabbed him by the sleeve, and to his horror started dragging Moronic Maurice towards the one patient in the place he didn't recognize. Maurice realized it was the moment for honesty. "Sir," he said solemnly, "I feel I must inform you that I have already had an opportunity to examine this particular case in the hospital." "Very truthful of you, my lad", the old boy said. "Come and have a look at one of these over here instead." So he got through.'

'Quite. Now if you'll explain what new villainy you're up to – '

'By the way, I forgot to mention we're both out of debt to that trio of sabre-toothed tigers, Wilson, Willowick, and Wellbeloved.'

'Both?'

'I strode in there the other day to fling their filthy lucre in their faces. It was such a pleasant experience I flung a bit more for you, too. Here are the IOUs. We might have a pretty little ceremony burning them in the Piccadilly Bar, don't you think?'

'Look here,' I said in alarm. 'You're not doing anything dishonest, are you? I mean, false certificates and abortions and things?'

Grimsdyke looked pained. 'Have you ever known me try anything underhand outside the examination hall? No, old lad, it's simple. I'll let you into the secret. Through family influence, I've got myself a good job. Personal doctor to old Lady Howkins – you know, widow of the bloke that grabbed half Johannesburg and has been digging up useful little bits of gold ever since. She lives in a ruddy great house near Gloucester. She's as mean as a tax collector in the usual way, but she's pretty lavish with the cash to yours truly – '

'You mean you're a sort of clinical gigolo?'

Grimsdyke slapped down his glass in annoyance. 'Damn it, I pay your bloody debts – '

'I'm sorry. But you must admit it looks fishy on the face of it. Even you wouldn't admit you're a second Lord Horder.'

'Look, Lady Howkins is ninety-four, and to my mind as crazy as a coot. But fortunately, like my grandmother, she's crazy about doctors. All I do is recite to her the miracles of modern medicine, some of which I know and some of which I mug up in the *Reader's Digest*, and she thinks it's wonderful. She's fascinated by technical stuff. She knows more about things like isotopes and gastroscopes than I do. And she's bound to kick the bucket any day now.'

'And you'll be out of a job.'

'Yes, and no. I have it on good authority she's left me a terrific packet in her will. Think of it, old lad! Thousands of quids in the kitty, tax-free just like the football pools! And that's where you come in. I thought we might go off for a nose round the Bahamas or somewhere, and set up a little clinic for tired newspaper owners, film stars, and so forth. You'd do the medicine, with your Park Lane touch, and I'd fix the business side – you must admit, even though I may not know an appendix from an adenoid, I've a sharp eye for juggling the cash. What do you say?'

'Say? Damn it, this is a bit startling – '

'Think it over. Coming to the hospital dinner next month?'

I nodded.

'We'll discuss it again then. Don't think you're going to use ill-gotten gains, old lad, because they're not. I dance attendance like any other G.P., and call in specialists to the old dear as needed. If it wasn't for me she might be shared by dozens of Harley Street sharks. Lots of people leave money to their doctors, anyway. Must be damn brave,' he added reflectively. 'Have another?'

I shook my head. 'I've got to see some patients. One thing I've learned in general practice, if you smell faintly of alcohol just once, the word goes round by next morning that the doctor's a drunkard.'

'Have one of these.' Grimsdyke said, producing a tube of tablets. 'Chlorophyll removes all unpleasant odours. Fools patients and policemen alike.'

'Don't delude yourself. The goats round here eat it all day, and you should have a sniff at them.'

*

123

The St Swithin's reunion dinner was held every year in the Moorish Room of a huge banquet factory off Piccadilly Circus, and was anticipated by most of the guests as eagerly as Christmas in an orphanage. The majority of St Swithin's graduates were hardworking G.P.s scattered across the country, who faced ruin by being seen in the local pub or having more than two small ones in the golf club; the reunion dinner was their only chance to shed their inhibitions and splash for a while in the delightful anonymity of London.

I had arranged to meet Grimsdyke in the Piccadilly Bar before the dinner, which was five weeks later. He arrived in a new dinner-jacket with a red carnation in the buttonhole, smoking a cigar and looking jubilant.

'Well, old lad?' he demanded at once. 'Have you decided?'

'I've thought the matter over very carefully,' I told him. 'I must admit I'm a bit scared of the scheme, but my present system of casual employment is precarious, and I see no future for myself anywhere in England as a surgeon. So I'll come with you.'

'Capital!'

'The only snag seems to be that this patient of yours might quite easily live to be a hundred, and by that time will certainly have found out that you are simply an unprincipled – '

'But haven't you heard, old lad? Haven't you heard? The old dear snuffed it last week. Frightful pity of course, but who wants to live longer than ninety-four? And look at this – ' He pulled a long letter from his pocket, typed on solicitor's paper. 'It came this morning – ten thousand quid! Ten thousand! Think of it! All for yours truly. Don't bother to read it all now, it's full of legal stuff. Shove it in your pocket. What an evening we're going to have! Barman! Champagne – the best in the house!'

We arrived in high spirits at the dinner, and found the Byzantine ante-room full of prosperous-looking middle-aged gentlemen in dinner-jackets, all drinking like pirates. The function always followed a strict ritual, and at eight o'clock the Dean himself climbed on a table and announced that dinner was served. This was a signal for the middle-aged gentlemen to cry 'Limerick! Limerick!' until the Dean coughed, and obliged tradition by reciting in his lecture-room voice:

> '*Ah – There was an old man of Manchuria*
> *Who had the most painful dysuria.*
> *The unfortunate chap*
> *Had not only got clap*
> *But haematoporphyrinuria.*'

This brought the house down.

Grimsdyke and myself, with our old friends Tony Benskin and Taffy Evans, sat round the foot of one table with Mr Hubert Cambridge, who was one of the most popular of St Swithin's surgeons through being entertainingly eccentric. While the waiter with the chronic sinusitis was serving the chemical soup, Grimsdyke insisted on ordering champagne for all five of us.

'But, my dear boy, can you afford it?' Mr Cambridge asked. 'I assure you that pale ale is good enough for me.'

'Sir,' Grimsdyke said solemnly, 'it is a token of our appreciation of your tuition at St Swithin's. Within an hour the champagne will be carbon dioxide and water – but your teaching will remain with us all our lives.'

'And the Dean says the standard of our students is dropping!' he said, rubbing his hands. 'Tell me, what are the names of your excellent young men?'

After the soup came the mummified turbot, wearing its funeral wreath of shrivelled shrimps; next, the poor arthritic chicken, the devitaminized cabbage, the vulcanized potatoes; then the deliquescent ice and the strange compost on toast. Afterwards, we faced with British composure the stern British discipline which emphasizes that life is not all feasting and gaiety – the speeches. They were always long at the St Swithin's dinner, because the speakers were in the habit of lecturing for a full hour at a time to their students without fear of interruption. First the Dean told us what jolly good chaps St Swithin's men were; then the visiting medical Lord told us what a jolly good chap the Dean was; then the Senior Surgeon told us what jolly good chaps everyone was. After that we were released into the Gothic Smoking Room to sing the old student songs, while the Dean played the piano and the visiting Lord conducted with a loaf of French bread. We sang about the unfortunate adventures of The Baker's Boy Who to the Chandler's Went, The Honest Woman and the Rogue, The Man Who went Fishing With Line and Rod, and of the wildly psychopathic evening in Kerriemuir. It was difficult to see anyone in the room ever gripping their lapels and declaring, 'No starchy foods, no alcohol, and no smoking – the human body's not a machine, y'know.' But all of them would be saying it tomorrow morning, sterner than ever.

In the excitement of the evening I had almost forgotten that I was committed to an alarming medico-commercial adventure. I was paying the waiter for a round of drinks when Grimsdyke's letter fell from my pocket. Concentrating, I began to read it in the light of one of the Tudor wall-lanterns.

Grimsdyke had just reached the top note in the

St Swithin's version of 'She Was Poor But She Was Honest,' when I drew him carefully to one side.

'Are you sure you've read this letter through?' I asked.

'Of course I've read it,' he said crossly. 'Every word. All that guff about my being a dedicated young physician and all that.'

I nodded. 'Perhaps you'd better look at the last line again.'

'Last line? What are you up to, old lad? Some sort of joke?' He took the letter. 'It looks absolutely straightforward to me – "In recognition of your devoted service bequeaths to you the sum of ten thousand pounds – "' His voice trailed off. Like a man uttering his last words while suffering death in the garrotte he finished the sentence: ' "... for you to donate in its entirety within six months to the hospital performing medical research you consider the most rewarding." '

The letter fell to the floor.

'Hard luck, Grim,' I said sorrowfully. I summoned a waiter. 'You'd better swallow the rest of that tube of chlorophyll.'

13

THE reunion dinner nevertheless ended in a gust of ill wind that blew Grimsdyke and myself a little good. Long after we had sadly staggered back to our lodgings, Mike Kelly, a heavy young man who had captained the first fifteen for several years and was now Mr Hubert Cambridge's house surgeon, found himself standing on the empty pavement in his dinner-jacket with only tenpence in his pocket. He resigned himself to walking back to the hospital, deciding to go by way of Covent Garden because he had heard that the pubs opened in the early hours to slake the thirsts of the busy fruiterers. Unfortunately, alcohol always had a confusing effect on Mike Kelly, and after trying to buy a drink in St Peter's Hospital for Stone and Stricture under the impression that it was the Strand Palace Hotel, he demonstrated his belief that the Royal Opera House was a gentlemen's convenience. When a policeman shouted at him unnecessarily, ''Ere! What do you think you're doing?' Mike Kelly made what he thought at the time to be the smartest remark of his life. Beaming at the constable he announced benignly, 'Officer, I am picking bloody gooseberries.'

Mike was then taken to nearby Bow Street and charged with being drunk and disorderly. As his head began to clear in the sobering surroundings, he remembered the only fact that had ever struck him as useful in his forensic medicine lectures: if you are charged with being drunk, you can choose your own doctor to come and examine you. 'Disorderly, yes,' he said sternly to the sergeant. 'Drunk, definitely no. I bet my blood-alcohol isn't even point one per cent. I demand my own doctor at once.'

'All right by us. It'll save the police surgeon getting out of bed. And who is your doctor?'

'Doctor – ' Mike Kelly drew himself to add dignity to his words – 'John Harcourt Bottle, Master of Arts at the University of Cambridge, Licentiate of the Royal College of Physicians of London, member of the Royal College of Surgeons – '

'All right, all right. Where's he to be found?'

'Ring the Resident Medical Staff Quarters at St Swithin's Hospital. Ask for', continued Mike, deflating slightly, 'the Assistant Junior Resident Anaesthetist.'

John Bottle, who had been continuing the party with the other residents in his room on the top floor of the Staff Quarters, expressed himself indignant over the telephone that the police should have submitted a member of the medical profession to such shame. He spoke at some length, giving the sergeant his opinion on his conduct, demanding an immediate apology, hinting at substantial compensation, and threatening to write to his M.P. He then declared that he would summon a taxi and appear immediately to put this regrettable matter to rights. The result of his intervention was not one doctor being charged with being drunk and disorderly in Bow Street that night, but two.

This was too much, even for St Swithin's, whose staff and governors showed remarkable tolerance towards purple paint on the statues, cart-horses in the quadrangle, and cami-knickers flying from the flag-staff on the morning of the Lord Mayor's visit. To avoid disproportionate damage to their careers the Staff Committee sent Kelly and Bottle on unpaid leave for the rest of their appointment, leaving two gaps on the resident staff until the next batch of students qualified in three months' time. As Mike Kelly had brought himself to his confused state by sympathizing with Grimsdyke at the dinner, he suggested his misfortune might at least be turned to the gain of his friends. Grimsdyke and I hurried to St Swithin's to see Mr Cambridge, and introduced ourselves as the charming young gentlemen who had been so appreciative of his teaching the night before. The next day I had become his temporary senior house surgeon and Grimsdyke was assistant junior resident to the hospital's anaesthetics department.

'I'm only a ruddy stuffist,' Grimsdyke complained. 'But by George! we're lucky to get paid work at all in our present state. It's hard luck on old Mike, though.'

I too was sorry for our former classmates, but I was overwhelmingly delighted to be back in St Swithin's. The disappointment of my earlier departure was wiped out. I was at last a senior house surgeon, if not an official one; there were hopes of resuscitating my moribund surgical career; and it would be a delicious affront to Bingham.

I returned to the Staff Quarters, the tall, cold, sooty building between the hospital laundry and the mortuary that had been used as the ear, nose, and throat wards until condemned by the Governors as unfit for the housing of patients. Mike Kelly's room was next to the one allotted Bingham, who was hurrying down the corridor in his white coat as I struggled in with my luggage.

He pulled up short. We had not met since the incident in the lift. He seemed uncertain what to say. He looked more boyish, more untidy, more pimply than ever, and his stethoscope seemed to have increased in size until it entwined his neck like a rubbery vine.

'Hello, Bingham,' I said.

He swallowed. 'Hello, old chap. Heard you were coming back.'

'Look here,' I said, dropping my suitcase and holding out my hand. 'I'm sorry about that business of the bananas in the lift. It was damn bad manners on my part, but I was a bit upset at the time. About not getting the job, you know. Not that I'm saying you didn't deserve the promotion. But we've got to live next door to each other for a bit, so can't we forget the whole thing?'

'Of course, old chap,' Bingham said awkwardly. There was a short silence. 'I'm – er, sorry if I hogged all the cases in cas., and all that.'

'You deserved them, too.'

We shook. 'If you want any tips about the work, old chap,' Bingham went on, 'I can put you right. Only if you ask, of course,' he added quickly. 'The Prof.'s been jolly decent, and letting me try quite a bit off my own bat. I've done a couple of hernias and some piles already, and there's a nice excision of warts on the list for me tomorrow. Must buzz off now, old chap, there's a query tib. and fib. just come into cas. See you at supper.'

I went to my room feeling like the head girl at St Agatha's making it up with the lacrosse skipper.

My job as a senior house surgeon in St Swithin's was looking after the day-to-day needs of the patients in the wards, assisting in the operating theatre, and acting as a clinical valet to Mr Cambridge. This was my most difficult duty, because Mr Cambridge, though an excellent surgeon who had plucked more stomachs than anyone else in the hemisphere, was alarmingly absent-minded. His professional memory was excellent: he never forgot a stomach. Socially, he couldn't remember the day of the week, whether he had come out in his overcoat, what he was supposed to be doing in the afternoon, and if he had already had lunch. As a young surgeon he had arrived at St Swithin's from his lodgings one winter's morning to operate as usual, and was aware as he scrubbed up of a strange loneliness about the place. Not only was the surgeon's room silent, but peeping into the theatre itself he found it deserted, with the table under a dust-sheet. At first he thought he was in the wrong operating block, but there was his name on his locker, as plain as ever. Next, he wondered if it might be Sunday; but he was certain it was Wednesday, because he paid his landlady every Tuesday and he remembered that he had forgotten to give her the cheque yesterday. It then occurred to him that he had noticed a strangeness about the streets while driving to the hospital. Was there a sudden general strike, perhaps, sweeping up the doctors and nurses as it hurricaned upon them? He padded down the corridor in his operating clothes, white rubber boots, and surgical mask, to seek information. At the ward door he stopped short. It was most extraordinary. There appeared to be some sort of riot inside, with nurses and patients dancing round the beds. Clearly, revolution had broken out in St Swithin's. 'Why, hello, Mr Cambridge!' called the Sister from the door. 'Merry Christmas!'

My first morning on duty I waited in the quadrangle for Mr Cambridge's arrival, according to hospital tradition standing beneath the statue to its famous former surgeon, Sir Benjamin Bone.

'The Chief's getting late,' I said to the Registrar, a tall, thin, serious, but pleasant young man called Hatrick, who already had his F.R.C.S.

'There's nothing much you can do about it,' he said

gloomily. 'The last time the old boy didn't turn up I found he'd gone on an American lecture tour.

We were due to begin operating at nine, but it was almost half-past when Mr Cambridge came cheerily through the main gates on foot.

'Ah, good morning, my dear Mr Er – er, and my dear Mr Ah – ah,' he greeted us. He could never remember the names of his assistants, and I was thankful that he had managed to recall mine twelve hours after the reunion dinner. 'Sorry I'm late. Got my notes?' I handed him three or four envelopes, addressed in his own barely legible handwriting. Whenever he thought of anything he ought to remember the next day, he wrote it on a card and immediately posted it to himself at St Swithin's. 'Let's see, we operate this morning, don't we?' he continued, as we marched towards the surgical block. 'There's a most interesting gastrocolic fistula I'd like you to inspect Mr Er – And of course you too, Mr Ah – '

There followed one of the most painful mornings since I qualified. As a medical student I had occasionally been ordered to scrub-up, dress in a sterile gown, and join the surgeon's assistants, but once at the operating table I only played dummy in the surgical quartet. Occasionally I would be given a retractor and told, 'Hang on to that, boy!' but usually I was edged away as the surgeon became more interested in the operation and spent most of the time watching nothing more illuminating than the buckle on the back of his braces. But as a house surgeon I was a necessary member of the surgical team, responsible for cutting the stitches, clipping off the bleeding points, and fixing the dressings. Conscious of this, I pulled on my rubber gloves with unusual determination, and split them from thumb to cuff.

'Nurse!' The sister's voice rang across the theatre. 'Another pair of gloves for Mr Gordon!'

A small nurse, muffled in her theatre clothes, darted across the floor and drew a white glove packet from the sterile drum with a pair of long forceps.

'Thank you,' I mumbled. I was now so flustered that I forgot to powder my damp hands with the small gauze bag of talc, and could hardly force them inside the rubber at all. I seemed to have two fingers jammed in the thumb space, while the end of the glove danced about like seaweed in a strong tide.

'A case of multipollices, isn't it?' murmured the small nurse.

This increased my agitation, and I pulled the glove in two.

'Nurse!' cried the theatre Sister, more loudly. '*Another* pair of gloves for Mr Gordon.'

I pulled on the third pair intact, though there was a small empty space like the teat of a baby's bottle at the end of each finger. I anxiously made towards the table, pushing aside a surgical trolley in my way.

'That trolley is *unsterile*,' declared the theatre Sister, louder than ever. 'Nurse! A complete change of clothes for Mr Gordon!'

When I reached the patient the operation was almost over. Mr Cambridge merely murmured, 'Hello, Mr Er —ah – Will you take the second retractor from Mr Ah – er – ?' I determined to do my best and recover from the bad start, but I cut the stitches the wrong length, let the retractors slip, jammed my fingers in the handles of artery clips, and dropped several small instruments on the floor. Mr Cambridge seemed to take no notice. I decided that he was not only the politest surgeon in the hospital, but one of the cleverest in allowing for the assistance of fumbling house surgeons when planning his operating technique.

My only consolation that morning was watching Grimsdyke out of the corner of my eye. He was having a worse time than I was. When I had asked him at breakfast how he felt about giving anaesthetics he had replied lightly, 'Doing dopes? There's nothing to it. It's all done by machines these days – none of the old rag-and-bottle business any more. Just like driving a car. You twiddle a knob here, twiddle a knob there, and you're away.'

'Possibly – but supposing you make the mixture too rich?

'Too much choke, you mean? He started to laugh, but said, 'Sorry, old lad. Didn't mean it at breakfast. Anyway, it's perfectly simple to a chap with a mechanical mind like myself.'

'I suppose you've read up all the stages of anaesthesia, and so on?'

'Old lad, as far as I'm concerned there are only three stages of anaesthesia – awake, asleep, and dead.'

It was now clear that Grimsdyke knew nothing about the administration of anaesthesia whatever. He was sitting at the head of the table beside a large chromium-plated trolley thick with dials, and though only his eye and forehead were showing I had never seen him looking so worried since one of the pretty girls in the X-ray Department thought she was in the family way. Every now and then he hopefully turned a coloured tap, or buried under the sterile towels to look up Macintosh's *Essentials of Anaesthesia*, which he had propped against the unconscious patient's nose. Grimsdyke had come to the theatre confident that he would be expected only to assist the consultant anaesthetist, a cheerful fat man with the best stock of rude stories in London: but the consultant had the habit of returning to the surgeon's room and solving *The Times* crossword as soon as the patient was on the table, leaving his assistant at the controls.

Unlike most of the surgeons at St Swithin's, Mr Cambridge was considerate and polite to his anaesthetist. He made no remark about the grunts coming from beneath Grimsdyke's fingers, and an unexpected paroxysm of coughing from the patient left him unperturbed. Towards the end of the operation I was alarmed to feel something stir beneath the sterile towels. I glanced at Grimsdyke, but he had now given up the struggle and was leaning on the trolley with his eyes shut. To my horror the patient's arm came slowly into the air. 'Mr Anaesthetist,' said Mr Cambridge quietly, 'if the patient can keep awake during the operation, don't you think you might, too?'

When operating on other people's stomachs Mr Cambridge disregarded his own. As gastrectomy followed gastrectomy my fumbling became worse and I began to long for the release of lunch. After the fourth case the theatre Sister announced firmly as she handed me the dressing, 'We are stopping for an hour now, sir. It's two o'clock.'

'Two o'clock? Already? How the morning flies, Sister.'

'And there is a detective to see you.'

'Ah, yes. Which one this time?'

'Sergeant Flannagan.'

'Flannagan? Can't say I recall the name. What's he like?'

'Big and red-faced, sir,' said Hatrick.

'I know him very well. I'll be out directly. Just clean up the incision, will you Mr Ah – er – '

136

Mr Cambridge was well known to the Metropolitan Police because he was continually losing his car. As soon as he felt his feet as a surgeon he had bought the customary Bentley, but he either forgot where he had parked it, wondered if he had come out in it at all, or threw open the garage doors in the morning and found it wasn't there.

'This time I'm certain it's been stolen,' he explained to the policeman in the surgeon's room, as Hatrick, Grimsdyke, and I began tucking in to our cold congealed mutton stew. 'I came in by tube this morning, and I didn't have it out yesterday – I don't think so, anyway. But the day before, Sergeant Um – um, I distinctly remember I had it parked outside my rooms in Harley Street. When I came out I'm absolutely certain it was gone.'

The sergeant coughed. 'But why didn't you inform the police at the time, sir?'

'Well, you see, when I saw it had gone I was certain I hadn't brought it with me. You follow?'

'Quite,' said the sergeant.

Mr Cambridge disappeared after lunch to remove stomachs in another part of London, leaving Hatrick and myself to finish the list. As the consultant anaesthetist accompanied the surgeon, Hatrick pointedly told Grimsdyke that he would do the remaining minor operations under local. Grimsdyke took this as a slight, murmured something about, 'Any bloody fool with a sharp knife can be a surgeon,' and left the operating theatre in a huff. As the students had drifted away with the loss of their main attraction, and a milder staff nurse was substituted for the theatre Sister, the pair of us operated peacefully until nightfall. After the morning's exhibition I was then certain that I would never become a surgeon; but under Hatrick's gentle tuition I began to gain confidence.

'Always steady the blade of the scissors with your finger when you cut,' he murmured as I fumbled round the incision. 'Tuck them into the palm of your hand when you're not using them. Take the artery forceps with the *tips* of your fingers, so, then you won't get stuck. Tie a surgical knot like *this*, and you'll only have to use one hand. Never worry about cutaneous bleeding – it always stops. And use the *handle* of your scapel if in doubt – it does less damage.'

When we returned to the surgeon's room as the last case was wheeled away, we found Sergeant Flannagan waiting.

'Mr Cambridge has left the hospital,' I told him. 'Is there any message?'

'Yes. There is. We've found his car.'

'Oh, really? And where was it in the end?'

'Locked in his ruddy garage at home.'

14

MR CAMBRDIGE had charge of two wards at St Swithin's – Fortitude for men and Constancy for women – where my duties, though less exciting than in the operating theatre, were of more value to the hospital. Mr Cambridge himself skipped round the beds every Tuesday morning, his bedside manner consisting largely of poking a patient hard in the tummy and saying cheerfully, 'You'll be much better with it out.' Hatrick tidied up all the surgical odd jobs, and I was left in charge of the more domestic side of hospitalization. The patients were less concerned with the feats of surgery performed upon them under anaesthesia than the discovery that they were unable to sleep, their bowels wouldn't work, the fish for supper was cold, and there was a draught all day from the window opposite, all faults that I was expected to rectify. As I was obliged to make my rounds twice daily the patients saw far more of me than the other members of the surgical firm, and sometimes embarrassed me by imagining that I was the brilliant young doctor in charge. 'Which surgeon are you under?' I overheard one of them being asked in the X-ray Department downstairs.

'Dr Gordon.'

'I mean, who's the head surgeon in your ward?'

'Why, Dr Gordon,' said the patient in amazement. 'You know – the young feller.'

'Is there any *other* doctor?'

The patient thought for a time. 'There's another

youngish chap called Hatrick what Dr Gordon gets to help him sometimes – '

'Yes, yes, yes! But who else?'

The patient tried to remember. 'No one else except an old man Dr Gordon asks in every so often out of the kindness of his heart. But he's past it, I reckon,' he added confidentially.

As the Professor's wards were immediately below mine in the surgical block, I saw a good deal of Bingham. We treated each other with aggressive politeness: Bingham markedly avoided the lift when we went downstairs together, and I pointedly asked his advice, as the senior surgeon by six months, about my difficult cases. Whenever our professional interests conflicted, we drenched each other in courtesy.

'Hello, old chap,' he said, coming to the duty operating theatre one evening. 'Just finished a case?'

'Well, er, no. Actually, I was just going to scrub up for a stitch abscess from the ward. But if you want the theatre first – '

'Not a bit, old chap, not a bit,' he said quickly. 'We *are* on duty tonight, I admit, and we do have priority in the theatre and all that, but I wouldn't dream of standing in your way. It's only a F.B. in the pop. foss., and that can wait.'

'No no, my dear Bingham! After all, I'm a septic case, so you should come first.'

'Well, that's terribly d. of you, old chap, but really – I know,' he announced, his eyes lighting up at the gentlemanly solution to this impasse, 'you shall have our centrifuge all tomorrow afternoon.'

'Really, I couldn't – '

'Yes, old chap. Absolutely insist.'

'That's awfully kind of you, Bingham.'

'Don't mench, old chap.'

A month passed like a fine April day. Then a strange feeling of depression began to creep over me. At first it puzzled me; my career was progressing splendidly, but I had the vague feeling of something missing from my life. I wondered if I were developing some dark psychological complaint, and mentioned this to Grimsdyke one evening over a pint of beer in the King George pub opposite.

'I don't know what it is exactly,' I told him. 'It's a sort of – well, unsatisfied feeling. Lord knows why. I love the work, I really feel I'm learning a bit of surgery at last, it's fun living in the hospital with the boys, and I haven't seen Bingham for two days. What more could I want? Do you think I ought to take an interest in art or music or something?'

Grimsdyke laughed. 'You don't want music, old lad, you want women. Or one woman at least.'

I was surprised. 'Do you really think so?'

'Absolutely certain. Can't miss the diagnosis. We're not run-around students any more, however much we try and pretend we are on Saturday nights. We're worthy citizens, God help us. "It is a truth universally acknowledged, that a single man in possession of a good fortune, must be in want of a wife." Jane Austen.'

'A wife!' I cried in horror.

'Well, I wouldn't go as far as that,' he added, finishing his beer. 'But you get the idea.'

I thought carefully about Grimsdyke's diagnosis, and decided that he was right. Fortunately, the treatment would be simple. Since returning to St Swithin's as a doctor, I had sensed a different relationship between myself and the hundreds of young women that the place was obliged to employ. Apart from the nurses, there were

141

the buxom dieticians, the cheerful girls in X-ray, the neat secretaries, the occupational therapists in sandals and folk-weave belts, the laboratory assistants, the speech therapists, the child-guidance workers, and the statuesque physiotherapists in the massage department who were known as the 'slap-and-tickle honeys'. As students, these ladies had treated us like well-brought-up Wrens dealing with fresh ratings; but now that we were qualified and therefore pressingly marriageable the iron hand was eased a little from the velvet glove.

The sister of Mr Cambridge's female ward had resigned shortly before I arrived, leaving the patients in charge of the staff nurse until the matron could make another promotion. This was Nurse Plumtree, a pale, thin, dark, snub-nosed girl, passably pretty except for her hair, which appeared to be attended by a gardener in a spare second while occupied with the hedge-clippers. From my first entrance to the ward Nurse Plumtree clearly looked upon me as her own property. This was correct hospital etiquette, for the staff nurse was always allowed first bite at the new houseman; but Nurse Plumtree, perhaps because she was in supreme authority over the others, took pains to make this obvious. I preferred her second-in-command, a bright, red-headed, freckled Scots girl, to whom I chatted if Nurse Plumtree was out of the ward; when she returned she would cross directly to us with an extra briskness in her step, look her professional sister squarely in the eye, and order her to check the laundry. One afternoon, Nurse Plumtree came back from lunch to find the pair of us giggling over a joke in the sluice-room, and afterwards rarely took any time off at all. She insisted that this was through her devotion to duty; but it was clear to every-one else that it was through her devotion to me.

'Have you any socks that need mending?' she asked one morning. 'If you'll bring them up I'll darn them for you. I've nothing else to do in the evenings. I never go out.'

We were sitting alone in the Sister's private sitting-room, a small apartment fierce with yellow chintz and brassware next to the ward. Every day I was invited there for a cup of milky coffee served timidly by the junior probationer, while Nurse Plumtree took a tin of her own chocolate biscuits from the bureau, put her feet up on the rushwork stool, and lit a cigarette. 'In fact,' she went on, 'I've got an evening off tomorrow. From five o'clock. I don't know what on earth to do with it.'

'Really? Well, er – perhaps something may turn up,' I said warily. 'Who knows?'

She sipped her coffee sorrowfully.

The morning after my talk with Grimsdyke she threw into her conversation, 'I've got a half-day on Wednesday. Starting at twelve o'clock. And I'm due for a late pass till midnight. But I don't expect I shall take them. There just doesn't seem anything to do.'

I already knew this, having sneaked a glance at the nurses' off-duty book kept with the insurance certificates on her desk. I had made up my mind. Nurse Plumtree was presentable and pleasant; besides, there was not the faintest chance of being snubbed.

I coughed.

'If you're really without plans, perhaps you'd like to come to the pictures, or something?'

For an instant her eyes widened. 'I'm not sure if I can really leave the ward. Nurse Macpherson isn't very experienced.'

'Of course not.'

'As well as being a lot too familiar with the patients –'

'So I've noticed.'

'And anyway, she's far too interested in one of the students for the good of her work.'

'Really? Do try and come. I'll see you at six,' I said, rising. 'Outside the dental department.'

15

My romance with Nurse Plumtree caused no more surprise in the hospital than the annual blooming of the geraniums outside the Secretary's office in summer. My colleagues grinned more widely the more I asked them to stand-in for me during the evenings, and Nurse Macpherson once winked at me over a ward screen; but to most people at St Swithin's we were simply another staff nurse and houseman obeying the local laws of biology.

Like many other young couples with no money in London, we sat at the back in the Festival Hall and the Empress Hall, we dined at Lyons, and we drank in the cosy saloon bars of tucked-away pubs, of which my medical education had left me with a more precise knowledge than of human anatomy. Often Nurse Plumtree paid for herself and sometimes she paid for us both. She was an easy girl to entertain, because she was fond of long silences during which she would stare at the opposite wall as if recalling the faces of friends long dead; and her conversation, when it came, was almost wholly about the hospital. As my few former girl friends had all been nurses this failure to throw off the cap and apron did not discourage me, and I consoled myself that another companion might have talked only about ponies or Proust; but after a few weeks I found myself irresistibly wishing that she would stop telling me exactly what was happening to number twenty-two's blood chlorides, and the bright retort she had made to Nurse Macpherson when informed that the ward's allocation of liquid paraffin had been used up in a week.

There was another more disheartening impediment in my relationship with Nurse Plumtree. I confessed this late one evening to Grimsdyke, when he came into my room to scrounge cigarettes.

'How's the sex life?' he asked cheerfully. 'Feeling more contented?'

'Well – yes and no.'

'What? You mean the course of true love hasn't run smooth?'

'Too smoothly, if anything,' I told him. 'You know how it is with nurses – we go to a flick or a concert or something, then I rush her back to the hospital before her late pass expires, we have a quick neck among half the medical school outside the mortuary gate, then I push her into the Nurses' Home on the stroke of eleven. If I kept her out another minute her good name would be ruined for ever, so it seems.'

'Frustrating.'

'You don't have to read Freud and Kinsey to know it doesn't do a chap much good. But what's the alternative? Apart from holding hands in Hyde Park?'

'How about a little intramural love life?'

'In St Swithin's, where they separate the sexes like a Victorian swimming-bath?'

'There's always the fire-escape.'

'Ah, the fire-escape!' This ugly zigzag up the wall of the Residents' Quarters was a monument to the victory of the insurance company's prudence over that of the matron. By climbing the darkened floors of the empty out-patients' block at night, crossing the roof of the physiotherapy department, and dodging past the night porter's mess-room, we could smuggle a nurse into our forbidden corridors. This risky adventure was rarely suggested, for the nurse, if discovered, was regarded by the Matron to be fit for nothing more but the Chamber of Horrors.

'There's nothing to it, old lad,' Grimsdyke went on, as I looked at him dubiously. 'Wait for a dark night, lay in a bottle of courting sherry, have a decent shave, and you're all set for a cosy evening. So much warmer than Hyde Park, too.'

At our next meeting I mentioned the fire-escape to Nurse Plumtree. As I expected, she looked sad, sniffed, and said, 'Oh, Richard!'

Feeling I should provide some excuse, I went on quickly, 'But I mean, I thought we could just have a cup of coffee, and I could show you my microscope slides of gastric ulcers that I've been telling you about. I mean, it would be quite – well, you know, all right –'

'Oh, Richard! It would spoil everything.'

'What, you mean just looking at my slides? They're most interesting, and of course I have to borrow a microscope from one of the other residents, so I can't very well show them to you elsewhere. But of course, if you don't want to –'

She sighed deeply, and looked away. I felt that Grimsdyke would have managed the invitation much better! I had tempted her only with the pathological equivalent of etchings. There was another of her silences, then we talked about the best way of treating post-operative thrombosis.

Our affair jogged along for several weeks. There was no alternative, for she now simply told me when she was next off duty and assumed that I would be waiting to take her out. It was a relationship with many concrete advantages, for Nurse Plumtree was a tender-hearted girl

whose motherly instincts were not wholly absorbed by
her profession. From our first outing she had mended
my shirts, lent me books, and provided currant cake with
the morning coffee; now she bought me ties and bars of
chocolate, pressed on me handfuls of vitamins from the
medicine cupboard, knitted me a muffler, and made me
wear braces instead of an old rugger club tie for keeping
up my trousers, which she pressed proudly every Sunday
with her iron in the Nurses' Home. My friends thought
I had not looked so tidy or so well fed for a long
time.

Two events disturbed the placid current of this romance. The first was Nurse Macpherson's transference to
night duty.

In the printed charge handed to him by the hospital
Secretary on his appointment, each senior house surgeon
at St Swithin's was enjoined 'to visit your wards at least
once nightly before retiring, to take the report from the
senior night nurse and attend to the needs of the patients,
at whatever hour that might be'. This night round was
the most conscientiously performed of all the house
surgeons' duties, for night nurses, who have to sleep all
day and work alone all night, are lonely souls who suffer
from a deficiency of masculine companionship. For this
reason the most untidy and unromantic houseman is
confident of a welcome in the darkened ward, even if he
has just been thrown out of the King George and
arrives, like my predecessor, wearing the head porter's
hat and riding a bicycle. Besides, all nurses are good
cooks and without the ward sister counting the rations
over their shoulders gladly provide peckish housemen
with bacon and eggs at midnight.

My night rounds had so far been dull, because the
nurse on Fortitude was a newly-promoted girl who

breathlessly read me the ward report with one timid eye on the door for the visit of the surgical night sister; on Constancy, the night nurse was a thin, spectacled woman with a faint moustache, who in the half-light reminded me of Groucho Marx. One night I came up the empty corridor after seeing Nurse Plumtree into the Nurses' Home as usual, and found Nurse Macpherson frying bacon and eggs and smoking a cigarette in the small kitchen next to the ward.

'What on earth are you doing here?' I asked in surprise.

'Why, hello, there! For three months I'm to be Queen of the Night, tra-la! Didn't Plumtree tell you?'

I shook my head.

'How about some eggs and bacon? Or would you prefer' – she opened a box on the diet trolley– 'some egg custard and puréed spinach?'

'As a matter of fact I could do with a bite. As usual, they gave us a rotten supper in the Residency. You know, that brawn stuff the patients won't eat.'

She nooded. 'How well I do! It would pass unnoticed in a pathology exam with "Draw, Label, and Identify this Tissue" stuck on it. There's a bottle of beer in the comforts cupboard,' she went on, breaking a couple more eggs. 'Help yourself and pour me a glass.'

'Aren't you worried about the night sister?' I asked, hesitating.

'What, old Muggsy Munson? She's got her feet up in the Sister's room with a nice cup of tea reading the *Washerwoman's Weekly*, I'll bet. She comes round as regularly as the hands of a clock.'

I sat down at the ward table, wondering why a nurse smoking in uniform always presented such a curiously abandoned appearance. Then I remembered that I had just kissed my girl-friend good night. 'How are the patients, Nurse?' I asked, trying to re-establish our professional relationship.

'Please, *please*, don't talk about them out of the ward, I beg.' She forked bacon from the pan. 'I cannot talk shop with my meals. The Nurses' Home is ghastly – it's mastoids with the mince, mumps with the macaroni, membranes with the mash. That's one of the things I've got against Plumtree – ' She bit her lip. 'I shouldn't have said that, I suppose?'

'Not said it?' I tried to sound as indifferent as possible. 'Why?'

'Well – everyone knows that you and Plumtree – I mean, she's a very good sort at heart.'

'She certainly strikes me as being a decent sort of girl, I must say.'

'Oh, yes, very nice. Such a pity about her acne.'

'Acne?' I recalled that Nurse Plumtree's face was occasionally marred by a small square of sticking-plaster.

'Yes, all over her back. But of course – ' She giggled. 'You wouldn't know about that, would you? But she's a nice placid person.'

'I happen to dislike chattering women,' I said, a little stiffly.

'She's no chatterbox. Why, sometimes she sits for hours and hours without saying anything, just looking into the middle distance.'

'I find her quite an interesting companion, anyway,' I insisted.

'So do we in the Home, these days. The things she tells us about you! My, my! I want to blush sometimes. Did you really go as far as that on the Inner Circle the other night?'

'Good God, did she tell you *that*?'

'That's only half of it. How many eggs '

I ate my bacon and eggs in silence. I was disillusioned. I had thought Nurse Plumtree above the common feminine habit of describing an evening out in the spirit of a boastful Grenadier in a pub after Waterloo.

When I met her the following evening I was more careful in my conversation and behaviour. This did not seem to disturb her, but as we came home I had to admit that her silences seemed longer and longer, and now extended from Piccadilly Circus to Russell Square on the Tube; and as she turned to allow me to kiss her good night I was sure I saw incipient acne all over her cheeks.

'I suppose you know Macpherson's on nights?' she said.

I murmured that I had noticed her while dashing through the ward on my night round.

'I'm asking the office to get her moved,' Nurse Plumtree went on. 'She's incompetent. Do you know that this morning she gave the high-protein diets to the low-proteins? And she mixed up the extra vitamins with the salt-deficients?'

'Oh, really? It doesn't seem to have done them much harm, anyway?'

She twisted the top button of my overcoat. 'Richard, I've got an evening tomorrow. Will you come to dinner at home?'

'Home?' I was startled. I had never thought of Nurse Plumtree having any home except the one provided by St Swithin's.

'It's only down in Mitcham. Mummy and Daddy would love to see you.' I hesitated. 'Please, Richard.'

I thought quickly. Dining with the parents would certainly be a trial. I could see it – gruff father, who I believed was a retired colonel, and sharp-eyed mother, both suspicious of my intentions towards their daughter. Still, Nurse Plumtree had been a kind companion to me, and I owed her some repayment – besides, I was running short of money, and it would mean a free meal.

'All right,' I said. 'I'll meet you at the usual place at six, if I can get away.'

The clock struck then, and she disappeared through the closing doors of the Nurses' Home.

'How's Plumtree?' Nurse Macpherson asked cheerfully, as I arrived in the ward kitchen two minutes later.

'Oh, all right.' I sat on the edge of the table, lit a cigarette, and swung my legs.

'You don't sound very enthusiastic about it, I must say.'

'Oh, don't I?'

She put down a bowl of eggs she was beating and went on, 'Be a darling and lend me a cigarette. I left mine in the Home.'

She came across to me as I pulled a packet from my jacket pocket. When I lit her cigarette with the end of mine she gripped my hand tightly and said, 'You know what's wrong with Plumtree, don't you? She's under-sexed.'

For a moment I looked at her. Nurse Plumtree was pale and dark, Nurse Macpherson red-headed and freckled. Nurse Plumtree always looked faintly ill, and Nurse Macpherson always buoyantly healthy, with a stride recalling a moor on a frosty morning and arms suggesting the tennis racket and the hockey stick. Nurse Plumtree was introverted and Nurse Macpherson extroverted, and if one was undersexed then the other was certainly oversexed. Before I realized what I was doing, I had kissed her.

152

'Ummm,' she said, nestling into my arms. 'Not quite the Nightingale spirit, but give me more.'

'What about the ward?' I gasped.

'The pro's looking after it.'

I kissed her again.

'But the night sister?'

'Not due for hours. Besides, I've got my cap on. That's the important thing. If they found a nurse stark naked with her cap on, it would still be respectable.'

It was late as I walked slowly up the stairs of the Residents' Quarters. I felt smugly sheikish. I now had two girl friends: one for companionship and comfort during the day, and one for excitement at night. As long as I could keep them reasonably separated and do without too much sleep, I was in for an interesting time.

16

THE second disturbance to my romance with Nurse Plumtree was the dinner at home.

'Mummy and Daddy are very sweet really,' she said as I drove Haemorrhagic Hilda down to Mitcham.

'I'm sure they are.'

'Forgive Daddy if he's a little crotchety sometimes. He's been rather like that since he retired from the Army. And Mummy's arthritis sometimes upsets her in weather like this. But I'm sure you'll like them very much. Just be youself,' she advised me.

The Plumtrees lived in a small house called 'Blenheim' that stood in a neat garden containing a row of yews shaped into horses' heads, with a miniature brass cannon by the steps and a notice on the door saying CIVIL DEFENCE – CHIEF WARDEN. She rang the bell, which had the effect of a bomb going off in a zoo. Immediately there was an outburst of barking, caterwauling and human shouting from inside, and I waited nervously on the mat wondering if it was a pair of lions who were scratching hungrily for me inside the door.

'I do love animals so,' Nurse Plumtree said.

The door burst open, and two Great Danes sprang at me, put their paws on my shoulders and began licking my face.

'Alexander! Montgomery!' cried someone inside. 'Mind what you're doing to the Doctor.'

'Don't worry,' said Nurse Plumtree calmly. 'They're only puppies.'

The dogs were pulled off, I staggered through the hall, and found myself in a sitting-room decorated with long photographs of regimental groups, a pair of crossed swords, a tiger-skin rug, and several ceremonial helmets under glass domes like forced rhubarb. The room seemed to be filled with human beings and animals. There were dogs in the corners, cats on the cushions, birds in the windows, and a tank of fish over the fireplace; scattered among them were a thin, stooping man with a white moustache, a fat dark woman in a purple dress, and a young man and a girl who both looked strongly like Nurse Plumtree.

'My dear, dear, Doctor,' said the Colonel, advancing with outstretched hand. 'How very pleased we are to see you! Edna has told us so much about you. May I introduce Edna's mother?'

As I shook hands she said warmly, 'Edna's told me so much about you, too.'

The young man held out his hand and said, 'Hel-lo. Name's Ian. I'm at the BBC. Sweet of you to come, old thing. This is Joan. We're Edna's brother and sister, and we've heard so much about you it isn't true.'

Joan said, 'Smashing you could come. Always hearing about you.'

I began to feel annoyed. I had expected the evening to be a quiet dinner, and it had been turned into a gathering of the clan.

'Naughty, Cromwell,' Joan said, picking up a wire-haired terrier which had sprung from the hearthrug to start biting my ankles. 'Naughty, naughty Cromwell! Did oo want to eat the Doctor, then?' She buried her nose in the struggling dog's neck. 'Don't you think he's got a lovely face?'

'He's getting married tomorrow,' Ian explained. 'Which makes him rather excited.'

'Now let's have a cocktail, Doctor,' said the Colonel, rubbing his hands. He smiled at me. 'Or I'd better call you Richard, hadn't I?'

'If you like, sir, of course.'

For some reason this made everyone roar with laughter. Before long I could not help mellowing in the warmth of my reception. I had come prepared for suspicious tolerance at best, and now Edna Plumtree's father was treating me like the man bringing the winnings from Littlewoods. Even conversation at dinner was easier than I had feared, because the Plumtree family, like many others, believed that the only way to make a doctor feel at home was to narrate their ailments since childhood in a richness of clinical detail more suitable for the operating table than the dining table. First Colonel Plumtree described the pelvic wound he had suffered at Dunkirk, starting with a short sketch of the military situation leading up to it and finishing with an account of the croquet lawn of his convalescent hospital in Torquay. Mrs Plumtree took up the surgical saga by relating all the events occurring both outside and inside her from the moment of entering hospital for a cholecystectomy. Joan Plumtree was bursting to begin the story of the carbuncle she had as a child which had to be squeezed of pus every morning, when Ian put his head in his hands and groaned, '*Not* your beastly boils again, Joan darling, *please!*'

They all looked at him in surprise.

'But Richard's a doctor,' Joan said.

'I know,' Ian shakily reached for his glass. 'But I'm not. It makes me go all over and over inside. If you don't stop I'll throw up, really I will!'

The family stared at the brother like passengers on a business-man's train watching a parson come aboard in the middle of a good story.

'I can't even stand *talking* about blood,' Ian went on to me. 'It's one of my things. I've got all sorts of things. I've got a thing about heights, and a thing about being trapped in the Underground and it filling up with water and everyone being drowned, and a thing about suffocating when I'm asleep. In fact, I'm all things. It all started when I had a nasty experience in a beastly prep school in Broadstairs – ' He went on to give a full history of his neurosis, and those of several of his friends in Broadcasting House.

For most of the meal Nurse Plumtree had remained silent. But as the sweet arrived the family ran out of clinical material, and kept the conversation going by asking her to repeat once more the story of the morning she put Mr Cambridge in his place, or the day she settled the Matron's hash in front of the whole hospital. It was soon clear that Colonel and Mrs Plumtree believed their daughter dominated the nursing staff at St Swithin's, in the same fond way that the parents of the spottiest fourth-form dunce imagine their child is the school's sparking-plug. I noticed that they afforded me similar status in the surgical department, and began asking my opinion on medical matters of the day. So far nothing had been expected of me beyond sympathetic 'Umms' and 'Really's' at long intervals, but the Colonel had provided a good bottle of Burgundy and I was feeling in the mood to let myself expand a little. After addressing them for some time like the President of the Royal College of Surgeons, I ended by giving a stitch-by-stitch description of removing a kidney, which brought Ian's face into his hands again but left me confident that

I had been an overwhelming success with the rest of the family.

'Well,' said Colonel Plumtree as I finished, 'that was most interesting, Richard. Absolutely fascinating. And now, I expect the ladies would like to retire.'

The three women left us, followed by Ian, who murmured that he wanted to lie down. Colonel Plumtree brought a decanter of port from the sideboard and said genially, 'This is a drop I've been saving. It's from the old Regiment. I think you'll like it, my boy.'

'That's very good of you, sir. But I hope you haven't decanted it specially for me?'

'Not a bit, Richard, not a bit. Special occasion, special port, eh? Cigar?'

'Thank you, sir.'

Feeling that a medical qualification was worth the hard work if it could occasion such handsome treatment in a staff nurse's home, I lit my cigar and settled myself at the head of the table close to the Colonel.

'You haven't known Edna long really, have you?' he asked.

'No, not very long. I only started on her ward a few months ago.'

'That doesn't seem to matter,' he said and roared with laughter.

To be polite I laughed, too.

'Tell me something about your career,' he went on. 'By all accounts you're a rather brilliant young man.'

'Oh, not really, you know,' I said, feeling flattered. 'There's nothing much to tell. I got qualified, did a spell in general practice, and now I'm at St Swithin's again. My ambition is to be a surgeon, of course.'

'Capital!'

He poured me some more port.

'If you'll forgive a more personal question,' Colonel Plumtree continued. 'About – ah, how much are you making at the moment?'

'I don't mind telling you at all.' I enjoyed giving inside information about the National Health Service. 'All we poor housemen get is about three hundred a year, when they've knocked off the board and lodging. But, of course, it soon goes up. In another four years or so I should be well inside the four-figure bracket.'

He nodded thoughtfully over his cigar. 'That's pretty reasonable, on the whole.'

'Not too bad at all, I'd say.'

'But you'll probably find yourself a bit short of cash at the moment, eh? After all, you've got to pay for the ring.'

'The ring?'

What on earth was he talking about? I had said nothing about amateur boxing? The circus, perhaps? Opera? Or bookmakers?

He nudged me. 'Her mother insisted on diamonds,' he chuckled.

The room spun round. The port boiled in my mouth. The cigar shot from my fingers like a torpedo.

'Steady on, old chap, steady on!' The Colonel patted me heartily on the back. 'Something go down the wrong way?'

It was almost a minute before I managed to speak. 'The port – perhaps a little strong – '

'Of course, my boy. Mustn't have you choke to death just now, eh? Ha, ha! Come along in and join the family.'

I followed father into the sitting-room, looking like Ian having one of his things.

The rest of the evening passed in a sickly blur, as though I were recovering from a bad anaesthetic. Joan said she

159

hoped we'd be jolly good pals, and Ian thought I'd like to meet his interesting chum Lionel at the BBC. Father showed us his photographs from the war, and mother kept pressing my hand, murmuring 'I'm so glad,' and bursting into tears. As soon as I dared I pleaded a headache, lack of sleep, and early duty. There were disappointed cries, and I bought my freedom with false pledges of returning for Sunday tea to meet the aunts and dining next week at Daddy's club.

We drove away in silence. 'Poor Richard,' said Edna, wrapping my muffler tenderly round me. 'Daddy's Regimental port *is* rather strong. But don't worry – you made an awfully good impression on the family. It really was time they knew about *us*, wasn't it?'

17

I BURST into Grimsdyke's room as soon as I reached the hospital.

'Good God, what's the matter?' he asked in alarm. He jumped from his bed, where he was lying in his crimson silk dressing-gown. 'Been frightened by the ghost of a blighted patient, or something?'

'A drink!' I fell into his armchair. 'At once!'

'Coming up right away. You look so bloody awful you make me want one, too.'

He threw aside the novel he was reading and brought a bottle of gin from the commode thoughtfully provided by St Swithin's. After we had both drunk deeply from his tooth-glasses he screwed his monocle into his eye and said, 'Now tell the doctor all.'

I gave him the story of my tragic evening, and he roared with laughter.

'I can't see anything funny in it,' I said crossly. 'Damn it all, I treat this girl with perfectly normal good manners and affability, and what happens? Before I know what's happening I'm surrounded by her bloody family patting me on the back and saying how nice it will be to have grandchildren. What the devil can she have been telling them all this time? She must think like a story in a woman's magazine.'

'I'll admit you're in a bit of a fix,' Grimsdyke said cheerfully.

'Bit of a fix! I know that without your help. The question is, what the hell can I do about it?'

Grimsdyke took a long drink. 'I should think the easiest way out is to go ahead and marry the girl.'

'Marry her? Marry her? Are you mad too, man? Apart from anything else, have you seen her family? I wouldn't share the same railway carriage with that bunch, let alone marry into them.'

'Have another drink,' Grimsdyke said.

'Thanks. I will.'

'Let's suppose you did marry Nurse Plumtree,' he continued in a reflective tone, lying down again. 'The worst part's over of course – being inspected by the family. Think yourself lucky. Many fellows have gone down to the old folks busting with love, and found themselves kicked into the rhododendrons before the fruit and coffee came round. You were a great success.'

I grunted.

'Then, as Father observed, you'd need a ring. Terribly expensive, engagement rings. The thing the best man loses in church is a brassy job worth a couple of quid, but the one you choose together in Mappin and Webb's is a sort of down payment on delivery of goods. You'll have to put it in *The Times* of course – you pay for that too – which will load your post for weeks afterwards with advertisements for photographers, florists, and contraceptives. All your bachelor chums will slap you on the back and tell you what a lucky chap you are, clearly implying what lucky chaps *they* are. They stand you drinks, I admit, but you don't get much chance for drinking because you spend all your spare time sitting on the edge of the sofa in her front parlour discussing the wedding. By now you may have decided that you don't want to marry the girl after all – '

'Must you go on?' I demanded. 'This isn't a bit funny.'

'. . . but that won't do you the slightest good because once you've set the terrible machinery of marriage in motion you stand as much chance as a crate of eggs under a pile-driver. You'll soon discover that marriage is nothing to do with the fusion of two souls, but an excuse for women to buy lots of expensive clothes. The bride is decked out to ride in triumph round the social circus, to the delight of her relations, the relief of her married friends, and the gratifying jealousy of those still single. You, of course, will be the horse. But I anticipate rather, because for several months you'll be forced to listen politely to exhaustive discussions about whether the bridesmaids should wear Juliet caps and if the bride can go to the altar in her usual undies. Incidentally the bridesmaids themselves – whom you'll later have to reward handsomely – will apparently be recruited from a home for female morons, while your own best man will be as socially acceptable to the bride, mother, and steering committee of aunts as Jack the Ripper. Your last loophole of escape is meanwhile blocked by a land-slide of saucepans, teaspoons, egg-cups, gravy-ladles, toasting forks, and hand-embroidered tea-cosies, for all of which you will have to write a letter extending over at least one page beginning, "Dear Uncle Augustus and Aunt Beatrice. Thank you a thousand times for your delightful contribution to our new little home." '

Grimsdyke took another drink, and staring at the ceiling continued: 'Brightly dawns your wedding day. You have a terrible hangover as you climb into the outfit you've hired from Moss Bros and you still can't find your collar when the best man arrives to collect you. He generally tries to cheer you up with a few funny jokes. The last thing you want to do in the world is get married, but before you know what's happening you're in church with your eyes on the level of the clergyman's boots. The reception afterwards will be upstairs in a tea-shop, there won't be nearly enough to drink and everyone will make speeches – some of the uncles twice – several of the aunts will be in tears, and only the waiters will at all be mellowed by alcohol. Then the "going-away" – frightfully pagan and primitive really, old shoes and tin cans on the back of the car in the middle of the High Street on a Saturday afternoon. This brings me to the honeymoon. There you are, arriving at St Ives in a snowstorm in your best clothes, trying to pretend you've been married for years and feeling that everyone is looking at you as though you were performing one of those *expositions* in the back streets of Marseille. However, I will skip all that. I next see you and Edna Plumtree-that-was strolling from your villa on a Sunday morning with the pram and two – possibly three? – walking along beside – '

I smashed his glass on the floor and walked out.

*

The next morning was my most miserable since the final examinations. The newspapers seemed concerned only with actions for breach of promise, judges' remarks about broken homes, and advertisements for cheap wedding rings. I could hardly eat any breakfast and hurried across the quadrangle to the surgical block feeling that every nurse in the hospital was pointing her finger at me and giggling. As I scrambled into my operating trousers I wondered if Nurse Plumtree had already spread the news around the Nurses' Home or was waiting for the Matron's blessing and a ring.

In the operating theatre it was one of those mornings. The Sister was in a bad temper, the catgut broke, the artery forceps slipped, the transfusion needles came adrift, the scissors were blunt, the swabs were lost. My own assistance was so clumsy that even mild Mr Cambridge was moved to murmur, 'My dear Mr Er – er, couldn't you do something more helpful to the patient than gaze at his umbilicus?'

Hatrick screwed up his eyes as he grinned and said through his mask, 'He must be in love, sir.'

I almost wept into the wound.

As I grasped my retractor through the long surgical morning I glanced at Grimsdyke, who was sitting smugly at my right elbow, and wondered if he was perhaps right. Should I give in and marry Nurse Plumtree? After all, I was past the facile flirtations of a penniless medical student, and almost every morning *The Times* proclaimed the virtuous love of one of my classmates. Nurse Plumtree would at least never be a nagger or a gossip, she was a tolerably good cook, and genuinely anxious to look after me. As the years rolled by I might be able to tolerate her brother and sister, while thankfully her parents could not live for ever.

Lunch was later, colder, and soggier than usual. Afterwards I made an excuse about discussing the next anaesthetic and managed to have a word with Grimsdyke alone.

'Sorry I was rather unsympathetic last night,' he said cheerfully in the anaesthetic room, gripping the chin of a freshly-unconscious patient. 'But your cosy little evening *chez* Plumtree sounded so bloody funny I couldn't spoil the joke.'

'I think I may take your advice after all,' I announced.

'What? Marry the woman? But you're not even in love with her, are you?'

I shrugged my shoulders, and started fiddling with an

ampoule of pentothal. 'What's love?' I said. 'It merely means that a certain system of genes in my chromosomes is about to be placed in relationship to an arrangement of genes in hers. To this biological end certain endocrine cells in her and myself pour out secretions that produce our secondary sex characteristics, such as the full bosom and rounded hips of Nurse Plumtree and the deep voice and hair on the chest of myself. I don't see that there's any more to it – '

'What disgusting nonsense! Anyway, you can't possibly marry a nurse. They make your life a horror of purgatives.'

'Then what the devil *am* I to do?' I asked him anxiously. 'So far you've been as useless as a letter-box on a tombstone.'

'The answer's simple, old lad. Have a bash at another woman. Hadn't you thought of it before?'

They wheeled the patient into the theatre then, but I finished the operating list in a happier frame of mind. In the emotional stress of the last two days I had forgotten Nurse Macpherson, and it cheered me to think that I could choose the primrose path to escape.

18

I saw little of Nurse Plumtree that day, for the operating list ended in a string of hernias, varicose veins, lipomas, biopsies, and cystoscopies that kept Hatrick and myself in the theatre until eight at night. I threw a white coat over my blood-smudged theatre clothes and hurried down to the wards, which on operating evenings resembled the French lines after Agincourt. Outside Constancy I was surprised to run into Nurse Plumtree in her cloak.

'I've got a strep. throat,' she said gazing at me sadly. 'I've got to go off duty.'

'Oh, hard luck.' I tried not to sound delighted. 'At least, it's nothing serious. I'll go round the ward with Nurse Summers instead. I couldn't have met you to-night anyway, not after that colossal list.'

'Don't give too much responsibility to that Nurse Macpherson,' she warned me. 'She's quite unreliable. Only this morning she mixed up the castor oils with the blanket baths. And don't stay up too late writing your notes. Promise?'

I nodded vigorously.

'I must go off to the path. lab. for a swab.' she ended softly. 'Good night, Richard, dear.'

'Good night. Hope you get better in no time, and all that.'

I went into the ward praying that her throat swab would reveal as sturdy a penicillin-resistant streptococcus as the bacteriologists had seen. It was a selfish thought, but at present complete isolation was the ideal state for Nurse Plumtree.

It was late before I left the ward with an armful of patients' notes to complete in my room. I ate my cold supper alone in the gloomy dining-room, found a bottle of beer in Grimsdyke's commode, and settled down at my small desk to reduce Mr Cambridge's surgical bravura to black and white. After midnight I wrote for the last time, 'Haemostasis secured and· abdomen closed in layers,' collected the folders, and began to think constructively about Nurse Macpherson. As I walked across the quadrangle to the entrance of the surgical block, I prepared my plan. I would get her cosily into the corner of the ward kitchen, kiss her against the bread-cutting machine, and ask her out next Friday. She would accept delightedly, and the news would seep into the innermost cell of the nurses' isolation block by breakfast. I felt this was hardly the behaviour of a gentleman, but consoled myself by remembering that desperate ills need desperate remedies.

I was glad to find her in the ward kitchen as usual, alone.

'My, my, you're late!' she greeted me. 'Today's victims are all doing splendidly, and old Muggsy's sent up a couple of extras to help me cope. Hungry?'

'Phew!' I waved the air in front of my face. 'Have you been fumigating the mattresses or something?'

'Oh, that must be Jimmy Bingham's tobacco. How many eggs?'

I stiffened. Now I recognized unmistakably the foul breath of Bingham's pipe, which he lit with the air of a clumsy father on Guy Fawkes Night after every meal.

'Bingham has been up here, has he?'

'Been up! He's eaten me out of house and home.'

My eyes caught the plate on the table, polished clean except for a rim of egg and a few forlorn rinds of bacon.

'And what was he doing in my ward?' I demanded.

She laughed. 'Oh, Jimmy comes up every night after you've gone – didn't you know? I was in the Professor's ward before I was sent here on days. We got to know each other pretty well.'

'Oh. I see.'

I had not allowed for a rival in my calculations and I felt outraged that this complication should take the form of Bingham. Deciding quickly that no sane woman could award him greater sex-appeal than a fourth-form schoolboy, I continued my plan.

'Here! What's the idea?' she demanded, as I wedged her into a corner.

'I only wanted to kiss you.'

'Oh, you did, did you? Well you can get that out of your mind to start with.'

'But you let me yesterday,' I said in surprise.

'Well, I won't today.'

'Come out on Friday.'

'No.'

'Why?'

'Because I'm going out with Jimmy Bingham. Now if you'd like the ward report, Mr Gordon, you may have it.'

I drew in my breath.

'Thank you, Nurse Macpherson. I should.'

I rose the next morning a bitter man. Not only had Bingham condemned me to a lifetime of living with Nurse Plumtree, but his rivalry for the favours of Nurse Macpherson had the familiar psychological effect of making her wildly desirable. It also brought to an end the professional honeymoon that Bingham and I had enjoyed since my return to the hospital. My toleration was already stretched thin, because of his unendearing social habits. There was only one bathroom on our floor, where he came to shave every morning while I was taking my bath. On my first day in the Staff Quarters he had greeted me heartily with, 'Good morning, old chap. While there's life there's soap, eh?' which was passably funny as a before-breakfast pleasantry, but when he repeated it the next morning, the morning after that, and every morning for the following weeks, I was ready to slit his throat with his own razor.

At meals, Bingham made a point of sitting next to me to emphasize our new chumminess, and though he was too careful about money to let slip a technicality and incur a fine he found it difficult to keep his thoughts away from his work while eating. 'Perirenal fat, hylum, medulla, and pelvis,' he murmured during supper one evening.

'Look out,' I whispered. 'If the Senior Resident hears you, you'll be down half a crown.'

'But I'm not talking shop, old chap,' he said, wide-eyed. 'See this – ' He stuck his fork into the middle of his steak-and-kidney pie. 'Nicest piece of dissected kidney I've seen for a long time. Young, too – look at those lobulations.'

Shortly afterwards I pointedly offered him the bananas, and I was glad to find he took the rest of his meals on the other side of the table.

I wondered at first if I was hypersensitive, but Bingham had already established his unpopularity with the rest of the Residency by taking all the magazines up to his bedroom, reading the *Lancet* at breakfast, and being unable to glance through a paper without leaving it fit only for wrapping chips. Although he glared furiously at anyone who talked in the common-room while he was listening to the Third Programme, he was unable to afford similar respect to his companions' ideas of evening entertainment. The brewer who had given the new surgical wing to the hospital had admirably topped off his donation with a supply of free beer to the resident doctors, so we never found ourselves short of an excuse for a party. These generally brought Bingham down in his dressing-gown, complaining, 'I say, let a chap sleep, won't you?' until one noisy evening he wrote to the hospital Secretary saying that he would be obliged for a room elsewhere as his colleagues were apparently tearing up the common-room immediately below. The Secretary hurried round the next morning to find the room looking as though it had been charged by a rhinoceros, locked the door, pocketed the key, and angrily strode off to find the Dean. We had an hour of dangerous climbing round the fire-escape and hard work with pails and brushes, but when the Secretary indignantly threw open the door the Dean found the room as neat as a barracks, with an aspidistra drooping from a brass pot on the piano and an open Bible on the table. But this did nothing to increase Bingham's like-ability.

The crisis came the morning after my frustration by Nurse Macpherson, when I strode into the ward after breakfast and found five strange faces in the beds.

'Where did those patients come from?' I demanded from Nurse Summers in astonishment. 'They weren't here last night.'

'They're Mr Bingham's.'

'Bingham's? But damn it, they were my only empty beds! I've got five gastrectomies coming in this morning. What right has he got to put his patients in my beds?'

'They were the duty firm last night. They're allowed to board out patients if they're swamped with emergencies.'

'What's wrong with them, anyway?'

She picked up the diagnosis board from the Sister's desk. 'They're all in for observation.'

'Observation!'

After examining all five, I concluded that one was suffering from severe constipation and the rest had nothing wrong with them at all.

'Bingham!' I called, as I spotted him in the corridor, 'what the devil do you mean by cluttering up my ward with your cases?'

He stiffened. 'I've a perfect right to, old chap.'

'Perfect right my foot! There's nothing wrong with any of them. I bet you only admitted them because you couldn't decide if they had acute abdomens. You were scared stiff of chucking them into the street.'

'That is a very unprofessional remark,' Bingham hissed. He stepped into the lift and slammed the gates. Unfortunately, this time it worked.

'It's so damnably irritating,' I told Grimsdyke in his room that evening. 'Here's this blasted Bingham, who's a walking disgrace to the medical profession, and here's this first-rate girl squandering her precious nights off duty at his feet. I can't believe it.'

'No accounting for the taste of women, old lad.' He stretched himself thoughtfully on his bed. 'Frightful gargoyles and crooks they fall for sometimes. You've only got to look through the wedding photos in the *Tatler*.'

'But this – this Caliban, Bingham. What on earth can she see in him?'

Grimsdyke screwed his monocle into his eye and stared at the ceiling. 'Let us not lose sight of the object of the treatment. You wish to purge yourself of the hookworm

Plumtree. Right? You intend to administer Macpherson for this purpose. But why not try some other anthelmintic? The hospital's full of nurses ready to quiver at a houseman's smile.'

I was silent for a second. 'As a matter of fact, I'm rather fond of Nan Macpherson.'

'Balderdash! Simple psychology – you wish to assert your superiority over Bingham by nabbing his mate. It's happening to chaps all the time.'

'You don't understand. She's a terrific girl, really. Tremendous vitality and good looks, with a wonderful sense of humour.'

'Delusions, delusions, delusions,' Grimsdyke murmured, putting his finger-tips together.

'Anyway, what do you know about psychology? All your patients are asleep.'

'If you don't believe me, try the experiment in reverse. Dangle Plumtree in front of Macpherson. Make her think she's wrecking the home. I guarantee she'll act like a thirsty cat with a saucer of milk.'

Although I had no faith in Grimsdyke's ability as a psychiatrist, I decided to take his advice because he was a more experienced man of the world than myself. Unfortunately the next day was Friday, and Nurse Macpherson was placed beyond reach by her official three nights off duty. She had clearly hinted to Bingham of my rejection in his favour, because he met me in the quadrangle at lunch-time with a broad grin, slapped me on the back, and said, 'By the way, old chap. Do you think you'll need me for anything tomorrow night? I mean, to give you a hand with a drip for a perf. or something?'

'Why should I?' I asked coldly. 'I never have done.'

'No, but just in case. I mean to say, Duckworth's H.S.

is standing in for me. I'm going out,' he added, as though announcing he was about to swim the Channel.

'I hope you enjoy yourself.'

He giggled. 'I shall, old chap. Don't go out much you know, but this is something special.' He slapped his thigh, grinned again, and winked. 'Eh, old chap?'

'If you make your intentions as obvious to Nurse Macpherson as you do to me,' I said sourly, 'you won't get her out of the Nurses' Home. Good afternoon.'

I strode angrily into the nearest doorway, feeling sick.

My determination to win Nurse Macpherson was fanned by Bingham's grinning at me, rubbing his hands, and declaring, 'Lovely life, eh?' every time I met him the next day. Meanwhile, I was glad to hear from the Junior Pathology Demonstrator that Nurse Plumtree was richly infected with *streptococcus pyogenes*, and would be off duty for at least a week. I sent her a letter of sympathy and a bunch of flowers, and patiently waited for the return of her rival.

The campaign was easier than I had expected. I apologized for my behaviour at our last meeting, and explained that her overwhelming attraction had swept me away from Nurse Plumtree, where my thoughts must henceforward dutifully repose. I murmured that, of course, Nurse Plumtree was a delightful girl, but if only Nurse Macpherson had been the staff nurse instead. . . . I passed on all the remarks that Nurse Plumtree had made about her, and prepared to sit in the ward kitchen every night and wait.

That was on Monday. By Wednesday she had agreed to come out to dinner on her night off – as long as I breathed not a word to Bingham – and by Friday she was inviting me to help her look for lost tea-cloths in the small, dark, cosy linen cupboard behind the ward. On Sunday I decided that I was in love with her; and on Monday more exciting ideas began to take shape in my mind.

'You know, I've been getting on damn well with Nan Macpherson, thanks to your advice,' I said to Grimsdyke. 'Do you think that – I mean, what would you say the chances were of her – well, being as cooperative on a grander scale, as it were?'

'Pretty good, I should think,' he replied thoughtfully. 'She has what the nurses call "a reputation". Though that might merely mean she paints her toenails red and uses mascara.'

'Do you think I dare ask?'

'Why not? At the worst, she can only kick your teeth in.'

After a brief and breathless spell in the linen cupboard that night, I began, 'Nan, about next week. Instead of just dinner, how about – ' I swallowed. I had dismissed the fire-escape as impracticable, because of Bingham. 'How about nipping out to the country somewhere, you know, and, well, you know?'

There was a surprised pause. 'Doctor, Doctor!' she said playfully. 'Is that an indecent proposal?'

'It's a pretty decent one, as far as I can see,' I said brightly. 'I'm sorry, I didn't mean to be funny about it. But if you'd feel inclined – '

'You'll have to go. Night sister'll be here in a minute.'

'But about next week –?'

'I'll see,' she said, laying her finger on my lips.

'I promise I wouldn't tell a soul. Especially Bingham. He hasn't done the same sort of thing, has he?' I asked, with sudden horror.

She laughed. 'Jimmy isn't out of the mistletoe stage.'

'Do say yes,' I implored. 'I can't stand suspense.'

'You must *go*, Richard! Night sister's due any second.'

175

'I won't go till you tell me.'

'Oh, well – I suppose I was going to buy a new toothbrush anyway.'

'Nan, darling! How wonderful – '

'Shhh! And remember – not a soul.'

'How could you think I'd breathe a word?'

I immediately woke up Grimsdyke.

'Can you imagine it, Grim?' I said excitedly. 'What luck! She's agreed. We're nipping off for a dirty weekend. Or a dirty night, anyway,' I corrected myself.

'You've woken me up to tell me this disgusting piece of news – '

'I want your advice. You see, I haven't had any experience of – of this sort of thing. Where do we go, for instance? Brighton? What do we sign in the visitors book – Smith or Jones? Supposing they ask for our marriage licence or something – '

'There's a sort of country hotel called The Judge's Arms, on the way north, which is very romantic I've heard. You could try that. Now for God's sake let me get some sleep.'

'The Judge's Arms. Thanks a million times, old fellow.'

'I suppose you're going to these lengths to unload Miss Plumtree?' he asked sleepily, turning over.

'Good Lord! I'd completely forgotten about her.'

'I don't like it,' Grimsdyke muttered, dropping off. 'I don't like it a bit.'

For the next few days Bingham and I both slapped each other on the back like brothers. What the psychology was behind it I didn't dare to work out.

19

THE stubborn streptococcus in Nurse Plumtree's throat refused to budge. She soon felt well again, but as no nurse could be let loose to spray penicillin-resistant organisms over the patients, second opinions were summoned. The senior ear, nose, and throat surgeon recommended that he remove her tonsils, excise her nasal septum, scrape out her sinuses, and extract all her teeth; the Professor of Bacteriology, a simpler-minded man, advised a week's holiday. This was thought to be the most convenient course for everybody, and the next day she left the hospital for Mitcham with an armful of home-building magazines.

'We'll announce it when I get back,' she declared as I saw her off. 'So far, I haven't told a soul – except my best friends, of course. It'll be nice to have the date fixed for the wedding, won't it? Now don't forget – no late nights while I'm away.'

A couple of afternoons later, in a state of devilish excitement, I started Haemorrhagic Hilda and drove from the hospital car park to pick up Nurse Macpherson.

Our plans had been laid the night before, over a cup of Ovaltine. I had left my junior house surgeon on duty for me, asking Mr Cambridge for permission to spend the night away from the hospital; she had told Bingham that duty to her parents demanded a visit. To allay suspicion, I arranged to meet her outside the Zoo.

She was waiting with her attaché-case by the main gates.

'Hello, hello, hello!' I called, drawing up and un-hooking the loop of string that restrained the near-side door. 'What a cad I am! Fancy keeping a girl waiting on an occasion like this.'

I noticed that she was staring at me in amazement. 'What's the matter?' I asked in alarm. 'Is my suit all right? It's my second best.'

'My God! Am I supposed to travel in *that?*'

I remembered that she hadn't seen Haemorrhagic Hilda before. 'It's a remarkably good motor car,' I told her stoutly. 'As reliable as a London bus and with a lot of charm about it. You wait till we get going.'

'Oh, it's charming all right. Like one of Emett's railway engines. How do I get aboard – do you let down a pair of steps?'

I helped her into the car, and she settled in the Windsor chair I had lashed specially to the floorboards beside me. I felt nettled. I was proud of Haemorrhagic Hilda, and even if she looked as startling on the road as George Stevenson's *Rocket*, such mockery hurt. But refusing to allow the start of a great adventure to be marred by the petty pride of ownership, I called cheerfully, 'Hang on!' and performed the rapid manipulation of the choke, ignition, throttle, brake, gear-lever, and hand petrol pump necessary to put Haemorrhagic Hilda in motion. 'Off we go to the wide open spaces!'

'By the way,' she said lighting a cigarette. 'I've got to go to Oxford Street first.'

'Oxford Street! But that's miles out of our way. What on earth do you want to go there for?'

'I simply must do my shopping. I've got to get a length of curtain material for my room – I can't stand the hospital stuff any longer – and a birthday present for Cissy Jenkins, and some kirbigrips and some linen buttons for my uniform and a tea-pot and some soap.'

'But couldn't you do it another time? I mean to say –
Apart from anything else, I'd like to get there in daylight. The headlamps aren't terribly efficient.'

'What other time? You seem to forget I'm a working
girl, my dear young man.'

'Oh, sorry. No offence, of course.'

She left me for an hour and a quarter in Oxford Street,
though the time passed quickly enough because I spent
it driving through side-streets looking for somewhere to
park and anxiously peering out for policemen, as though
I were about to hold up a bank. She rejoined me with a
Christmas Eve load of parcels, which she threw on to
the sofa in the back, and said, 'Phew! What a bloody
tussle! Drive on, James.'

'Are you sure you've got everything?' I asked stiffly.

'Except some cigarettes. But that doesn't matter. I
can smoke yours.'

My spirits had dropped badly since leaving St
Swithin's, and now it occurred to me that I had never
seen Nurse Macpherson out of uniform before. Indeed,
I had never seen her in daylight at all for several weeks.
She was unfortunately one of those nurses who are flattered by the starched severity of their dress, and she had
chosen for our escapade an odd orange knitted outfit
that recalled the woollen suits worn at one period by
Mr Bernard Shaw. Her face, too, suffered away from
the night-club dimness of a sleeping ward. Her make-up
was careless, the freckles that had enchanted me across
the Night Report Book now reminded me of a dozen
skin diseases, and I reflected that she must have begun
her nursing training comparatively late, because she
was clearly several years older than I was.

My mood was darkened further by the weather, which

had turned from a lunch-time of brittle blue sky and sharp-edged sun to an afternoon in which the clouds and the twilight were already conspiring to make me confess Hilda's deficient headlights. On top of this, I was getting a sore throat. Nurse Plumtree's streptococcus, breathed into our farewell kiss, was already breeding generations of grandchildren across the mucous membrane of my pharynx. I had left the hospital with a half-perceived tickling in the back of my throat, and now I felt like a fire-eater after a bad performance.

Fortunately, Nurse Macpherson became more romantic as we left the outskirts of London, and began stroking my arm against the steering-wheel while murmuring that she felt deliciously abandoned. She even managed a few flattering words about Hilda, expressing surprise that the car had managed to travel so far without stopping or coming off the road. This was encouraging, but I was too busy to listen attentively through contending with the traffic on the Great North Road, which that afternoon was composed only of cars driven by men late for important interviews, bicycles propelled by blind imbeciles, and lorries carrying boilers for ocean liners. But we progressed without breakdown or accident, and when darkness fell I was delighted to find that the headlights shone more brightly than before, sometimes both of them at once. By the time The Judge's Arms appeared in front of us I began to feel more cheerful and more appreciative of the unusual treat in store for me.

'Here we are, Nan,' I said, as I pulled up at the front door.

She peered through the cracked window. 'Are you sure? It looks like a municipal lunatic asylum to me.'

'It's very romantic inside. And – according to a friend

of mine who ought to know – they're very broad-minded.'

My heart was beginning to beat more quickly. 'Sure you've got the ring on the right finger?' I asked nervously.

'Of course I have. Put these parcels in your case, will you? I can't possibly get them in mine.'

We got out of the car.

When I had asked Grimsdyke more about The Judge's Arms he had murmured that it was 'a coaching inn in the best English tradition'. It was in the English inn-keeping tradition, right enough, but the most wide-spread rather than the best. The walls of the hall sprouted thickly the heads of deer, otters, badgers, foxes, ferrets, stoats, and weasels, among the glazed bodies of pike, salmon, trout, perch, and bream in generous glass coffins; in the corner a pair of rigid snipe huddled beneath a glass dome, and over the stairs was impaled the horned skull of a buffalo. The place was so dark, empty, and musty that it immediately reminded me of a corner in the Natural History Museum in Cromwell Road.

On one side of the hall was a door with a cracked frosted-glass panel embossed with the words 'Coffee Room' in curly letters; opposite was a similar door marked 'Lounge'. In the corner, carefully hidden by a spiky palm leaning in a large brass pot, was a hatch with a panel inviting 'Inquiries'. In front of the hatch was a ledge bearing a small brass hand-bell, secured to the wall by a length of chain.

'Cosy place,' murmured Nurse Macpherson.

'It's bound to be rather quiet,' I said, feeling I ought to defend the hotel as well as Haemorrhagic Hilda. 'We're in the country, you know.'

She made no reply, so I set down our cases, picked up

the bell, and gave a timid tinkle. She began to make up her face, and I read a large notice in a black frame explaining that it was your own fault if anyone walked off with your valuables. As no one appeared, I rang the bell again.

Not a sound came from the hotel.

'I suppose they haven't all been scared away?' said Nurse Macpherson, snapping her compact closed. 'You know, like the *Marie Celeste?*'

'It's just a sleepy part of the world,' I told her testily, for my throat was beginning to hurt badly. 'We're not in Piccadilly Circus, you know.'

'I can see it now,' she went on, gazing at the sooty ceiling where it was gathered round the root of the tarnished chandelier. 'We shall find every room empty, meals half-eaten on the tables, baths filled, beds turned down, fires burning in the grates. Some awful thing came through the front door, perhaps from Mars. Everyone has fled except for one corpse in the garden, with its features twisted into an expression of spine-chilling terror. What a wonderful story for the newspapers! We'll phone the *Daily Express*, and in no time there'll be reporters and photographers and these tedious little men from television saying, "Now, Doctor, will you explain how you happened to be here with a trained nurse – " '

'Please be quiet for a minute. I'm doing my best.'

I rang the bell again, as though vending muffins. With the other hand I rapped the frosted glass, and Nurse Macpherson tapped a large and greasy gong with her foot.

'Yes?'

The coffee-room door had opened. Through it poked the head of an old man, in no collar and a railway-porter's waistcoat.

'We want a room.'

'I'll fetch Mrs Digby,' he said, disappearing.

We waited in silence for some minutes. I was beginning to wonder whether it would be less trouble to bundle Nurse Macpherson into Haemorrhagic Hilda and turn her out at the Nurses' Home, when the glass suddenly shot up beside me.

'Yes?'

I turned to meet one of the most disagreeable-looking women I had seen in my life. She had a thin peaky face, cropped hair, a gold pince-nez on a chain, and a dress apparently made from an old schoolmaster's gown.

'Oh, er, good evening. You're Mrs Digby?'

'Yes.'

'Good. Well, you see, I wanted a room.'

'Yes?'

'You have a room?'

'Yes.'

I was now plainly nervous, for we had reached the point in our adventure that I had rehearsed the most in the secrecy of my room. It all seemed so easy in novels and the Sunday papers: once the initial difficulty of persuading the girl was overcome, the rest of the trip was sheer enjoyment. I had hoped at least for a genial boniface at the reception desk, but now I felt more confident of seducing a hundred women than convincing this sharp-eyed shrew that we were married.

'What name?' she demanded, opening a ledger like the Domesday Book.

'Phillimore,' I said. I had decided that was the most natural-sounding alias I could imagine.

'Sign here.'

She handed me a pen, and spattering ink freely over the page I anxiously filled in the name, address, and nationality. I noticed that the last column left a space for 'Remarks.'

The manageress blotted the book. 'Which of you's Framleigh?' she asked, frowning.

'Eh? Oh, yes, of course, I am. I'm Framleigh. Mr Framleigh. The young lady's Phillimore. Miss Phillimore.'

I cursed myself. Framleigh had been my second choice of *nom d'amour*, and in my agitation I had scrawled it over the visitor's book. Mrs Digby was now looking at me like Hamlet sizing up his uncle.

I tried to smile. 'We want two rooms,' I said.

'And I should think so, too!'

I put my hands in my pockets, took them out, and scratched the back of my head.

'The young lady must register.'

Mrs Digby handed the pen to Nurse Macpherson, who coolly wrote across the page 'Hortense Phillimore. Park Lane, London. Manx.' Feeling I should offer some innocent explanation of a young unmarried couple arriving for a single night in an unfrequented hotel in mid-winter, I said, 'We happened to be travelling north. We're cousins, you see. We're going to our uncle's funeral. Charming old gentleman, in the brass business. You may have heard of him. We both work in London, and to save the expense we decided to come up together by car, and we asked a man on the road for a good hotel – '

'Er-nest!' Mrs Digby poked her head out of the hatch like a cuckoo-clock. 'Er-nest! Where are you, Er-nest?'

The head reappeared from the coffee-room. 'Yes?'

'Ernest take up the baggage.'

Ernest, who looked unfit to carry anything heavier than a letter, creaked arthritically across the floor.

'The lady's in number three,' said Mrs Digby, taking

from the rack behind her a key secured to a steel flag nine inches long. 'And the gentleman – ' She carefully went to the far end of the rack. 'Is in number ninety-four.'

'Right, said Ernest, picking up our cases. 'Foller me.'

'We happen to be cousins,' I told him as he stumbled up the stairs. 'We're going north for our uncle's funeral. He used to be in the brass business, poor fellow. We happen to work in London, so Miss Phillimore and I decided to come up together. On the road we met a man, and I asked him to recommend a good hotel, He said, "You can't beat The Judge's Arms – " ' '

'Number three!' Ernest interrupted, as though announcing the winner of a raffle. He threw open the door and switched on the light. We found ourselves in an apartment the size of a billiard-room, lined with dark-brown wallpaper and containing a pair of marble-topped tables, a bowl of waxed fruit, a dressing-table ornamented with cherubs, a wash-stand with a mauve jug and basin, and sufficient solid wardrobes to lock up a gang of burglars. In the centre of the room was a large knob-garnished brass bedstead.

Nurse Macpherson, who had said nothing since signing the register, drew in her breath.

'I don't believe it,' she muttered.

'Foller me,' Ernest repeated.

'I'll see you downstairs in five minutes for a drink,' I said. 'Hope you'll be comfortable.'

'Oh, I'll be comfortable all right. I'm used to sleeping in the middle of St Paul's.'

'Foller me!' Ernest insisted.

Number three was on the first floor, but my room appeared to be at the far end of the latest extension to the building, several of which had been added with floors at different levels.

'Don't know why she put you up here,' Ernest grumbled, pausing for breath half-way up a narrow staircase. 'There ain't been no one in ninety-four since the Farmers' Union.'

Number ninety-four was immediately under the roof, a narrow, cold, low, damp room, with a bed, a commode, and a wash-stand topped with a marble slab that reminded me of the post-mortem room. I gave Ernest a shilling, which he looked at carefully before saying, 'Good night!' and disappearing. I sat heavily on the bed. If this was romance, I could understand why Casanovas flourished only in warm climates.

20

I REACHED the ground floor before Nurse Macpherson.
As the hotel had resumed the sullen silence with which
it had greeted us, I decided to explore the door marked
'Lounge'. This led to a small room with some furniture
arranged haphazardly, like the bodies of mountaineers
frozen to death where they stood. There were three or
four more palms, and in the corner was an iron grate,
bare of fire irons, in which a tiny fire blushed with shame.

I was now feeling really ill and I needed a drink
desperately. There was a bell by the fireplace labelled
'Service', but knowing the hotel I supplemented a ring
on this by opening the door and shouting, 'Hoy!'
several times loudly.

From the coffee-room, which was now lighted as a
preparation for dinner, came a thin, dark, short young
man in a tail-suit that stretched almost to his heels.
'What'll you be wanting?' he asked, with the amiability
of citizens of the Irish Republic.

'I want a drink.'

'Sure, you can have a drink if you want to.'

'What have you got?'

'Oh, anything at all,' he told me expansively. 'There's
gin, whisky, rum, Guinness, crème de menthe, port, egg
nogg –'

'I'll have whisky. Two doubles, in one glass. And
have you any aspirin?'

'Wouldn't you be feeling well?'

'I'd be feeling bloody awful. And please hurry up.'

By the time Nurse Macpherson appeared I had downed my quadruple whisky and twenty grains of aspirin, while the waiter found some coal and brought the poker from the office. 'We have to be careful over the fires,' he explained to me. 'Some of them commercial gentlemen pile it up as though they were stoking the *Queen Mary*.'

'Nan, my dear,' I greeted her more cheerfully. 'You're looking very beautiful.'

'My God, I could do with a drink, too. That room up there's absolutely freezing.'

'That would be number three?' asked the waiter sympathetically. 'Oh, that's a terrible room that is. It's a wonder they put humans in it at all. I'd rather sleep in the tent of a circus, that I would.'

'We want some more drinks.'

'Would the lady like a cocktail, now? I could do her a good cocktail, and very reasonable.'

'Two large whiskies will do.'

As he left and we sat down on each side of the fire I began to feel better. 'It's a pity about the single rooms,' I said, looking shiftily to see if the door was shut. 'That old buzzard in the office quite put me off my stride.'

'It doesn't matter,' she said, lighting a cigarette. 'You can creep down as soon as everyone goes to bed. It saves a lot of bother in the long run.'

'You've had some experience of this – this sort of thing?' I asked.

'Really, darling, I wasn't born yesterday.' She glanced round her. 'What a bloody hole you've taken me to, if you don't mind my saying so. This place looks like a waiting-room got up for the wake of a dead station-master.'

'I'm sorry. Really I am.' I reached for her hand. 'But I've never done anything like this before. And – and I did so much want to do it with you, Nan.'

She smiled, and squeezed my fingers. 'You're really very, very sweet.'

The waiter then returned with the drinks.

'I was looking you up in the visitors book, and I see you're from London,' he said. 'What sort of line of business would you be in, now?'

'I'm a doctor.'

I bit my lip; it was my second idiotic slip. Apart from the danger of discovery by confessing my profession, I was now the target for everyone's intimacies.

'Are you now? And that's very interesting.' The waiter settled himself, leaning on his up-ended tray. 'I've a great admiration for the medical profession myself, Doctor. It must be a great work, a great work. I had a brother, now, and he started off to be a doctor, but he had some sort of trouble with the authorities. Now he's an oyster-opener in one of the big hotels in O'Connell Street. Oh, he would have been a fine doctor, he would, a lovely pair of hands he had on him. And the lady wouldn't be a nurse, would she?'

'It happens that we are cousins,' I told him firmly. 'Our uncle, who was in the brass business, has unfortunately died suddenly. We are attending his funeral. The reason we are travelling together is that we both work in London, and it is obviously more convenient for us to share the same car. The reason we are in this hotel is that we met a man on the road – '

'Now it's a very convenient thing that you should have come tonight, Doctor, because I was having a lot of trouble with my feet, you see, and I was meaning to go to a doctor tomorrow. But now you're here, it'll save me

189

the journey. I think that the arches must be dropped, or something, but I get a sort of burning pain along here which sort of moves round and round – '

'I'll hear about your feet later, if you really want me to. Will you please get us two more drinks.'

'But you've only just started those.'

'I know. But we shall have finished them before you can turn round.'

'I've had some trouble with my kidneys, too, I'd like to talk to you about, Doctor.'

'Yes, yes! Later if you like. But drinks now.'

'Just as you please, Doctor. I don't mind at all.'

We had several more drinks, after which Nurse Macpherson became more romantic. The waiter fortunately had to go and serve dinner.

'How about some food,' I suggested.

'Ummm! I'm ravenous. And there's a good three hours to kill before we can decently disappear.' I kissed her, and she began to laugh. 'I wonder how old Plumtree is?' she asked. Both laughing, we entered the coffee-room.

*

I later decided that the decline of the evening really started with dinner. The coffee-room itself instantly damped our spirits. It was a long, cold place, decorated only with pictures of horses in heavy gilt frames. Most of the tables were bare, those laid for dinner being huddled round a small fire in a large grate at one end. Our fellow diners were a pair of old ladies at a table thickly covered with patent-medicine bottles, an elderly couple, a red-faced, fat man with a ginger moustache, and a thin, white-haired man who was drinking soup and reading the paper propped against a bottle of beer. Everyone was silent and eating steadily, as though they were anxious to get back to the unknown corners of the hotel where they lurked.

'If you please, Doctor, over here, Doctor,' said the waiter loudly, interrupting his service and clattering a vegetable dish on the table. 'I've put you nice and near the fire, Doctor.' He crossed to a small table almost in the hearth and began beating the seat of a chair violently with his napkin. 'There you are, Doctor. And the young lady, too, now, Doctor. Nice and cosy, would it be?'

Coming from a land where only the Church and the medical profession are venerated, the waiter had automatically made us his favourites. This was good for the service, but it immediately made everyone in the room fix us with their fiercest attention.

'And what would you be having, Doctor?' he continued as we sat down.

I looked at the menu. 'I'll have some of the Potage Dubarry,' I said, trying to appear unaware of the spectators.

'Oh, I wouldn't have any of that, Doctor.'

'Very well,' I glanced at Nurse Macpherson. 'We'll try the steamed plaice with pommes vapeur and cabbage.'

The waiter, who had his order-pad in one hand, scratched his head with the butt of his pencil. 'I wouldn't touch the fish if I was you, Doctor. Mind, it's not a thing I'd tell anybody, but even the cats downstairs are refusing the fish.'

'How about the casserole de mouton? And we'll have some wine.' He looked blank, so I added, 'You have some wine?'

'Sure, we've got wine. I'll bring you a bottle.'

'Red wine,' I insisted. 'I'd like to choose a Burgundy, if you've got one ready at room temperature.'

'You just leave it to me, Doctor.'

'Did I understand, sir,' said the man with the ginger moustache, 'that you are a medical man?'

I nodded.

'My name is Major Porter,' he continued. 'If I may effect an introduction to your good self and your lady wife – '

'I'm a lady, but no wife,' Nurse Macpherson said tartly.

'We're cousins, as it happens,' I explained. 'We have an uncle in the lead business in Scotland, who died, and we've been to his funeral. So we came together because we both work in London. I mean, we're going to his funeral. Poor fellow.' I felt that my whisky before dinner had made the story mildly confused, so to clarify it I added, 'He wasn't in the lead business, I mean the brass business.'

I noticed Nurse Macpherson's mouth harden.

'I hope you won't mind my saying so,' Major Porter continued, 'but I don't believe in doctors. I've nothing against doctors individually, mind – not a thing. Some of my best friends are doctors. I've no faith in the medical profession as a whole.'

'Neither have I,' said Nurse Macpherson, with the frankness of the slightly tipsy.

'Really, madam? I'm interested to hear it. Are you – forgive me if I ask – at all connected with medical work?'

'Yes, I'm a member of a Sisterhood of Druids. We use a good deal of mistletoe, and aren't past sacrifice at sunrise. Can I do anything for your warts?'

Major Porter seemed surprised, but continued, 'I'm sure you'll be interested in my case, Doctor. In fact, I'd like your opinion on it. Not that I expect you to approve of my treatment.' He looked at me slyly. 'You fellows stick together, eh? There's no closed shop like the doctors' shop, I often say. I mean no offence, of course. Now would you believe it, Doctor,' he said, drawing back his coat and protruding his abdomen proudly, 'at the age of five I was given only six months to live?'

I recognized wearily the doctor's second social blight: worse than the men who insist on telling you about their orthodox illnesses are the people cured by faith, herbs, and osteopathy. Major Porter addressed the coffee-room about his miraculous lease of life while we ate our mutton stew and drank our wine, boiling hot from under the stillroom tap. By the time the waiter reverently bore us the porcelain slab with the remains of the cheese, the Major was tugging up his trousers and pointing to the scar of his old tibial osteomyelitis. The white-haired man, who like the Major was a commercial traveller, joined in with the story of the remarkable cure effected by a man in Catford on his sister-in-law who came out all over when she ate strawberries. Then the waiter made himself comfortable leaning against the fireplace and began talking about his kidneys.

'What you need for your kidneys', declared Nurse Macpherson, with slight slurring, 'is pure water. Flush them. Drink water – several gallons a day.'

'That's a damn silly remark,' I said. I was beginning to have a hangover, my throat was raw, and I was starting to shiver. 'That treatment went out with pneumonia-jackets and ice-bags. You restrict fluids and give 'em a high protein intake.'

She looked at me steadily. 'Have you ever nursed a case of nephritis?' she demanded.

'You don't have to know any medicine to be a nurse, my dear. Any more than you have to know dietetics to be a good cook.'

She was about to reply, when the old gentleman said, 'Doctor and nurse, eh? What brings you to this part of the world?'

'We met a man on the road who recommended the hotel. You see, we're cousins. We're going to the funeral of our uncle in the brass business – '

'For God's sake!' shouted Nurse Macpherson. 'Not again!' She stood up. 'I'm going to bed.'

Bed! I suddenly remembered what we were there for.

'I'm going in a minute, too,' I said, as she stalked from the room.

'It isn't ten yet,' said the Major. 'Let's have a drink.'

'No thanks.' I turned to the waiter, who was rubbing his loins thoughtfully under his coat. 'Bring me what's left in the whisky bottle. I'll take it to my room.'

I sat on the edge of my bed feeling miserable. I wished I were tucked up in a ward at St Swithin's, with someone bringing me throat lozenges every half-hour. But I would have to go through with it. Nurse Macpherson, the un-ruffled heroine of a dozen such adventures, would roast me in her contempt if I didn't. After waiting for the hotel to become silent I slowly undressed and put on my dressing-gown. Carefully I opened the door. I began to creep down the stairs towards the first floor.

The effect of fever, excitement, and alcohol raised my pulse rate alarmingly as I felt my way along the darkened corridor towards room number three. I had carefully memorized my landmarks before dinner, and I remembered that you turned left by the fire-extinguisher, went down three steep stairs, and reached the first-floor landing. I was checking my position by feeling for a marble statuette of Britannia when the light went on.

'Yes?'

Mrs Digby, in hair-net and dressing-gown, stood at her bedroom door.

I tried to smile again. 'Good evening.'

She said nothing.

'I was looking for the bathroom.'

'There's a bathroom on your floor.'

'Oh, really? Is there? I didn't notice it.'

'It is opposite your room. There is "Bath" written on the door in large white letters.'

'Thank you. Thank you very much. Stupid of me, coming all this way. Should have seen it. All conveniences, what? Good hotel. Capital!'

She made no reply, so I made my way back along the passage. She waited at her open door until I had disappeared, then put the light out. I tried to creep back after shivering on the upper landing for ten minutes, but she opened her door again before I had reached the foot of the stairs.

'Did you say opposite my room?' I asked. 'With "Bath" on it?'

'Yes.'

'Well. Thanks. Good night to you. A very good night to you.'

I went back to my bedroom and drank the rest of the whisky. It was then eleven-thirty. Clearly I should have to wait another hour, or even two, before operating my risky sortie. I lay down on top of my bed and picked up the *Lancet*, which I had somehow included in my packing.

When I woke up it was eight-thirty in the morning.

'God Almighty!' I said. I already saw myself the laughing-stock of St Swithin's. I dressed quickly, dashed downstairs, and threw open the door of Nurse Macpherson's room. It was empty, with her pink nightie rumpled on the bed. So was the hall below, and the coffee-room.

'If you're looking for the lady,' said the waiter, 'she's gone out for a walk with the Major.'

*

Nurse Macpherson and I said little on the journey home. When we were nearing the Zoo again she began to laugh.

'I don't really see there's anything very funny in it,' I told her sourly. 'I've been extremely unwell all the time, I've got a roaring temperature, and how did I know what the bloody place was like?'

'I'm not blaming you about the hotel I was just thinking what a laugh the girls will get in the Nurses' Home.'

'You wouldn't tell them?' I asked anxiously.

'Why not? A nurse's life is a dull one. It can always do with brightening up.'

'If you breathe a word about this to your friends,' I said savagely, 'I'll spill it all round the Residency.'

She laughed again. 'You wouldn't dare.'

'I damn well would.'

But I knew she was right.

Nurse Plumtree never spoke to me again. Two weeks later Nurse Macpherson became engaged to Bingham.

21

'It was hard luck, old lad,' Grimsdyke said sympathetically. 'Still, it might have been worse. There was one fellow I knew who took a girl away for a week-end to Torquay. Best hotel, no expense spared and so on. They'd just got to their room and he'd opened the windows to have a breath of sea air, when what do you think he saw? Her whole bloody family arriving for their summer holidays at the front door, ma, pa, and several small sisters and brothers. Phew!'

We were sitting in his room some time later. I stared gloomily at my drink in his toothglass; my throat was better, but my pride would wear its scars for a lifetime.

'My trouble', I said solemnly, 'is women.'

'Come, come, Richard! A less flighty citizen than you would be hard to discover. Disregarding the pocket harem you were running until this disaster, I've never thought of you as one of nature's bottom-pinchers.'

'I don't go chasing women right and left, I admit. But ever since I qualified I seem to keep getting involved with them just the same. First it was the shocking female married to Hockett. Then there was that smooth piece of goods in Park Lane. Next Plumtree. Then that frightful nympho Macpherson.'

'Personally, I'm all for getting in the clutches of unscrupulous women now and then,' Grimsdyke said cheerfully. 'Rather fun.'

'But it was never like this when we were students!'

'You underestimate the fatal allure of a medical qualification, old lad. In a quiet way, it's about ten times as powerful as any uniform.'

'You think so?'

'Sure of it. Look at all these chaps that get hauled in front of the G.M.C. Why do you suppose every text-book starts by telling you to have a nurse handy when examining any female from nine to ninety? Then look at the medical profession as a whole. A more pug-ugly collection of badly-dressed social misfits would be difficult to find.'

'True,' I admitted.

'Allure, old lad. Remember it. Have another drink.'

'The unpleasant truth', I said, 'is that I've shirked the responsibility of my ambitions. I'm not saying I've been a good-time Charlie, but now it's a year since I qualified and I haven't gone far towards becoming a surgeon.'

'You've learnt a lot about men and women, as opposed to male and female patients, though.'

'Unfortunately that cuts no ice with the Fellowship examiners. There's no easy way out. I'll have to buckle down to the books again.'

'How about a job?'

I sighed. My appointment at St Swithin's had only another week to run. 'I'll have to start on those beastly interviews again, I suppose. This time, I'll address the committee "Dear Sir or Madam".'

The next few days were sad ones. I would be sorry to lose the companionship of the Residency, and to leave at last the hospital that had been the centre of my life for seven years. But there was no alternative: under the hospital rules I had to make way for the junior men just qualified, and I could never gain promotion to become a registrar like Hatrick without my Fellowship. I could only say good-bye to St Swithin's as cheerfully as possible, turn again to the back pages of the *B.M.J.*, and mark the date of the next reunion dinner in my diary.

Then hope appeared, outlandishly embodied in the Professor of Surgery.

I had gone to his laboratory behind the surgical block to fetch the notes of one of our patients, when he unexpectedly appeared from his office.

'Gordon!'

'Sir?'

'Will you step inside a minute?'

Licking my lips nervously, I followed him into his tiny room, which was filled with ungainly physiological apparatus, pickled things in pots, piles of text-books, journals in several languages, and the forbidding photographs of his predecessors in the Chair.

'Sit down,' he commanded.

I gingerly took the edge of a packing-case marked RADIOACTIVE MATERIAL, while he sat in his swivel chair and pulled his white coat tightly round him. I wondered what was coming. I had carefully avoided the Professor since my return, but every time I caught his eye I had felt him mentally signing my Certificate of Lunacy.

'I had lunch with my friend Mr Justice Hopcroft today,' he began.

I said nothing.

'We recalled that incident when you were my Casualty H.S.'

'I had hoped, sir, he might have forgotten it.'

'On the contrary, we laughed about it heartily. Most amusing in retrospect. Hopcroft has a lively sense of humour, you know. Some of his remarks when passing sentence have caused many a chuckle in the Bar.'

'I'm sure they have, sir.'

There was silence, while the Professor stared hard at a pair of kidneys mounted in a glass jar.

'I was perhaps rather hasty with you, Gordon,' he confessed.

'It's kind of you to say so, sir.'

'Unfair, even.'

'Not at all, sir.' The interview was developing more comfortably than I had imagined. 'I deserved it,' I added indulgently.

'I might say it has worried me somewhat since. If one's judgement once becomes clouded by one's emotions, there's no telling where it will end.'

There was another silence.

'Bingham' said the Professor.

'Yes, sir?'

A friend of yours?'

'Hardly a close one, sir.'

'I will confess, Gordon – in confidence – that Bingham has been something of a disappointment to me. The young man has ability, I'm not denying it, But I sometimes have a little difficulty in the operating theatre deciding which of us is the Professor of Surgery.'

'Quite so, sir,' I said.

'I gather he is not one of the most popular members of the Residency?'

'Not the most popular, sir.'

'A job on the Unit here has come up unexpectedly,' the Professor went on. 'The resident pathologist – Shiradee – has had to return to Bombay. It's a fairly leisurely job, which would give a man plenty of time to work for his Fellowship. Some minor research would be expected, of course. The appointment will be made with the others at the Committee on Wednesday evening – naturally it's my duty to support Bingham for the job. But I can't answer for the rest of the Committee. And in the present state of my relations with Bingham I assure you it would not take a great deal to make me change my mind. In short, Gordon, if you agree, I'd like to make up for my somewhat high-handed treatment of you earlier in your career by at least offering you a chance of the job. Will you apply on the usual form?'

I was so excited that I was almost unable to sleep for the rest of the week. In the operating theatre, where I now approached the table with the confidence of Robert Liston in his prime, I began fumbling so badly that Hatrick declared wearily that I was again in love.

Every time I saw Bingham approaching I avoided him: indeed, I had hardly spoken to him at all since his engagement, apart from stumbling out my congratulations with the rest. But on the evening before the meeting I was forced to seek his company. I was sitting in my room after dinner writing up my case notes, when I became aware of an unpleasant smell. As I sniffed, it grew stronger. From a whiff of the Southend mudflats it rapidly turned into the odour of a faulty sewage farm, and within a few minutes it appeared that some large animal was decomposing in the room next door. Holding my handkerchief over my nose, I banged on Bingham's door.

'Come in!'

Bingham was in his shirt-sleeves, boiling something in a glass beaker over a spirit-lamp.

'Good God, man!' I exclaimed. 'What the devil are you cooking?'

'What, this? Oh, it's manure, old chap,' he said calmly

'Manure!'

'Yes, old chap. Ordinary horse manure. You see, the Prof.'s very interested in the enzymes present in the manure of different animals. Pure research, you know. I've studied it a bit, and it might easily throw a good bit of light on the old human guts. Interesting, eh?' He blew out the lamp. 'I've collected specimens of all sorts of animal manure,' he continued proudly, picking up a row of small test-tubes. 'This one's dog, that's cat, that's pigeon, and the end one's ferret. I just caught the horse when I saw a carter's van stop outside casualty.'

'And what, may I ask, is all this in aid of, Bingham?'

'If you can keep a secret, old chap. I'll tell you. Fact is, I've put in for the path. job on the Unit. Knowing the Prof.'s interested in this line of research, I had a go at it. I've had one or two interesting ideas which I've put to him already, as a matter of fact.'

'And you think you'll get this job do you?'

'Don't want to boast, old chap,' said Bingham, rubbing his hands, 'but I fancy my chances a bit. It happens that the Prof. of Bacteriology and a few of the consultant surgeons have heard of this research I'm doing off my own bat, and it seems to have impressed them. As for the Prof., he's tickled pink. For some reason he particularly wanted to study the elephant's manure, and was talking about cabling to Africa, when I said, "What's wrong with the Zoo?" I've asked them to send a specimen round to him.' He sat down on his bed, and pulled out his pipe. 'By the way, old chap,' he continued, with a sheepish grin. 'Best man win, and all that?'

'Eh?'

He nudged me. 'Know what I mean, old chap, don't you? Don't worry, I'm as broadminded as the next. About Nan. You were a bit sweet on her yourself, eh? When she went on nights, I mean. You couldn't blind me to it. Still, no hard feelings. Only one of us could be chosen, couldn't he, old chap? I hope the fact that you didn't make any headway doesn't prevent our shaking hands?'

'It certainly doesn't,' I said shaking.

'She tells me you tried to kiss her once,' he added, nudging me again. 'But no ill will, old chap.'

'One of us, Bingham, is a very, very lucky man,' I told him, laying a hand on his shoulder.

'Very decent of you, old chap.'

'Not a bit,' I said. 'Old chap.'

The next twenty-four hours were worrying. Knowing Bingham's ability to worm his way into the estimation of his seniors, I was increasingly despondent about my chances of stealing the pathology job from under his nose. As the morning of Wednesday passed I felt that I was again waiting for the result of an examination, with the recollection of having made one certain boner in the middle of the fourth question.

'It's no good worrying,' Grimsdyke said, as we sat in my room before supper. 'The old boys will gather for the meeting in about an hour's time, and you'll either be in or you won't. And anyone with half an eye can tell that Bingham's a first-class tapeworm.'

'But he's a damn clever tapeworm,' I insisted. 'Look how he bamboozled the Prof. in the first place. Now he's playing mother's little helpmeet over this research business. Oh, blast Bingham!' I said with sudden bad temper. 'He did me out of the first job, and now he'll dish me with this one. I wouldn't mind if he was a decent human being, but of all the nasty, grovelling, slimy – '

The telephone began ringing in the room next door. As it continued, I yelled, 'And now I have to answer his bloody phone for him!'

When I came back I was grinning.

'I think I'm going to get that job,' I told Grimsdyke. 'You do? And why?'

'That was the Prof. The Zoo have sent him his specimen of elephant's manure all right. Seven tons of it. They've unloaded it in his front garden.'

*

I was appointed Resident Pathologist to the Surgical Professional Unit, and at the same meeting Grimsdyke was promoted to Senior Resident Anaesthetist.

'Very gratifying,' he said, as we strolled contentedly into the Residency after the pubs had shut that night. 'Very, very gratifying. Virtue triumphant, vice confounded and all that.'

'I can't believe it,' I said. 'I just can't believe it! It means we've got another whole year to enjoy the hospitality of dear old St Swithin's. We will grow old together, old lad. But I didn't know you were putting in for the anaesthetics job. You never told me.'

'Didn't I?' He screwed in his monocle. 'Must have forgotten to mention it. The fact is – and far be it from a Grimsdyke to express any liking for the toil that earns his daily bread – but I'm getting quite interested in doing dopes. Also – I fancy myself – I'm getting the hang of it right and left. Did you notice that endotracheal tube I passed this morning? Very pretty.'

'You're as bad as Bingham,' I said laughing.

'Ah, Bingham! I might add that, in case my sterling qualities as an anaesthetist were overlooked at tonight's meeting, yesterday I handed that old trout's cheque for ten thousand quid to the senior anaesthetist to buy himself some research. I fancied that might strengthen the old boy's determination if voices were raised against me.'

'You're *worse* than Bingham!'

I found Bingham in his room, starting to pack.

'Well, old chap,' he said, trying to look pleasant, 'you got the better of me this time, eh?'

'I'm afraid so, Bingham. No ill will, I hope?'

'Oh, no. Not a bit, old chap. We've always been chums, haven't we? Besides, I have something which you can never have.'

Deciding that he was referring to Nurse Macpherson, I said, 'Too true.'

'I think I'll have a go at general practice,' Bingham went on. 'Just for a spell, of course, before I get my Fellowship. Does a chap good.'

'Have you anywhere in mind?'

'Not exactly,' he continued, folding his trousers. 'But there's a jolly smart agency I'm going to tomorrow called Wilson, Willowick, and Wellbeloved. They'll fix me up.'

'Yes, they'll fix you up, all right.'

'There's just one thing,' he continued. He grinned sheepishly. 'Fact is, not getting this job's a blessing in disguise. In G.P. I can afford to get married a bit earlier, and – well, Nan and I will probably be man and wife by the end of next week. It's jolly good, and I'm jolly pleased, of course, but it's a bit of a rush. Hasn't given me time to arrange anything. Thing is, old chap, where's a good and fairly inexpensive place to spend the – ah, honeymoon? Do you know of anywhere?'

'The Judge's Arms,' I said immediately. 'It's a hotel on the way north. Very romantic.'

'Thanks, old chap. I'll remember that.'

'There's just one thing. I'd make a surprise of it – keep it quiet where you're going until you actually arrive. A chum of mine did, and claims it gives you something to talk about in the painful journey from the reception.'

'By jove, old chap, what a terrif. idea! I'll certainly do that. Well, thanks a lot, old chap.'

'Don't mench, old chap,' I said. My happiness was complete.

Written by Robert Savage

Published by Thomas Cook Publishing
A division of Thomas Cook Tour Operations Limited
Company registration no. 3772199 England
The Thomas Cook Business Park, Unit 9, Coningsby Road,
Peterborough PE3 8SB, United Kingdom
Email: books@thomascook.com, Tel: +44 (0) 1733 416477
www.thomascookpublishing.com

Produced by Cambridge Publishing Management Limited
Burr Elm Court, Main Street, Caldecote CB23 7NU
www.cambridgepm.co.uk

ISBN: 978-1-84848-494-8

This first edition © 2011 Thomas Cook Publishing
Text © Thomas Cook Publishing
Cartography supplied by Redmoor Design, Tavistock, Devon
Map data © OpenStreetMap contributors CC-BY-SA, www.openstreetmap.org,
www.creativecommons.org

Series Editor: Karen Beaulah
Production/DTP: Steven Collins

Printed and bound in Spain by GraphyCems

Cover photography © Patrick Ward/Alamy

As one of the world's longest establ[...]
and best-known travel [...]
Thomas Cook are the experts in tr[...]

For more than 135 years our
guidebooks have unlocked the secrets
of destinations around the world,
sharing with travellers a wealth of
experience and a passion for travel.

**Rely on Thomas Cook as your
travelling companion on your next trip
and benefit from our unique heritage.**

Thomas Cook **pocket** guides

WINDSOR

CONTENTS

SYMBOLS KEY

The following symbols are used throughout this book:

ⓐ address ☏ telephone ⓦ website address ⓔ email
🕒 opening times Ⓝ public transport connections ❶ important

The following symbols are used on the maps:

i information office ▪ point of interest
✚ hospital ═ motorway
🛡 police station — main road
🚌 bus station minor road
🚆 railway station — railway
✝ cathedral
❶ numbers denote featured cafés, restaurants & venues

PRICE CATEGORIES

The ratings below indicate average price rates for a double
room per night, including breakfast:

£ under £99 ££ £100–£150 £££ over £150

The typical cost for a three-course meal without drinks
is as follows:

£ under £20 ££ £20–30 £££ over £30

▶ *It's not hard to imagine why this is the Queen's favourite weekend home*

INTRODUCING
Windsor

Introduction

You can't say the word Windsor without conjuring up images of the grand **Windsor Castle**, the royal family, horse racing and **Eton College**. The **Changing of the Guard**, the humongous hats designed for **Royal Ascot** and horse-drawn carriages dashing through the cobbled streets are common sights here, and the town thrives on this rich cultural heritage.

Residents of the Royal Borough are proud of their town and with good reason. Windsor is after all one of the most popular tourist destinations in the United Kingdom, and indeed the world. A stroll along the banks of the **River Thames** and a meander through the historic town centre will explain in seconds why so many travellers are drawn here, and just how quintessentially British the town is.

The international landscape might have changed since William the Conqueror established the town, but most of the amazing architecture, the parks and the town's rich cultural inheritance remain.

The shop where H G Wells worked on *The War of the Worlds* and the castle library where Shakespeare wrote *The Merry Wives of Windsor* exemplify Windsor's literary legacy, and you won't go far without recognising a familiar scene from one of the many Hollywood blockbusters that have been filmed in the town.

The River Thames is a big part of local life and hundreds of spectators are drawn down to its banks when the rowing teams from Eton College take to the water, and when the celebrities who own a home on White Lilies Island come to town. Windsor isn't just a holiday home for the Queen, after all.

The permanent residents are a big part of the town's charm too, and you won't be left looking at a map for long before a passer-by stops to offer guidance. Add to this an abundance of quaint one-of-a-kind shops, a local culinary scene headed up by the likes of Heston Blumenthal and the excellent shows taking to the stage at the Theatre Royal, and you have a reasonable idea of the treats that lie in store for you in Windsor.

⬤ *The Changing of the Guard is a world-famous tradition*

When to go

The jam-packed annual events calendar in Windsor means that there's always something going on in the area to suit all tastes and budgets. From the free polo matches on **Smith's Lawn** in **Windsor Great Park** between April and September to the big **Windsor Festival** in September and October, there really is something here for everyone. The weather, like many of the attractions in the Royal Borough, is typically British and can change in a moment, so expect unexpected sunshine and always bring an umbrella. The summer months are particularly popular with outdoor sport enthusiasts, who flock to the area to enjoy the facilities built for the **2012 Olympic Games**.

ANNUAL EVENTS

January–March In January the biggest celebrations in town are the New Year and Chinese New Year parties – the latter sometimes falling in February instead. These are soon followed by the popular Flippin' Windsor and Eton Pancake Challenge. In March look out for the Windsor Festival Spring Weekend, the Italian Market and the opening day of Legoland.

April–June April is all about the Easter events on the High Street and in Windsor Great Park, not to mention the celebrations surrounding the Queen's birthday. May brings with it the Royal Windsor Tattoo and Horse Show, and June kick-starts the summer with Tango on the Bridge, the Royal Windsor Triathlon and Garter Day at the castle. The biggest event of June, however, is Royal Ascot – four days of horse racing attended by the royal family.

July–September In July make time for Cartier International Polo in Windsor Great Park and in August enjoy the Windsor Beer and Jazz Festival in Alexandra Gardens. September brings the Windsor Half Marathon and the first half of the annual Windsor Festival.

October–December After the Windsor Festival wraps up, calendar highlights in October include the Willmott Dixon Day – with a food fair and racing at Ascot. In November the Christmas Shopping Village arrives and the Christmas lights are switched on in Windsor and Eton. In December The Savill Garden leads the festive charge with a packed events programme, the Windsor Reindeer Parade trots through town and the Christmas markets arrive.

🔺 *Windsor High Street plays host to many a celebration*

History

The history of Windsor – which lies less than 34 km (21 miles) away from London – is one of a settlement that has enjoyed many powerful, often royal, connections, including such major figures as William the Conqueror, Henry VIII, Queen Victoria and the current royal family. The town is very much part of Britain's historical fabric.

Windsor has played a crucial role in the evolution of Great Britain – a role that can be traced back to the Battle of Hastings in 1066. William the Conqueror's rapid military success left him with the problem of occupying a foreign land with a hostile population. His forces were spread too thin to accomplish this by numbers alone and so a secure network of fortresses was constructed in order to provide security, and maintain his authority.

Three fortresses, including the Tower of London, were built around the British capital, and in turn were reinforced by another ring of battlements – approximately 32 km (20 miles) or one day's march away. Windsor was the site of one such fortress: occupying an easily defendable chalk outcrop high above the River Thames. The river's proximity was an important part of the decision to choose Windsor as a second line of defence – given its use for transportation and as an essential lifeline to London.

William's Saxon predecessors had constructed their defences nearby in the ancient settlement of Windlesora, now known as Old Windsor. This was later abandoned, but the name was transferred to the newer settlement and shortened over time. Over the years the castle evolved from a wooden fortress to the solid stone

🔼 *The town boasts a long history of royal connections*

building it is today and, in the ten centuries that it has been occupied, the castle has only been laid siege to on two occasions.

The town around the castle also evolved – an accomplishment all the more remarkable given the absence of any manufacturing industry. In fact, to this day, the majority of industry in the area is found in the neighbouring town of Slough. This includes the Mars Bar factory, a facility capable of producing millions upon millions of chocolate bars every year.

Today the town thrives on its cultural legacy and the visitors this attracts – a prosperity threatened only by events such as the devastating fire that almost destroyed Windsor Castle in 1992. The rebuilding work took many years and a staggering £37 million, but the newly restored castle still stands proud over the Royal Borough of Windsor and Maidenhead.

Culture

The most famous facet of Windsor's culture is undeniably the family that takes its name from the town – the Windsors. It is, after all, the royal family that attracts visitors from all over the world to see the artworks, extravagant gifts from foreign heads of state and the coats of armour on display in the living quarters, dressing rooms, galleries and corridors of Windsor Castle. Add to that the spectacular Changing of the Guard, the Queen's penchant for horse racing at Royal Ascot and royal weddings at the Guildhall, and it becomes clear how intrinsic the Windsors are to the culture of the town.

The **Theatre Royal** is also a key component in the culture of Windsor, but the Queen and her family might find it more difficult than usual to see one of the many excellent local productions and West End shows here; ironically, the theatre has no 'royal box'.

The ever-changing multimedia exhibitions and live performances at **The Firestation Centre for Arts and Culture** are a real treat for entertainment seekers, and over the river in Eton the abundant art galleries are filled with contemporary masterpieces. The competition fever that surrounds the boat-racing clubs from Eton College is also a huge part of the town's make-up, and serves as a further cultural enticement.

To top it all off, visitors will be delighted to discover a vibrant culinary culture that thrives on both sides of the Thames and guarantees to satisfy all palates and budgets.

▶ *The castle sits in beautiful and extensive grounds*

MAKING THE MOST OF
Windsor

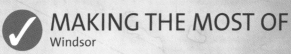

Shopping

Shopping might not seem like the most obvious pastime for visitors to Windsor, but with the sheer volume of specialist retailers, travelling markets and one-of-a-kind shops throughout the town, it's hard not to set aside some time for a spot of retail therapy.

Peascod Street is the best place to start for shopaholics visiting Windsor for the first time and it's on this car-free street where you can find the best mix of high-street brands, including Marks & Spencer, and local department stores such as Daniel. There's also a Fenwick department store in the area known as **King Edward Court**. This runs parallel to Peascod Street and is connected to Windsor & Eton Central Rail.

Heading along Peascod Street and away from the castle will take bargain hunters to **Lower Peascod Street** and **St Leonards Road**. Here local craft shops, fine food stores, jewellery makers and florists abound, and at every turn there's a quaint café offering sanctuary from those draining credit-card workouts. The **Windsor Royal Shopping** arcade also has a great range of outlets. As busy as the **high streets** in Eton and Windsor might be, the two shouldn't be overlooked, especially if you're on the hunt for locally produced woollens, pottery and other fine Windsor fare to take away as gifts.

If markets are more to your liking, then the **Ascot Farmers' Market** on the third Sunday of each month at Ascot Racecourse is a must. This is a highlight on the local shopping scene – similar in size and variety to the much-admired **Thames Valley Farmers' Co-operative Market**, which you'll find on St Leonards Road on the first Saturday of the month.

⬥ *The hub of Windsor's shopping scene*

Eating & drinking

If you like to eat well, then you are certain to find a café, restaurant or gastro-pub in Windsor that'll fill a hole and have you coming back for more. From top-quality treats at Michelin-rated restaurants to scrumptious budget eats at The Vansittart Arms (affectionately known as The Fancy Tart among locals), there are stops on Windsor's culinary circuit to suit all tastes.

Just like any other large town in the United Kingdom, you can expect to find your fair share of big-name chain restaurants in key locations across town, but mixed in among these you'll also find a good selection of unique establishments, serving up tasty local produce and extravagant afternoon tea – just as you'd expect in Royal Windsor.

If it's top-notch nosh that you're after, then be sure to phone ahead and try your luck in getting a reservation at The Fat Duck in the nearby village of Bray. The taster menu at Heston Blumenthal's restaurant doesn't come cheap, but it holds three Michelin stars and was voted Best Restaurant in the UK in the 2008 *Good Food Guide*. Or head for The Waterside Inn, also three-Michelin-starred and also in Bray, where the Roux dynasty has presided over exceptional cooking for more than 30 years.

For high-quality dining at a slightly more reasonable price, restaurants such as Strok's Restaurant and The House on the Bridge – both overlooking the River Thames – are a safe bet, and even if you're on a strict budget you can still eat like a king in some great locations. The Two Brewers pub is a prime example of this: located just seconds away from Windsor Great Park, it has a great-value menu.

If you're after a quick bite to eat, the cafés and sandwich shops along St Leonards Road offer a great selection of tasty treats. For something more substantial the arches surrounding Windsor & Eton Central Rail are a good bet, as are the many eateries along Eton High Street.

⬥ The Two Brewers, for good-value British pub grub (see page 67)

Entertainment

The entertainment on offer in Windsor is diverse and plentiful – to the extent that it really would pay dividends to sit down beforehand with a notebook and plan ahead for a day or night out on the town. From the family-friendly **Royal Windsor Wheel** to evening racing at the **Royal Windsor Racecourse**, you'll easily find something to suit all members of the family.

If you are visiting with children, or just want a chance to indulge your own inner child as you stride through exhibitions like a giant, head to **Legoland**, where visitors can learn to drive in fully functional Lego cars before watching the swashbuckling acrobatics of the modern-day Pirates of Skeleton Bay.

If, on the other hand, you prefer a spot of outdoor entertainment and long scenic walks, then **Alexandra Gardens**, **The Brocas**, **The Long Walk** between **Windsor Castle** and **Ascot**, **The Savill Garden** or **The Thames Path** will all serve you well.

If you take your music with a little bit of an edge, the live sets and bands at the **Old Ticket Hall** are super. The same venue also hosts a variety of stand-up comedy acts, that will appeal to many tastes.

If you feel like spending an uplifting evening in the company of some fine thespians, then the **Theatre Royal** is guaranteed to delight – it offers a great mix of West End shows, incredible local talent and international celebrities. Or you can aim to combine it all in one cultural hotspot with a visit to **The Firestation Centre for Arts and Culture**. This is a very contemporary venue where you'll find an amazing blend of films, music, comedy, dance, theatre and art on offer, not to mention good food. If you can't make it to the castle and you only have time for one cultural encounter when you're in town, make sure it's this.

🔺 *Head to the Theatre Royal for a cultural fix*

Sport & relaxation

Hiking & cycling

In addition to exploring Windsor Great Park and The Thames Path on foot, visitors can easily get around on a bicycle. Bikes are available to hire from the Windsor Roller Rink in Alexandra Gardens. And if you prefer to explore using a pair of roller blades or a skateboard, this is also an option. ⓐ Alexandra Gardens ⓣ 01753 830220

Horse riding

Watching the polo matches on Smith's Lawn is a real treat, but so is travelling the length of The Long Walk in Windsor Great Park in your own horse-drawn carriage. It is something of an indulgence and an outing that depends largely on the weather, but if you have your heart set on travelling in style you can arrange this with **Orchard Poyle Horse Carriage Hire** (ⓣ 01784 435983 ⓦ www.orchardpoyle.co.uk). Alternatively, **Ascot Carriages** offer equally exciting excursions and are based at ⓐ The Savill Garden ⓣ 07811 543019 ⓦ www.ascotcarriages.co.uk

Rowing

Eton College Boat Club is based on Dorney Lake, close to Windsor, where the public are always welcome to watch the rowing, canoeing and dragon-boating lessons. The lake also plays host to major sporting events, including the Rowing World Cup. In 2012 it will be a primary venue for the British Olympic and Paralympic Games. ⓐ Eton College Rowing Centre, Dorney ⓣ 01753 832756 ⓦ www.dorneylake.co.uk

Spa treatment

Everyone needs a little indulgence from time to time, and in Windsor one of the most luxurious outlets for such a service is **The Stables Spa** at The Harte and Garter Hotel. As you might gather from the name, the spa is housed in what used to be a stables – 200 years ago, that is. Today the top treatments here include deep-tissue therapy and skin-plumping facials.

ⓐ High Street, Windsor ⓣ 01753 863426
ⓦ www.akkeronhotels.com

🔺 *Anyone for polo?*

Accommodation

Because of Windsor's popularity on the international travel circuit, there are hotels, bed and breakfasts and apartments galore – at prices that will suit everyone. From luxurious hotel suites just over the road from the castle to quiet, chalet-style lodges on Eton High Street and tranquil, secluded offerings just a short distance away, the accommodation pickings are rich – and very often steeped in history, too.

HOTELS

Savill Court Hotel & Spa £–££ A ten-minute journey away from the historic centre of Windsor, the Savill Court Hotel is surrounded by the type of peace and quiet that only 9 ha (22 acres) of privately owned grounds can provide. The spa, with numerous treatment rooms and an indoor pool, is a recent addition to this superb red-brick building, and weekend guests may catch sight of a wedding taking place against the picturesque background. ❸ Bishopsgate, Windsor Great Park ❶ 01784 472000 ❿ www.savillcourt.com

The Christopher Hotel ££ This former coaching inn is conveniently located in and among the refined hustle and bustle of Eton High Street. The 34 bedrooms and suites on offer are all decorated to a standard well above the hotel's three-star rating and the beds are comfortable to the point where you'll never want to leave. The superb breakfast and chalet-chic suites are definite strong points at this hotel. ❸ Eton High Street ❶ 01753 852359 ❿ www.thechristopher.co.uk

Mercure Windsor Castle Hotel ££ The Mercure Windsor Castle Hotel offers a service that might well receive the royal seal of approval – that is if the Windsors ever grew tired of their castle lodgings. The rooms in this hotel offer a superb view during the Changing of the Guard – and what's on the inside is quite a sight to see, too. The painstakingly preserved Georgian architecture is flawlessly fused with all of the mod cons and, given its proximity to the comings and goings of the High Street, it's refreshingly soundproof too. ⓐ High Street, Windsor ⓣ 01753 851577 ⓦ www.mercure.com

The Oakley Court ££ This rather beautiful French Gothic-style, country house hotel can be found on the outskirts of Windsor, set in 15 ha (37 acres) of landscaped lawns. Guests here will enjoy the excellent selection of rooms, an impressive array of fitness facilities and the AA Rosette Dining Room, not to mention the terrace – a spot perfect for afternoon tea in the great outdoors during the warmer months. ⓐ Windsor Road, Water Oakley ⓣ 01753 609988 ⓦ www.principal-hayley.com

Pinewood Hotel ££ Not far from Windsor and still thoroughly fresh from its renovation in 2005, this four-star hotel offers a tranquil touch of luxury and plenty of space to breathe in its extensive parkland. ⓐ Wexham Park Lane, Slough ⓣ 01753 896400 ⓦ www.pinewoodhotel.co.uk

Royal Adelaide Hotel ££ The Royal Adelaide Hotel is not as close to the castle as some of its counterparts, but it more than makes up for this with the astoundingly good hospitality shown to guests by the staff. A two-minute conversation with the receptionist at this grand hotel will do more for your self-esteem than any self-help book. Recently refurbished bedrooms include flat-screen TVs and Wi-Fi access. ⓐ Kings Road, Windsor ⓣ 01753 863916 ⓦ www.theroyaladelaide.com

Macdonald Windsor Hotel ££–£££ Opened in the summer of 2010, this addition to the accommodation listings in the Royal Borough has been well received – thanks to the 120 luxurious bedrooms and suites, not to mention a key location just opposite the historic Guildhall. If you like boutique hotels that pack a modern punch, then you'll love the Macdonald Windsor Hotel, and the simple but amazing Caleys Lounge and Restaurant on the ground floor. ⓐ High Street, Windsor ⓣ 0844 879 9101 ⓦ www.macdonaldhotels.co.uk

Sir Christopher Wren's House Hotel ££–£££ This elegant town house began life as the home of the famous architect, Sir Christopher Wren (see page 51). Today it's a Grade II-listed building and a hotel that most certainly pushes the boat out. Unique features here include fine dining at the multi-award-winning Strok's Restaurant, and a massage at the Wren's Spa will ensure you feel well and truly relaxed. This is most certainly a high-end option but, nonetheless, a treat worth spending that little bit extra on. ⓐ Thames Street, Windsor ⓣ 01753 861354 ⓦ www.sirchristopherwren.co.uk

The Harte & Garter Hotel and Spa £££ There aren't many hotels where you can wake up from a good night's sleep and open the curtains to spectacular views of Windsor Castle, but that's exactly what you can expect at The Harte & Garter. After a thorough refurbishment in 2007, this four-star lodging offers guests a generous serving of the luxurious and a top location with direct access to the best attractions in town. ⓐ High Street, Windsor ⓣ 01753 863426 ⓦ www.akkeronhotels.com

BED & BREAKFAST

Park Farm £ If you prefer a cosy and informal B&B to a concierge-controlled hotel, you'll enjoy a stay at Park Farm. This family-run business is just off the main shopping strip in Windsor and offers en-suite facilities in every room, along with the option of self-catering accommodation. ⓐ St Leonards Road, Windsor ⓣ 01753 866823 ⓦ www.parkfarm.com

The Rutlands B&B £ The Rutlands B&B is very much all about the Victorian charm that can be found in every facet of this homely building. Whether it's the perfectly polished brass bed knobs or the painted period fireplaces, this terraced building with a balcony will bring a smile to your face. ⓐ St Leonards Road, Windsor ⓣ 01753 859533 ⓦ www.therutlandsbandb.co.uk

SELF-CATERING

Dorney Self-Catering Apartments £ These apartments are located in the beautiful village of Dorney, a few minutes away from Windsor. Guests who stay here will find themselves in the grounds of a picturesque Tudor house, surrounded by luscious and unspoilt English countryside. ⓐ The Old Place, Dorney ⓣ 01753 827037 ⓦ www.troppo.uk.com

THE BEST OF WINDSOR

Windsor is a city where you'll never be bored or stuck for something to do. In fact, there's so much going on that, in order to make the most of your trip, it really does pay to shortlist the cream of the crop.

TOP 10 ATTRACTIONS

- **Theatre Royal** Take in a show at this spectacular setting where, ironically, there's no royal box (see page 67).

- **Windsor Castle** A true beacon of British history, where visitors can explore the State Apartments, Queen Mary's giant Dolls' House and much more (see page 58).

- **Eton College** Established by Henry VI in 1440, Eton is one of the most prestigious, and expensive, schools in the world (see page 73).

- **Windsor Great Park** Over 405 ha (1,000 acres) of beautiful gardens, lakes and woodland span the distance between Windsor Castle and Ascot (see page 53).

- **Legoland** A real treat for all the family: a whole world created from the tiny plastic bricks that everyone loves (see page 56).

- **The Savill Garden** One of the finest ornamental gardens in the UK, home to an extraordinary mix of native and exotic species (see page 57).

- **Peascod Street** A true delight for shopaholics – this pedestrianised strip includes boutique treats and department store fare (see page 61).

- **Royal Ascot** An annual event where the presence of top hats, designer dresses and the royal family is just as important as the horse racing (see page 55).

- **The Thames Path** Britain's greatest river runs through the heart of Windsor, and by it you'll find many miles of beautiful walks and nature trails (see page 53).

- **Eton High Street** Unforgettable architecture, restaurants, one-of-a-kind pubs and more shops than you can shake a stick at (see page 69).

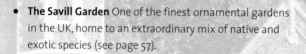
▼ *Illustrious Eton College*

Suggested itineraries

Tried, tested and tailor-made itineraries, showcasing what you can squeeze into your stay in Windsor.

HALF-DAY: WINDSOR IN A HURRY

If you can only spare a morning or an afternoon for sightseeing in Windsor, then use your time wisely by taking a tour of Windsor Castle and Windsor Great Park. The castle ticks every box with its grand fortress, royal walkways and impressive array of galleries. A stroll through the massive Windsor Great Park is the perfect way to round off any trip and the views of the castle's stone buttresses from The Long Walk – between Windsor Castle and Ascot – are truly superb.

1 DAY: TIME TO SEE A LITTLE MORE

After exploring the castle and the park, take the gate exit on Park Street, walk towards the town centre and stop en route for a drink at the traditional pub The Two Brewers or The Crooked House of Windsor. The latter, a quaint café, was constructed using damp timber; when it dried, it dried crooked. Explore the shops and restaurants in the Windsor Royal Shopping arcade, before returning to the High Street and proceeding down the hill and towards the river. Look out for Sir Christopher Wren's House before you cross the bridge over the water to Eton High Street. In Eton enjoy the art galleries, traditional shops and the beautiful buildings of Eton College, before grabbing a spot of supper from one of the many excellent restaurants nearby. Finish off your day with a show at the Theatre Royal.

2–3 DAYS: SHORT BREAK

In addition to the aforementioned activities, take a stroll along the beautiful Thames Path and linger at Eton College for a guided tour. A visit to Legoland and a horse-drawn carriage ride through Windsor Great Park both also come highly recommended.

LONGER: ENJOYING WINDSOR TO THE FULL

With a bit more time at your disposal, take a jaunt along the river to Maidenhead. For memorable day trips, Hampton Court Palace, the magnificent Cliveden Estate and the Royal Botanic Gardens at Kew are all within easy reach.

🔺 *Traditions die hard on Eton High Street (see page 71)*

Something for nothing

With a bit of local know-how it's easy to experience the best of Windsor – without spending a penny. **The Windsor Heritage Walking Trail** offers visitors a rich mix of sights, cultural inheritance and unique local experiences. From stunning views of the River Thames to historic secrets hidden in the cobbled streets of Guildhall Island, and from the Crooked House to the Curfew Tower – the turret that once housed Windsor Castle's dungeons and from which criminals used to be hanged – this self-guided walk is a real treat. A free guide detailing everything you need to know about the attractions you'll see along the way is available from the **Royal Windsor Information Centre** (ⓐ Windsor Royal Shopping ❶ 01753 743900), which is also where the trail begins.

If you enjoy fresh air and walking you are spoilt for choice in this area, with acres of fabulous parkland right on Windsor's doorstep, as well as the picturesque charms of **The Thames Path National Trail** (see page 53). Windsor Great Park and Richmond Park offer space aplenty for roaming and celebrity spotting, as well as stunning views of central London.

There are also plenty of riverside walks that can be enjoyed for free: start in Maidenhead and follow The Thames Path past the magnificent **Cliveden Estate** (see page 80) and on to Cookham and Marlow, attractive and lively towns in their own right. Just south of Maidenhead you can have fun trying out the spectacular **Sounding Arch** (see page 80), built by Isambard Kingdom Brunel – shout up into the bricks and listen to count how many times you can hear your voice echo.

Window shopping can be enjoyed for free, as can a smile at the hefty price tags on the artworks displayed in the galleries lining Eton High Street. The beautiful architecture and interesting shops are attractions in themselves and act as reminders of a more genteel age.

On the Eton side of Windsor Bridge, check out the millennium sculptures designed by Wendy Ramshaw OBE, which make an excellent viewing point across both sides of the river.

◆ *The intriguing sculptures built to celebrate the second millennium*

When it rains

When the great British weather strikes without warning and the heavens open – as they often do – there are plenty of options available for visitors to Windsor. The more prominent attractions include the indoor delights of Windsor Castle (see page 58), not to mention the sheltered itineraries offered by the **French Brothers' boat tours** and the **City Sightseeing bus tours** (see page 46).

Alternatively, you can enjoy a spot of indoor sport at **Windsor Leisure Centre**, where everyone is welcome to come along and participate in the daily classes and fitness events. If you're already soaked to the bone, then you might as well take it one step further and take advantage of the two pools; they appeal to both serious fitness swimmers and to families searching out a bit of fun with a wave machine.

Many visitors also follow the local example when wet weather strikes, by seeking shelter in the many homely cafés that are on offer in the centre of Windsor. St Leonards Road is a great place to go to really soak up the café culture, and offers an international atmosphere in addition to the traditional English tea rooms. Nearby, on Peascod Street, the Daniel department store is a popular indoor retail option.

If your solution to rainy days is to see a good movie, then The Firestation Centre for Arts and Culture (see page 55) offers a good selection of multimedia treats. But if you prefer to catch up with the most recent Hollywood blockbusters, the **Odeon** cinema in the neighbouring town of Maidenhead – a short bus or taxi journey away – is a safe bet.

On arrival

Windsor couldn't be easier to find your way around, and no matter what method of transportation you use to get there – be it train, coach, car or horse-drawn carriage – you'll soon discover that the best way to see the town is on foot. Windsor is perfect for pedestrians – the combination of cobbled streets, pedestrian-only shopping zones, parks and river walks keeps cars at bay and makes any trip here all the more pleasant. This scenic town is also a key spot for avid walkers arriving from the northwest or the southeast via The Thames Path, or embarking on a day's hike from here – but not before devouring a hearty meal at one of the many excellent riverside cafés and restaurants.

Despite the fact that Windsor is definitely geared to those on foot, there are still plenty of parking spaces available for visitors who choose to drive there. Motorists can leave their cars safely while they enjoy the stress-free streets. Furthermore, the many coaches that convey visitors between the town, central London and further afield, nip in and out of the town centre with ease.

It is very difficult to get lost in Windsor with the easy-to-spot, grand castle looming over so much of the town, but if you do become disorientated, or lose sight of the stone turrets as you head towards the bottom end of Peascod Street, don't hesitate to ask for help. The residents of Windsor are courteous through and through, so expect excellent manners, a polite perspective and plenty of assistance.

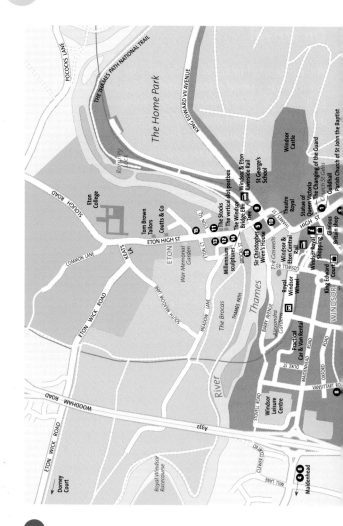

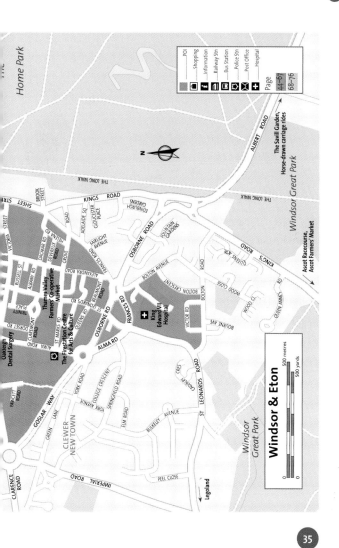

	POI
	Shopping
	Information
	Railway Stn
	Bus Station
	Police Stn
	Post Office
	Hospital

	Page
	44–67
	68–76

Windsor & Eton

0 — 500 metres
0 — 500 yards

ARRIVING

By air

The airport closest to Windsor just happens to be Heathrow, the busiest airport in the world. This has connections to pretty much everywhere that you might need or want to go to. Heathrow Airport is a mere fifteen-minute journey from the centre of the town. Both Gatwick and Luton Airports can also be reached within an hour from Windsor by road.

The most efficient way to travel directly from Heathrow Airport to Windsor is by coach. Express coach services operating on Route 77 provide a direct link between Windsor town centre and Terminal 5 at Heathrow Airport. Coaches between the two locations run every half an hour during the day and once every hour on Sundays and in the evenings. The service drops off and picks up passengers just opposite the parish church on Windsor High Street.

The coach company behind this service is called **First**. You can get more information about the airport transfer service, including timetables, by calling (☎ 0871 200 2233) or by checking online (Ⓦ www.firstgroup.com).

Alternatively, **National Express** coach services (Ⓦ www. nationalexpress.com) also offer direct airport transfers between Heathrow Airport and Windsor.

By rail

When you take a train to Windsor you will arrive at Windsor & Eton Central Rail or Windsor & Eton Riverside Rail. Both stations are centrally located and are just a few minutes away from the High Street and Windsor Castle.

Windsor & Eton Central Rail – a part of the Windsor Royal Shopping arcade – is the terminus point for a branch line that connects Windsor to the neighbouring borough of Slough. Passengers can change at Slough for frequent services to London Paddington and regular connections to Oxford and Reading. An average journey between London Paddington and Windsor & Eton Central Rail takes around 40 minutes.

Windsor & Eton Riverside Rail is, as the name suggests, located by the river. This is the terminus point for direct services between Windsor and London Waterloo. This route stops at several key locations between Windsor and London, including Richmond and Clapham Junction, the latter a station with a direct link to London's Gatwick Airport. The average journey time between the two ends of this line is one hour.

It should be noted that, even though the two stations are not notorious locations for pickpockets, they can become very crowded, thereby presenting thieves with the opportunity to take advantage of new arrivals. So it does pay to stay safe, and keep an eye on your valuables at all times.

By coach & bus

Travelling by coach is one of the most efficient ways of getting into and out of Windsor. The **Green Line** coach service is one example – it operates a popular and highly reliable service between London Victoria Coach Station and Windsor.
Stops along the route of the 701 and 702 Green Line coach services include Hyde Park Corner, Knightsbridge, Kensington and Hammersmith. After Windsor the coaches travel on to Legoland and Bracknell.

National Express coaches connect Windsor to the majority of UK cities and – like most coach services arriving in Windsor – drop off and pick up passengers just opposite the Parish Church on the High Street. There's also a dedicated coach park, used by a number of tour companies, next to Alexandra Gardens.

Local buses are also a very efficient part of Windsor's infrastructure; with an **Explorer FirstDay** ticket, travellers can take advantage of unlimited travel on First coaches and buses within the Royal Borough of Windsor and Maidenhead. The

◆ *Navigate Windsor atop the City Sightseeing bus*

same ticket can also be used on the local bus network to get as far as Heathrow, Staines, Slough, Bracknell and High Wycombe. Bus tickets, free route maps and more information are available from the Royal Windsor Information Centre.

By car

There's no denying that Windsor is the domain of the pedestrian, but visitors with cars are still well catered for.

Drivers arriving from the M4 motorway should take the junction 6 exit – signposted for Windsor. From the M25 the Windsor exit is junction 13, signposted Egham; on the M3 the exit for Windsor is junction 3, signposted Bagshot. Drivers approaching via the M40 should exit at junction 4, signposted Marlow, or junction 2, signposted Beaconsfield.

When you arrive in Windsor there are three primary car parks – promoted by local authorities – that cater for those who wish to stay in the town for more than two hours. These long-stay facilities work out cheaper than other local alternatives and all three are no more than a ten-minute walk away from Windsor Castle. These parking facilities are signposted on the approach to Windsor as Romney Lock, King Edward VII and Alexandra Gardens.

FINDING YOUR FEET

Windsor and Eton aren't difficult to navigate but, during your first trip to the towns, you never know when a map might be useful. This can be especially true when walking along the Peascod Street shopping strip, where eventually you'll lose sight of the castle, the principal guide to orientation.

New visitors should note that although crime levels in Windsor are relatively low, it's always best to take good care of your personal belongings in crowded places.

ORIENTATION

To get your bearings in Windsor, remember that when you're facing the High Street with the castle behind you, the river and Eton are to your right at the bottom of the hill, the shopping along Peascod Street is linked to the High Street from a road in front of you, and Windsor Great Park is to your left – as you follow the High Street to the point where it joins Park Street.

GETTING AROUND

Windsor and Eton are very easy to get around on foot; however, for journeys a little further afield the local bus services and taxi companies are excellent. The seasonal **City Sightseeing** bus tours also cover the majority of Windsor and Eton, with a hop-on, hop-off service that stops at a number of key locations.

You can catch a cab from the taxi rank on the High Street, just outside Windsor Castle. For advance bookings **Five Star Radio Cars** (☎ 01753 858888) and **Windsor Radio Cars** (☎ 01753 677677) are both recommended.

If you want to hire a car your best bet in the area is **Practical Car & Van Rental** (☎ Vansittart Industrial Estate ☎ 01753 833442 ✉ windsor@practical.co.uk).

▶ *The great bridge connecting Windsor to Eton*

THE CITY OF
Windsor

Introduction to city areas

The town of Windsor is 34 km (21 miles) west of Charing Cross train station in London and is bordered to the north by the River Thames. The river separates Windsor from the town of Eton, a short walk away over the Windsor Bridge. Eton and Windsor are key components in the Royal Borough of Windsor and Maidenhead, and experiencing the two areas together will give any traveller a much greater understanding of this historic part of Great Britain.

The first section covers **Windsor**. Seen from above, Windsor is contained in the east and in the north by the curve of the River Thames. Windsor Great Park occupies much of the town's eastern territory; to the south is Legoland and to the west is the village of Oakley Green. It's within these boundaries that visitors can experience Windsor's rich collection of historical landmarks, the influence of the royal family throughout the ages, extensive walking trails, beautiful parks and a melting pot of contemporary culture.

The second section turns its attention to **Eton**, which stands mere metres north of Windsor over the River Thames. This is a town known throughout the world for its ancient school, Eton College, and the many famous students who have graduated from this institution before going on to accomplish great things in politics, literature, engineering and countless other fields. The town of Eton follows the High Street, which stretches from the Windsor Bridge to the collection of college buildings and school grounds.

⬛ *A decidedly charming and rare Edwardian postbox*

Windsor

It is true that Windsor's biggest attraction is the castle and the historic gems contained within it, but there's also a great deal more to experience and enjoy among the cobbled streets, lovingly tended parks and riverside trails. There are beautiful monuments and stunning structures around every corner and, because of the town's historic importance, every building, walkway, street and sight is preserved, restored and safeguarded for future generations. The town is also home to some of the best international fashion designers, an instantly recognisable café culture and a theatre graced by some of the biggest names in the entertainment business.

SIGHTS & ATTRACTIONS

Alexandra Gardens

In August 1902 the land here was regenerated and trees were planted – an event tied into the celebrations surrounding the coronation of King Edward VII and his queen, Alexandra. A bandstand was also erected to provide a stage for the band of the Royal Horse Guards. Today, visitors can enjoy this protected green space, which includes a special sundial that anyone can use to tell the time by standing on the current month of the year and observing their shadow. Alexandra Gardens is also home to the Royal Windsor Wheel during the summer months and at Christmas. This Ferris wheel is similar in concept, if not in scale, to the London Eye. ⓐ Barry Avenue

The Changing of the Guard

This is a show of pomp and military precision that's unrivalled the world over. The procession of guards along the High Street and into Windsor Castle, where they replace those on duty, is accompanied by a band and culminates at the Guardroom in the castle's Lower Ward. Depending on the weather, the event can be enjoyed at 10.50 from the High Street, with the part of the ceremony that occurs inside the castle starting at 11.00. The old guards march back to their barracks at about 11.25. The parade takes place year-round, but never on a Sunday.

ⓐ High Street 🕐 10.50, 11.25 alternate days (Aug–Mar); Mon–Sat (Apr–July) ❶ Admission charge for the part that takes place in Windsor Castle

🔺 *Like clockwork, at 11.00*

TOURS

City Sightseeing bus tours

You can walk across Windsor town centre in less than 30 minutes, but a number of sights on the outskirts are not so easy to reach. The hop-on, hop-off bus tour takes passengers from Windsor Castle past the Guildhall, Windsor Great Park and the village of Datchet. The route passes through Eton and returns to the town centre via Thames Street. ⓐ High Street, Windsor ⓣ 01708 866000 ⓦ www.city-sightseeing.com ⓒ daily (Mar–Nov); for Dec–Feb listings, check online ⓘ Admission charge

French Brothers' boat tours

French Brothers offer a number of trips, but their 40-minute jaunt is a nice, bite-size treat. A major highlight is the sight of some of the small boats that bear the Cross of St George and the Crest of Dunkirk. These boats took part in Operation Dynamo – a last-minute mission that saved thousands of lives in World War II – when a flotilla of unarmed vessels ferried troops back from the failed 1940 landings in Dunkirk. Other tour highlights include Brunel's famous echoing railway bridge and a number of celebrity homes on White Lilies Island. This spot has been a home to Michael Caine and Natalie Imbruglia. ⓐ Clewer Boathouse, Clewer Court Road ⓣ 01753 851900 ⓦ www.boat-trips.co.uk ⓒ 10.00–17.00 (Apr–Oct); schedule subject to river conditions Nov–Mar ⓘ Admission charge

Horse-drawn carriage rides

The world-famous pictures of Queen Elizabeth riding through Windsor Great Park with President Ronald Reagan portray just how intrinsic horse riding is to the culture of Windsor. A carriage ride through the park is a highlight of any trip and **Ascot Carriages** stands out as a family-run business with a personal touch. Starting from the Savill Building, the ride takes in the beautiful water lilies on the Cow Pond, as well as Chapel Wood – populated by maple trees that turn a fiery red in autumn and an oak tree that's over 400 years old. The carriage used on the tour was passed on from Lt-Col Sir John Miller who was Her Majesty the Queen's Equerry and Horsemaster. ⓐ Wick Lane Englefield Green ⓣ 07811 543019 ⓦ www.ascotcarriages. co.uk ⓛ 11.00–16.00 daily; appointments by arrangement, weather permitting ⓘ Admission charge

Windsor Town Walks

The Windsor Town Walk guides are fonts of knowledge about every nook and cranny in Windsor and often extend the hour-long excursions at no extra cost – simply because they enjoy sharing what they know. They have a store of facts about everything from the madness of King George to the leading role of the royal family in British farming. ⓐ Royal Windsor Information Centre ⓣ 01753 743900 ⓦ www.windsor.gov.uk ⓛ 11.30 Sat & Sun (Apr–Aug), call ahead for availability ⓘ Admission charge

Church Street Gardens

Also known as the Heritage Gardens, this is the smallest public open space in Windsor. A cluster of cottages once occupied this site but, after a fire in 1800, all that remains are the fireplaces on the nearby wall. The gardens offer locals and visitors a cherished sanctuary away from the hustle and bustle of town. A stone hopscotch game displays the shields of the monarchs connected to Windsor. ⓐ Church Street, just off High Street

Glorious Britain shop

It's a little known fact that H G Wells was a resident of Windsor in the late 19th century. While here he worked as a draper's apprentice for Rodgers and Denyer, a company that once occupied what is now the Glorious Britain shop. At the same time Wells was also working on his influential science-fiction masterpiece, *The War of the Worlds*. ⓐ 26 High Street

The Goswells

This patch of land was once a slum. During Queen Victoria's reign it was cleared and developed as a grand and green open space with views of the castle and the river. Today it belongs to the National Trust and visitors can enjoy the bowling green – it is home to Windsor and Eton Bowling Club – and the free tennis courts. You'll also find the **Royal Windsor Maze** in here. ⓐ Goswell Road

Guildhall

This amazing building, designed by Sir Christopher Wren in the 17th century, is perhaps one of the most famous wedding venues in the world. It was in the Ascot Room here that Prince Charles married Camilla Parker Bowles, and where Sir Elton John tied the knot with David Furnish. The interior includes chandeliers on loan from Her Majesty the Queen and, outside, keen observers will spot four rather strange columns. When the building neared completion the local authorities refused to pay Sir Christopher Wren unless he added extra pillars to support the overhang. Despite Sir Christopher's argument that his designs held up thousands of tonnes of masonry in St Paul's Cathedral, his protests fell on deaf ears. He eventually gave in and added the columns – but if you look closely you'll see that they're separated from the ceiling by a very slight gap. The supports are purely aesthetic but the authorities were none the wiser and Sir Christopher got his fee. ❸ High Street

Guildhall Island

After the Guildhall became a prominent feature of the town in the 17th century, the cobbled streets around it, including Church Street, became known as Guildhall Island. In days gone by this was the town's main market area; in fact, until the 18th century, Church Street was known simply as Fyssh Street because of the quantity (and smell) of the fish that were sold here. The street also has royal connections: on the wall of The Old King's Head you'll find a copy of the death warrant issued for King Charles I (1600–1649), signed by Oliver Cromwell.

Park Street

This street in Windsor looks like any other collection of homes and businesses before you take account of who their next door

Founded In 1518

The Carpenters Arms

WELCOME

⬤ *Old-fashioned pubs deck the cobbled streets of Guildhall Island*

neighbour is. The fact that the British monarch resides only metres away means house prices here are astoundingly high.

The Royals' Royal Mail postboxes

At the High Street's junction with Park Street you'll notice two postboxes, one red and one blue. The blue box is one of the first airmail postboxes in the country. Neither is still in use, but they remain by royal decree. The same protection is behind the survival of the cobbled streets that crisscross Guildhall Island. The cobbles were replaced with a smooth surface decades ago; however, when faced with this affront to their national heritage, the British public turned to the Queen for support. Three weeks later the cobbles were back. The same thing happened when the red telephone boxes began to disappear. ❸ Park Street

St George's School

This school at the bottom of the Windsor Castle hill was created to provide choirboys for St George's Chapel within the castle. It has supplied the chapel with an uninterrupted line of choristers since 1352 and connects directly to the castle by the House of 100 Steps. ❸ Windsor Castle

Sir Christopher Wren's House

Sir Christopher Wren was a hugely successful architect in the 17th and 18th centuries and, as you'd expect, the house he built for himself mirrors many of his greatest professional achievements. Not much is known of the history of the Wren family in Windsor beyond projects such as the Guildhall and the role played in the community by Sir Christopher's father, the

Dean of Windsor. Today this Grade II-listed, red-brick building is a hotel (see page 24). ⓐ Thames Street

Statue of Queen Victoria

This grand bronze statue is an unmissable sight on the approach to Windsor and a great photo opportunity for anyone who wants to capture the royal spirit of the town, set against the grand backdrop of Windsor Castle. The statue was commissioned and erected to celebrate Queen Victoria's Golden Jubilee. It was designed by Sir Joseph Edgar Boehm and unveiled to the public in 1887, on the site formerly occupied by the town's market. ⓐ High Street

⬧ The towering statue of Queen Victoria

Taxi rank stoppers

Look down at the road by the taxi rank on the High Street and you'll notice a series of metal bars driven into the tarmac. In the days before handbrakes it was somewhat harder to keep a taxi stationary on this incline – especially taxis attached to horses. The bars were therefore installed to prevent the carriages from rolling backwards. ❷ High Street

The Thames Path National Trail

This popular walking trail follows the 296-km (184-mile) route of the River Thames – from its source in the Cotswolds to London. If you're determined, you can reach central London on foot within a day. If, however, you prefer to keep it local, a popular route stretches between Romney Lock, 4.8 km (3 miles) upriver from the Old Windsor Lock, and Bell Weir Lock, a similar distance downriver. ⓦ www.visitthames.co.uk

The Windsor Bridge Elm Tree

When Dutch elm disease destroyed over 25 million of the UK's elms the future of the tree seemed hopeless, until Prince Charles appealed to the USA and began importing a disease-resistant species from North Carolina. One of the first saplings was planted here in Windsor. ❷ Windsor Bridge

Windsor Castle & Windsor Great Park

Windsor Castle is undeniably a huge cultural component of the town, but it's also a major sight in its own right (see also Culture, page 58). The Round Tower at the centre dominates any snapshot and has been built up over the years in order to remain the highest point in Windsor. The castle is often likened to a town – given that it occupies 5.25 ha (13 acres) of land and contains a huge array of fascinating facets. The magnificent **State Apartments** and **St George's Chapel** have to be seen to be believed, and just outside of the castle walls **Windsor Great Park** is home to another battery of visual delights. A quick stroll along **The Long Walk** offers spectacular views towards to the castle, the statue of George III on **Snow Hill** and Ascot beyond. Also in the park, it's worth keeping an eye out for the spectacular polo matches on **Smith's Lawn** – between **The Savill Garden** and **The Valley Gardens**. ⓐ High Street

◔ *Superb views over the grounds and parks that surround the castle*

Windsor Parish Church of St John the Baptist

There's been a church on this spot for over 800 years and visitors can see Saxon arches and Norman architecture preserved in the underground vaults. The original church can be traced back to Henry I (1068–1135), when he moved the royal court from Old Windsor to the castle. Inside the building today, visitors will find a set of ornate glass doors – the Royal Borough's tribute to those who fell in World War II – and a rather famous painting: *The Last Supper* by Benjamin West, presented to the Royal Chapel in 1660 by Brian Duppa, Bishop of Winchester. ⓐ High Street

CULTURE

Ascot Racecourse

This is undoubtedly one of the most famous horse-racing venues in the world. Competitions are held here throughout the year, in addition to a healthy schedule of beer and wine festivals, family days and – of course – Royal Ascot. This event in June is attended by the Queen and many other members of the royal family, and it's during this time that spectators in Windsor Great Park can see the Queen and her horse-drawn entourage leave Windsor Castle and proceed to the racecourse. ⓐ Ascot ⓣ 0870 227 227 ⓦ www.ascot.co.uk ⓟ Admission charge

The Firestation Centre for Arts and Culture

There's been an arts centre in this old fire station for almost 40 consecutive years, and the current incarnation is home to an exciting array of films, music, comedy, dance, theatre and art.

Other attractions include monthly book-swap clubs and open-mic nights. ⓐ St Leonards Road ❶ 01753 866865 ⓦ www.fire stationartscentre.com ❹ 10.00–24.00 Mon–Sat, 11.00–23.00 Sun ❶ Admission charge

Legoland

This land of approximately 55 million Lego bricks is an attraction that brings out the inner child in everyone. Expect interactive exhibits, pirate acrobats and the world's most famous landmarks recreated in miniature. Legoland is worth a

⬣ *A veritable hotbed of all things entertaining*

trip if only to see the diminutive London skyline. ⓐ Winkfield Road
ⓣ 0871 222 2001 ⓦ www.legoland.co.uk ⓛ hours vary daily (Apr–
Nov); closed mid-Nov–Mar ⓝ Bus: shuttle buses operate from both
Windsor & Eton Central Rail and Windsor & Eton Riverside Rail;
Coach: Green Line 701 and 702 ⓘ Admission charge

Royal Windsor Racecourse

What sets Royal Windsor Racecourse apart from its well-known
counterpart in Ascot is the stunning riverside location and the
figure-of-eight layout – and that it stands on one of the largest
islands in the River Thames. There's even a yacht basin for those
arriving by boat. The course was featured in the 2001 film *Last
Orders* starring Bob Hoskins. It offers a year-round racing
schedule. ⓐ Maidenhead Road ⓣ 01753 498400 ⓦ www.
windsor-racecourse.co.uk ⓘ Admission charge

Royal Windsor Wheel

Standing 4 m (13 ft) taller than Nelson's Column, this popular
seasonal attraction is lit up at night by 60,000 LED lights.
The wheel offers great views of Windsor, Eton, the Berkshire
countryside, and even the sparkling skyline of London.
ⓐ Alexandra Gardens ⓣ 020 8241 9818 ⓦ www.royal
windsorwheel.com ⓛ 10.00–22.00 daily (May–Aug); closed
Sept–Apr (excluding Christmas) ⓘ Admission charge

The Savill Garden

A short taxi ride or an enthusiastic hike away from Windsor is
The Savill Garden, a collection that showcases some of the
United Kingdom's most impressive woodland and ornamental

garden species. Rare plants thrive in this 14-ha (35-acre) enclosure and visitors can expect everything from the golden grasslands of New Zealand to giant pumpkins. The 2010 Rose Garden is a beautiful addition to this scenic getaway. ⓐ Wick Lane, Englefield Green ⓣ 01784 435544 ⓦ www.theroyal landscape.co.uk ⓛ 10.00–18.00 daily (Mar–Oct); 10.00–16.30 daily (Nov–Feb) ⓘ Admission charge

Windsor Castle

Windsor's continued prosperity has a great deal to do with its castle. Known as the oldest and largest occupied castle on the planet, Windsor Castle is one of the Queen's favourite getaways, as evidenced by the frequency with which the monarch's personal standard flies from the Round Tower flagpole. The castle is approximately the same size as 268 tennis courts and feels more like a fortified town than a mere fortress. It's also a significant source of employment and military prowess, and has been a huge draw for sightseers for centuries.

An audio tour – narrated in part by The Prince of Wales – takes you around the castle's attractions in the order they're given below. As you begin, one of the first things pointed out is **The Royal Library**. This has been an integral part of the castle since the reign of King William IV (1830–1837) and is reputed to be the place where William Shakespeare wrote *The Merry Wives of Windsor* at the turn of the 17th century. Shakespeare wrote this in just two weeks after Queen Elizabeth I ordered the writer to create some comic relief, during a time of brutal fighting between Protestants and Catholics in Europe.

Shortly after The Royal Library, visitors reach the breathtaking sight of **Queen Mary's Dolls' House**. Built in 1924, this miniature aristocratic townhouse has running water, electricity and hundreds of accessories. There's even a garden designed by Gertrude Jekyll in a drawer below. In the display units around the house are two remarkable French dolls, presented to the young princesses Elizabeth and Margaret Rose in 1938, along with a number of couture outfits from Cartier and Hermès!

The China Museum is certainly worth a look, if only to admire the extraordinary Rockingham Service commissioned by King William IV in 1830. The intricate designs of the time reflect a sense of pride in the British Empire, with their palm trees, pineapples and coral features. The expense of this undertaking left Yorkshire's Rockingham Works bankrupt.

⬤ *The gorgeous architecture of Windsor Castle*

The **Grand Staircase** and the **Grand Vestibule** are located immediately after the museum. The Grand Staircase, which is adorned with beautifully preserved suits of armour and lit by a glazed gothic lantern roof, leads to the Grand Vestibule and the marble statue of Queen Victoria – depicted here with her favourite collie dog.

The **State Apartments** are a sequence of fine rooms that include the **King's Drawing Room**, the **Queen's Ballroom**, **St George's Hall**, the **Semi-State Apartments** and much more. The visitor exits into **Engine Court**.

Inside **St George's Chapel** all eyes are drawn to the stone, fan-vaulted ceiling, added by King Henry VII (1457–1509). A Perpendicular style dominates, with a huge window and soaring pillars. As you leave, look out for Edward III's 1.8-m (6-ft)-long sword. The daily evensong here at 17.15 is an unforgettable event.

The splendid **Albert Memorial Chapel** is one of the many grand projects commissioned by Queen Victoria as a memorial to her much-loved husband, Albert. It was originally built for Henry III in the 1240s and later altered by George Gilbert Scott at the request of Queen Victoria. Inside, visitors can admire the magnificent marble effigy of Prince Albert by Triqueti.

ⓐ Windsor Castle, High Street ⓣ 020 7766 7304
ⓦ www.royalcollection.org.uk ⓛ 09.45–17.15 daily (Mar–Oct); 09.45–16.15 daily (Nov–Feb) ⓘ Admission charge

RETAIL THERAPY

There are plenty of shopping opportunities to be had in Windsor and the fact that most of them can be enjoyed in car-free, pedestrianised streets is a real bonus. Most of the shops can be split into four key areas – **Windsor Royal Shopping**, **Peascod Street**, **St Leonards Road** and **King Edward Court**. There are also unique boutiques and markets dotted around the town, so anyone who likes a good old-fashioned spree is well catered for.

King Edward Court Running parallel to Peascod Street, and slightly removed from the hustle and bustle, King Edward Court offers a good mix of high-street brands, a large Waitrose supermarket and access to Windsor & Eton Central Rail. There's also a **Fenwick** department store here (ⓐ 10–11 King Edward Court ☎ 01753 855537 ⓦ www.fenwick.co.uk 🕐 09.00–18.00 Mon–Sat, 11.00–17.00 Sun).

Markets For stalls selling locally produced organic fare and international treats from farms across Europe, there are only two markets in Windsor worthy of your attention. The first is the **Ascot Farmers' Market**, held in car park three of the racecourse on the third Sunday of each month (🕐 09.30–13.00). This is a great place to buy the genetically unmodified produce championed by the Prince of Wales. The **Thames Valley Farmers' Co-operative Market** takes over St Leonards Road on the first Saturday of the month (🕐 09.00–13.00). Among the delights on offer, the cake stand is always a spectacular sight to see, smell and taste. Both markets take on a distinctively international feel over the Christmas and Easter holidays.

Peascod Street Ask any Windsor resident where the main shopping strip in Windsor is and they'll point you in the direction of Peascod Street. Here you'll find popular high-street brands including Marks & Spencer, HMV and River Island. There are also a number of stand-alone retail hot spots, equally worthy of your credit card's attention. **Daniel** department store (ⓐ 121–125 Peascod Street ⓣ 01753 801000 ⓦ www.danielstores.co.uk ⓛ 09.30–17.30 Mon & Tues, 09.15–17.30 Wed, 09.30–17.30 Thur–Sat, 11.00–17.00 Sun) has a concession within it to match all moods, and sells everything from thick-knit wool jumpers to celebrity cosmetics.

At **John Goodwin** designer clothes shop (ⓐ 95 Peascod Street ⓣ 01753 866116 ⓦ www.johngoodwin-online.com ⓛ 09.30–18.00 Mon–Sat, 11.00–17.00 Sun), customers can expect made-to-measure orders, home delivery and private evening parties.

🔺 *Treat yourself at the Thames Valley Farmers' Co-operative Market*

St Leonards Road Unusual, unique and irreplaceable is the order of the day at **Rules Antique Interiors** (@ 39 St Leonards Road ❶ 01753 833210 Ⓦ www.rulesantiques.co.uk ❶ 10.30–18.00 Mon–Sat, closed Sun), where the inventory includes everything from bird cages to weighing scales and antique door knockers to garden statuettes.

If you love cooking and the celebrity chef Anthony Worrall Thompson, then the **Windsor Larder** is a must (@ 59a St Leonards Road ❶ 01753 840272 Ⓦ www.awt restaurants.com/windsorlarder ❶ 08.00–17.30 Mon–Sat, closed Sun). The principle here is simple. You don't need to be a whizz in the kitchen to eat well, so most of what's sold here is ready to reheat and eat. Expect picnics and dinner parties to take away.

Windsor Royal Shopping This beautiful, historic and sheltered arcade is a great place to start your exploration of Windsor's retail scene. Windsor Royal Shopping is built around the Windsor & Eton Central Rail station and the carefully selected shops within cater for all wants and needs.

For a touch of childhood nostalgia, **Mr Simms Olde Sweet Shoppe** (@ Royal Station Parade Shopping Ⓦ www.mrsimms oldesweetshoppe.co.uk ❶ 09.00–18.00 Mon–Sat, 11.00–17.00 Sun) really hits the spot.

For everything to do with oils, vinegars, spirits, cocktails or liqueurs, head for **VoM Fass** (@ Royal Station Parade Shopping ❶ 01753 832173 Ⓦ www.vomfass.com ❶ 10.00–18.00 Mon–Sat, 11.00–17.00 Sun). The stock is stored in oak barrels and mind-boggling bottles.

TAKING A BREAK

CAFÉS

The Crooked House of Windsor £ ❶ Everyone who walks past this charming tea room does a double take because, as the name suggests, the building isn't straight. According to local experts, the extreme lean came about after the wet timber used to build the house warped as it dried. Aesthetics aside, this is a lovely, and safe, spot for tea and a toasted teacake. ⓐ 51 High Street ⓣ 01753 857534 ⓛ 10.00–17.30 Mon–Fri, 10.00–18.30 Sat & Sun

Avanti Bistro Bar Café £–££ ❷ The authentic Italian lasagne is a stand-out dish at this favourite spot for lunch. ⓐ 98 Peascod Street ⓣ 01753 866338 ⓦ www.avanti-bistro-cafe.co.uk ⓛ 08.30–18.00 Mon, 08.30–19.00 Tues–Sat, 09.00–18.00 Sun

RESTAURANTS

The Green Olive ££–£££ ❸ Match the size of your dish to your appetite at this meze-meal restaurant. Dishes include filo pastries stuffed with spinach and feta, beef casserole in a rich red-wine sauce and honey and walnut cake. ⓐ 10 High Street ⓣ 01753 866655 ⓦ www.green-olive.co.uk ⓛ 12.00–15.00, 18.00–22.30 Mon–Sat, 12.00–15.00, 18.00–22.00 Sun

The Fat Duck £££ ❹ This is the triple-Michelin-starred brainchild of Heston Blumenthal – a gastronomic hurricane who adores the science behind cooking. The tasting menu demands and deserves four hours; the price reflects the quality

◔ *The accidentally crooked timber-built tea room*

of unforgettable dishes such as salmon poached in liquorice gel and served with an artichoke vanilla mayonnaise. ⓐ High Street, Bray ⓣ 01628 580333 ⓦ www.thefatduck.co.uk ⓛ 12.00–14.00, 19.00–21.30 Tues–Sat, 12.00–14.00 Sun

Strok's Restaurant £££ ⓺ This superb restaurant offers amazing views over the river and a refined menu. Expect salads with a sherry dressing, succulent lamb dishes and scrumptious chocolate-box desserts. ⓐ Thames Street ⓣ 01753 861354 ⓦ www.sirchristopherwren.co.uk ⓛ 12.30–14.15, 18.30–21.45 daily

The Waterside Inn £££ ⓻ The Roux brothers have been cooking in England since the 1960s and this restaurant – now run by Michel's son Alain – personifies every aspect of the culinary excellence they champion. Dishes range from cocotte of oxtail

🔺 *Confound your tastebuds at The Fat Duck*

and beef cheek braised in Beaujolais wine to date soufflés flavoured with cognac, and served with coffee ice cream. @ Ferry Road, Bray ☏ 01628 620691 @ reservations@waterside-inn.co.uk ⏰ 12.00–14.00, 19.00–22.00 Wed–Sun (Feb–May & Sept–Dec), 12.00–14.00, 19.00–22.00 Tues–Sun (June–Aug); closed Jan

AFTER DARK

PUBS
The Two Brewers ❼ A homely setting for a quick pint and a cheeky pie. It features ancient oak beams, low ceilings and friendly family dogs. @ 34 Park Street ☏ 01753 855426 ⏰ 11.30–23.00 Mon–Thur, 11.30–23.30 Fri & Sat, 12.00–22.30 Sun

The Vansittart Arms ❽ Also affectionately known among locals as the Vanny and the Fancy Tart, this friendly pub welcomes all. In the winter patrons are warmed up by roaring, open fires. @ 105 Vansittart Road ☏ 01753 865988 ⏰ 12.00–23.00 Sun–Wed, 12.00–23.30 Thur, 12.00–24.00 Fri & Sat

THEATRE, MUSIC & COMEDY
The Old Ticket Hall ❾ A top venue for live music and stand-up comedy. @ Windsor & Eton Riverside Rail ☏ 01753 854554 ⓦ www.oldtickethall.co.uk ⏰ 19.00–02.00 Wed–Sat, 19.00–24.00 Sun, closed Mon & Tues

Theatre Royal ❿ This grand setting dates back to George III (1738–1820). @ Thames Street ☏ 01753 853888 ⓦ www.theatre royalwindsor.co.uk

Eton

Just over the river from Windsor, the small town of Eton offers visitors an insight into a way of life that hasn't changed all that much over the centuries. The famous Eton College is very much at the core of this community and the High Street is known far and wide for its collection of art galleries, fine dining, superior, tailor-made clothing and intimate bars.

SIGHTS & ATTRACTIONS

The Brocas
These riverbank meadows offer amazing views of Windsor, its castle and life along the River Thames. They're also a great spot for a quiet summer picnic. ⓐ Brocas Street

Coutts & Co
A bank might not seem a likely candidate for a sightseeing to-do list, but Coutts & Co is worthy of a look. Historically, the services of this bank were offered only to the landed gentry and, even though times have changed, prospective clients still need at least £500,000 in disposable funds to open an account. As you might guess from the crowns displayed in the bank's logo, the royal family have an account here. ⓐ Eton High Street

Eton College
Founded by Henry VI in 1440, this school has become one of the best private educational institutes in the world. The college is, of course, a key contributor to the culture of the town, but from

a purely aesthetic point of view a good deal of the school can be enjoyed and photographed without stepping through the front door. From Eton High Street the key sights include the **College Chapel** and the adjoining **Church Yard**, the **Cannon Yard** of the **Geography Department**, the beautiful dome of the **Library** and the **Burning Bush**, a nineteenth-century lamppost on the corner of Eton High Street and Common Lane. This has been a congregation point between lessons for teachers and students for centuries. ⓐ Eton High Street

Eton High Street

If you have 20 minutes to spare and you enjoy a leisurely stroll, a saunter from the beginning of the High Street by the river

◓ *Stroll down Eton's picturesque High Street*

and up to Eton College is an experience not to be missed. The classic architecture and perfectly preserved wooden shop fronts are a joy to behold and it's easy to lose yourself in the shop windows, which display fine food, antique books and contemporary art. After a few moments wandering along, Eton starts to feel less like a small 21st-century town and more like a quiet, 17th-century village where the pace of life is enjoyably slow.

Millennium sculptures

This series of stainless steel designs by Wendy Ramshaw OBE was commissioned to mark the year 2000. You'll find the stainless-steel bollard sculptures at the beginning of the bridge that connects the town to Windsor. There's also a stand-alone tower bollard with a viewing lens that visitors can aim towards Eton High Street. Take a look through this and see if you can fit in all the sights. Turn around on the same spot and you have a wonderful view of Windsor Castle, rising up over the town and the river below it. ⓐ Windsor Bridge

The Stocks

As you walk along Eton High Street it's not uncommon to see people stopping abruptly to take a second look at something just outside the Tiger Garden Indian restaurant. If you look closely you'll see a set of preserved wooden stocks with metal restraints attached – a device used in the past to incarcerate criminals in a public place. It was hoped that passers-by would think twice about committing a crime if it meant meeting such a humiliating fate! ⓐ 47–49 Eton High Street

Tom Brown Tailors

This traditional tailor's shop was first founded at Number One Eton High Street in 1784. Since then it's been the first port of call for parents looking to equip their children with the correct uniform before they embark on their education at Eton College. The colourful waistcoats designed for the college prefects are an attraction in their own right. ⓐ 1 Eton High Street

The vertical slot postbox

Because of the nearby royal connections, Eton enjoyed many modern conveniences ahead of the rest of the country. This included one of the earliest Victorian postboxes in England – easily identified by the distinct vertical slot. The postbox is still in service to this day, making it the ideal place from which to send a postcard. ⓐ Eton High Street

War Memorial Garden

This garden, halfway along Eton High Street, is dedicated to the memory of the men from Eton who gave their lives for their country in World War I and World War II. The garden is open to all, and more often than not is guarded by a black and white cat, notorious among locals for its daily patrols. ⓐ Eton High Street

CULTURE

Art galleries

Contemporary and classical art are a big part of life in Eton, as anyone who takes a walk along the High Street will soon discover. The price tags attached to some of the offerings on display in the galleries may well leave you breathless, but they are worth a look in all the same. There are plenty of galleries to choose from, but **The Contemporary Fine Art Gallery, The Barker Gallery** and **The Eton Gallery** are popular with residents and visitors alike. ❸ Eton High Street

Dorney Court
A short journey west of Eton and through the picturesque village of Eton Wick is Dorney Court, a Grade I-listed Tudor manor house. The house has been passed down through 13 generations of the Palmer family over 450 years and is still lived in to this day. Because of this it's only open to the public at certain times of the year, but if your trip to Windsor and Eton

🔺 *Eton is a hub for contemporary art*

happens to coincide, it's well worth the effort. The yearly open days are updated on the Dorney Court website. ❸ Court Lane, Dorney ☎ 01628 604638 ⓦ www.dorneycourt.co.uk ✉ palmer@dorneycourt.co.uk ❶ Admission charge

Eton College

Eton College is one of the oldest schools in the United Kingdom and, despite the annual £30,000 attendance fee, places here are fiercely coveted. The school was founded in 1440 by Henry VI to produce the next generation of high-flying scholars, politicians, engineers and explorers, and that's exactly what the college does to this day. Eton has educated 19 British prime ministers, as well as authors George Orwell and Ian Fleming, economist John Maynard Keynes and, more recently, the princes William and Harry – to name but a few. The guided tours of Eton give visitors access to the cobbled school yard, the magnificent **College Chapel**, the classrooms of the lower school and the **Museum of Eton Life**, housed in the former cellar of College Hall.

Certain aspects of the tour are sure to stick in your mind, including the memorials around the Cloisters dedicated to Etonians who gave their lives during wartime, the names of William and Harry etched into the woodwork in the long-standing tradition of graduation from Eton, and the extra-curricular pursuits offered to pupils by their individual tutors: non-examined subjects pursued by students in their spare time include law, medicine, car mechanics and opera! Add to this the cannon in the Geography Department courtyard that was captured in the battle of Sebastopol (1854–5) and the very rare first edition of the Gutenberg Bible (printed in the 1450s) in the college library, and you begin to understand just how special and resourceful Eton College is. ⓐ Eton High Street ⓣ 01753 671000 ⓦ www.etoncollege.com ⓛ Tour times vary, see website for details (Mar–Oct) ⓘ Admission charge

RETAIL THERAPY

Opportunities for a well-earned spot of retail therapy can be found along the full length of Eton High Street and, as you might expect, you'll find a mix of couture clothing, art galleries (serving champagne to their clients) and delicious delicatessens.

C J Reid This chemist and wine merchant is a kitsch treat for any shopper and a practical stop for over-the-counter medicines and remedies. ⓐ 30 Eton High Street ⓣ 01753 863819 ⓛ 09.00–18.00 Mon–Sat, closed Sun

Eton Antique Bookshop If rare and second-hand books are your thing, then the stacks of wonderfully aromatic treasures in this shop are guaranteed to excite. ⓐ 88 Eton High Street ⓣ 01753 855534 ⓛ 11.30–18.00 Mon–Fri, 11.00–19.00 Sat, 12.00–18.00 Sun (hours may vary)

Jack Wills The clothes on sale here are a mix of high-street chic and wonderfully posh casual attire. Expect thick-knit cashmere jumpers, polo shirts galore and effervescent underwear. ⓐ 17 Eton High Street ⓣ 01753 856112 ⓦ www.jackwills.com ⓛ 10.00–18.00 Mon–Sat, 11.00–17.00 Sun

TAKING A BREAK

Zero.3 £ ⓫ The menu at this coffee and sandwich bar offers a good selection of hearty fare and is great value for money. ⓐ 45 Eton High Street ⓣ 01753 864725 ⓛ 07.30–16.00 Mon–Fri, 08.30–17.00 Sat, 10.30–16.00 Sun

Tastes Delicatessen £–££ ⓬ This deli sells a mind-boggling variety of cooked meats, cheese, stuffed olives, tangy pickles and cake. There's also a good selection of gluten-, dairy- and nut-free dishes. ⓐ 92 Eton High Street ⓣ 01753 641557 ⓦ www.tastesdeli.co.uk ⓛ 10.30–18.00 Tues, 10.30–19.00 Wed, 10.30–18.00 Thur & Fri, 10.00–18.00 Sat, closed Sun & Mon

🔺 *A fashionable favourite for fine dining*

Gilbey's ££–£££ ⓳ *Vogue* magazine loves Gilbey's for a reason and that might be something to do with the fillet of Cornish hake roasted with coriander seed butter, the lemon pilaf and the fennel compôte, among other menu selections! ⓐ 82–83 Eton High Street ⓣ 01753 854921 ⓦ www.gilbeygroup.com ⓔ eton@gilbeygroup.com ⓛ 12.00–14.30, 18.00–21.30 Sun–Fri, 12.00–14.30, 18.00–22.00 Sat

AFTER DARK

The George Inn ⓮ If you're in town in the summer, then head for the terrace at The George Inn. This historic, 300-year-old pub is a great place for a glass of wine, a pint or, if you're feeling decadent, a chilled bottle of bubbly. ⓐ 77 Eton High Street ⓣ 01753 861797 ⓛ 10.00–23.30 Sun–Fri, 10.00–24.00 Sat

The Henry VI ⓯ With live music most weekends, a spacious beer garden and traditional British grub on the menu, The Henry VI is a popular everyday spot. ⓐ 37 Eton High Street ⓣ 01753 866051 ⓛ 12.00–23.30 Sun–Thur, 12.00–24.00 Fri & Sat

The Watermans Arms ⓰ Originally a workhouse back in 1542, this building became a makeshift mortuary during the Great Plague. Today it's a traditional English pub with a popular comedy club attached. ⓐ Brocas Street ⓣ 01753 861001 ⓦ www.watermans-eton.com ⓛ 18.00–24.00 Mon, 12.00–23.00 Tues–Fri, 12.00–24.00 Sat, 12.00–23.30 Sun

▶ *Cliveden Estate's beautifully manicured lawn*

OUT OF TOWN
trips

Maidenhead

Maidenhead is the largest town in the Royal Borough and, thanks to the well-developed transport links, it's easy to nip to for shopping, celebrity-spotting and gallery exhibitions.

GETTING THERE

By bus
Local buses are cost-effective and efficient. Bus No 6 goes to Maidenhead via Bray and takes just under an hour.

By car
Take the A308 from Windsor straight to Maidenhead. The drive should take less than 20 minutes.

Tourist information
The Maidenhead Information Centre has up-to-date listings for all of the cultural comings and goings in town. You'll find the centre in the Central Library. ⓐ St Ives Road ❶ 01628 796502 ⓔ maidenhead.tic@rbwm.gov.uk ⓛ 09.30–17.00 Mon, 09.30–20.00 Tues, 09.30–17.00 Wed, 09.30–20.00 Thur, 09.30–19.00 Fri, 09.30–16.00 Sat, closed Sun

SIGHTS & ATTRACTIONS

Boutler's Lock
This lock, dating back to 1772, is a popular spot for kayakers and canoeists. Regular buses connect this scenic area to

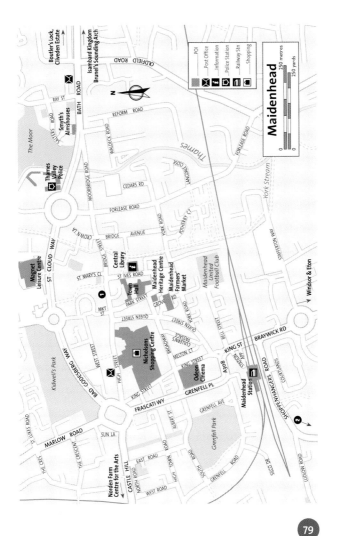

Maidenhead

POI
Post Office
Information
Police Station
Railway Stn
Shopping

0 ___ 250 metres
0 ___ 250 yards

Maidenhead town centre and, even if watersports aren't your thing, there are plenty of parkland attractions to be enjoyed nearby on Ray Mill Island. ⓐ Lower Cookham Road

Cliveden Estate

Close to Ray Mill Island, the estate is immediately recognisable by the beech woods on the steep cliffs, 200 m (650 ft) above the river. The house at Cliveden was made famous when Lady Astor lived there and today the 152-ha (376-acre) estate is protected and preserved by the National Trust. Highlights include a beautiful water garden and the spectacular views along the woodland walk. ⓐ Taplow ⓣ 01494 755562 ⓦ www.nationaltrust.org.uk/cliveden ⓘ Admission charge

Isambard Kingdom Brunel's Sounding Arch

This stunning brick railway bridge, designed by the famous civil engineer, was finished in 1838; it still carries trains over the River Thames. Over the towpath on the left, just downstream of Maidenhead Bridge, is the Sounding Arch – test how many times your voice echoes as you shout out beneath it. The bridge is commemorated in *Rain, Steam and Speed*, an 1844 painting by J M W Turner. ⓐ Downriver of Boulter's Lock, near Bath Road

Maidenhead river walks

A stroll along the riverbanks from Maidenhead will take keen hikers to the nearby villages of Cookham and Marlow (upstream) and Bray, Eton and Windsor (downstream). A walk through nearby Maidenhead Thicket is also worthwhile; it is known to have been the old haunt of highwayman Dick Turpin.

CULTURE

Maidenhead Heritage Centre

The Maidenhead Heritage Centre traces the story of the settlement back to the Romans. There are photo albums galore of days gone by, free lunchtime lectures twice a month and a number of exhibitions. This is also a great place to pick up local maps and books. ⓐ 18 Park Street ⓣ 01628 780555 ⓦ www.maidenheadheritage.org.uk ⓛ 10.00–16.00 Tues–Sat, 10.00–12.30 every second Sun of the month, closed Mon

Norden Farm Centre for the Arts

Ten years old in 2010, the Norden Farm Centre for the Arts is Maidenhead's cultural pride and joy. The venue offers a programme brimming with cutting-edge entertainment and performing arts. From touring productions and endorsements from Sir Michael Parkinson to literature festivals and dance societies, you'll find it here. Performances take place in the large Courtyard Theatre, the 100-person capacity Studio Theatre and the intimate Long Barn. There's also a free art gallery to the rear. ⓐ Altwood Road ⓣ 01628 682555 ⓦ www.nordenfarm.org ⓘ Admission charge

Odeon Cinema

This eight-screen movie theatre showcases all the latest Hollywood blockbusters, which you can enjoy from the comfort of the special, body-sculpted seats. ⓐ 42–44 King Street ⓣ 0871 224 4007 ⓦ www.odeon.co.uk ⓘ Admission charge

⬡ *Delightful sculptures in the grounds of Cliveden Estate*

RETAIL THERAPY

Maidenhead Farmers' Market This popular spot sells the best local produce, every second Sunday of the month. You'll find the 25 stalls in the Grove Road car park behind Maidenhead Town Hall between 10.00 and 13.00 – selling fresh fish, local meats, bakery treats, vegetables and cider. ⓐ Grove Road

Nicholsons Shopping Centre All of the big high-street brands can be found in this shopping centre. ⓐ Nicholsons Walk ⓣ 01628 783746 ⓦ www.nicholsonsshoppingcentre.co.uk ⓛ 09.00–17.30 Mon–Sat, 11.00–17.00 Sun

TAKING A BREAK

Hobgoblin £–££ ❶ This is a friendly and modern ale house with a pleasant garden and a lively atmosphere. It's also a popular spot on the local ghost-tour circuit, so keep an eye out for ghouls, especially when closing time approaches. ⓐ 34 High Street ⓣ 01628 784786 ⓛ 11.30–23.00 Mon–Sat, 11.00–23.00 Sun

Fredrick's Hotel ££–£££ ❷ The hotel restaurant Alfresco is a real treat, but it won't break the bank and the setting is perfect for any special occasion. From the classic house club sandwich to the prawn and chilli salsa and coconut rice parcels, there's a dish here to put a smile on your face. ⓐ Shoppenhangers Road ⓣ 01628 581000 ⓦ www.fredricks-hotel.co.uk ⓛ 07.00–09.30, 12.00–14.00, 19.00–21.30 Sun–Fri, 07.00–09.30, 19.00–21.30 Sat

Richmond upon Thames

If you like the scenery and the pace of life in Windsor, then you'll like this borough of London. Richmond upon Thames boasts a number of very special attractions, including Hampton Court Palace, Kew Gardens, the culture-rich Richmond Park and some stunning views of London.

GETTING THERE

By car

From Windsor take the M4 east until you reach the roundabout before junction 1. Follow Chiswick High Road, which becomes Kew Road, and go over the River Thames. Kew Road then becomes Twickenham Road, at which point you've reached Richmond upon Thames.

By train

From Windsor & Eton Riverside it is possible to travel direct to Richmond on the train destined ultimately for London Waterloo. The journey from Windsor to Richmond takes 36 minutes. From Richmond, London is only 15 minutes away by train.

Tourist information

You can find up-to-date information about everything in the borough at the **Richmond Visitor Information Centre**, located in the Old Town Hall. ⓐ Whittaker Avenue, just off George Street ⓣ 0208 734 3363 ⓦ www.visitrichmond.co.uk ⓔ info@visit richmond.co.uk ⓛ 10.00–17.00 Mon–Sat, closed Sun

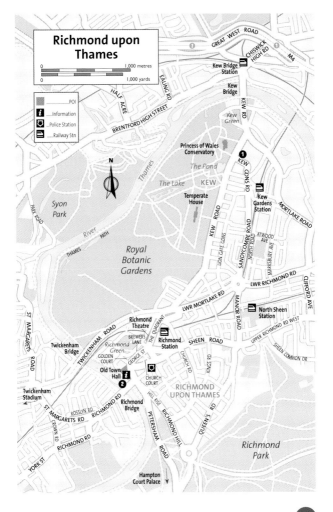

SIGHTS & ATTRACTIONS

Hampton Court Palace

This extraordinary building, lavishly rebuilt by Cardinal Wolsey in the early 16th century and acquired by King Henry VIII, is within easy striking distance of Richmond and is a must-see attraction. The 24 ha (60 acres) of beautiful riverside gardens, the world-famous maze and the sumptuous interiors are a magnificent snapshot in time of Henry's ostentatious character. Hampton Court Palace is a short journey south from Richmond. **ⓐ** Hampton Court Road **ⓦ** www.hrp.org.uk/hamptoncourt palace **ⓔ** hamptoncourt@hrp.org.uk **ⓛ** 10.00–18.00 daily (Apr–Sept); 10.00–16.30 daily (Oct–Mar) **ⓘ** Admission charge

Richmond Park

At 1,012 ha (2,500 acres), this is the largest royal park in London and home to 600 free-roaming deer. There's a golf course, and from King Henry's Mound there are spectacular views of St Paul's Cathedral and the London skyline, 16 km (10 miles) away. **ⓐ** Richmond Park **ⓣ** 020 8948 3209 **ⓦ** www.royalparks.org.uk **ⓛ** Dawn to dusk daily

Royal Botanic Gardens, Kew

You can't pass through Richmond without taking a trip to Kew Gardens – it has one of the most impressive collections of plant life in the world and is a certified World Heritage Site. In addition to the *ginormous* water lilies and the stunning greenhouse collections, the site is also an important botanical research centre, championing conservation around the world. **ⓐ** Kew Road

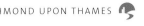

① 020 8332 5655 **Ⓦ** www.kew.org **Ⓛ** Opening times vary: see website for details **❶** Admission charge

CULTURE

Richmond Theatre

The interior of this beautiful red-brick and stone building is a mix of box seats, felt-covered chairs and carved cherubs. From Billie Piper in breakthrough roles to the hilarious Christmas pantomimes, the annual programme has something for everyone. The theatre is also popular with filmmakers and was featured in the films *Finding Neverland* and *Evita*. **ⓐ** The Green **①** 0870 060 6651 **Ⓦ** www.ambassador tickets.com/Richmond-Theatre **❶** Admission charge

▲ *Views across the enticing woodland of Richmond Park*

Twickenham Stadium

A real treat for any rugby union fan, this stadium can hold 82,000 spectators and is the undisputed home of English rugby union. It's also the biggest rugby union stadium on the planet and over the years has become a popular music venue, attracting big names and big crowds. Visitors here can also enjoy the **Museum of Rugby** and take part in stadium tours. ⓐ Rugby Road ⓣ 0871 222 2120 ⓦ www.rfu.com/TwickenhamStadium

RETAIL THERAPY

Visitors to Richmond are spoilt for choice with shops, boutiques, one-of-a-kind retailers and commercial art galleries galore. The highest concentration of such shops can be found in **Church Court**, **Hill Rise**, **Brewers Lane** and **Golden Court**.

TAKING A BREAK

The Original Maids of Honour £–££ ❶ You'll find this little tea room opposite Kew Gardens serving up an irresistible selection of cakes, cookies, tea and coffee. ⓐ 288 Kew Road, Kew ⓣ 020 8940 2752 ⓒ 09.00–18.00 Mon–Sat, 08.30–18.00 Sun

Tide Tables £–££ ❷ A scenic spot for vegetarian light bites or more substantial dishes under the arches of Richmond Bridge. The large outdoor terrace is lovely in summer. ⓐ Arch 2, Richmond Riverside ⓣ 020 8948 8285 ⓒ 08.30–18.30 daily

◔ *Even Windsor's information centre is delightfully housed*

PRACTICAL
information

Directory

GETTING THERE
By air

Because of Windsor's proximity to London, flying into town from destinations around the world – and indeed from within the UK – is simple. With the train links into the British capital, Luton, Stansted and Gatwick Airport are all within easy striking distance; however Heathrow Airport is the closest to Windsor. Heathrow is served by every major airline and many smaller operators. It is directly linked to Windsor by local bus services and by the National Express coach network.

British Airways ☎ 0844 493 0787 ⓦ www.britishairways.com
EasyJet ☎ 0871 244 2366 ⓦ www.easyjet.com
Thomas Cook ☎ 0871 230 2406
ⓦ http://book.flythomascook.com
Virgin Atlantic ☎ 0844 874 7747 ⓦ www.virgin-atlantic.com

Many people are aware that air travel emits CO_2, which contributes to climate change. You may be interested in lessening the environmental impact of your flight through the charity **Climate Care** (ⓦ www.jpmorganclimatecare.com), which offsets your CO_2 by funding environmental projects around the world.

By car

When you arrive in Windsor you'll soon discover that you don't really need a car to get around; however, the town is well connected to Britain's national road infrastructure. Windsor is linked to the M4 via junction 6, the M3 via junction 3, the M25 via junction 13 and the M40 via junction 4 or junction 2.

By train

Windsor is connected to the British railway network, with two stations linking the town to wherever you might need to go. With a quick change at Slough, London can be reached in less than 40 minutes, making Windsor a very attractive day-trip destination for visitors arriving into London's airports and the Eurostar terminus at King's Cross St Pancras. All timetables and information about which destinations are linked to Windsor by rail can be accessed through Network Rail. ☎ 0845 748 4950
🌐 www.networkrail.co.uk

By bus and coach

For travel information about local bus services operating in Windsor, Eton and the surrounding area, and to plan your journey in advance, go to the **First Group** website.
🌐 www.firstgroup.com

You can find out more about the Green Line coach service between London and Windsor by calling their help centre or looking online. The timetables, fares and booking facilities for National Express coach services operating in the area are also available online.
Green Line coach services ☎ 0844 801 7261
🌐 www.greenline.co.uk
National Express coach services 🌐 www.nationalexpress.com

HEALTH, SAFETY & CRIME

The NHS community hospital in Windsor is **King Edward VII Hospital** on St Leonards Road (☎ 01753 860441). If you require a General Practitioner try the **Dedworth Medical Centre** (🅐 300 Dedworth Road ☎ 01753 864545).

If you need police assistance you can find the station on **Alma Road** (☎ 08458 505505).

If you require a dentist during your trip to Windsor, try the **Oakleigh Dental Surgery** (🅐 34a Alma Road ☎ 01753 861161).

OPENING HOURS

The shops in Windsor are generally open between 09.30 and 18.00 from Monday to Saturday, with slightly shorter opening hours on a Sunday. It's not uncommon to find that smaller businesses are only open for one day over the weekend.

The primary tourist attractions in the town are usually open 10.00–17.00, closing slightly earlier on Sundays.

Banks in Windsor are normally open 09.00–17.00 Monday to Friday and 09.00–noon on Saturdays, closed on Sundays.

TOILETS

You can find toilets open to the public in the King Edward Court shopping area. Alternatively, head to the toilets inside the Fenwick department store, next to the hair salon.

CHILDREN

Many of the attractions in Windsor are suited to children, especially plastic-fantastic **Legoland** (see page 56). The following is also particularly good:

Windsor Leisure Centre A great riverside spot with a wave machine, a children's crèche and an adventure play-zone. ⓐ Stovell Road ☎ 01753 778566 🕒 10.00–21.30 Mon & Tues, 10.00–22.00 Wed, 10.00–21.30 Thur & Fri, 10.00–18.00 Sat, 10.00–16.00 Sun. Please note that from 18.15 to 22.00 the centre is open to over-21s only.

TRAVELLERS WITH DISABILITIES

Because of the historic nature of the Royal Borough, there are a number of inherent problems for travellers with disabilities. Many attractions, including Windsor Castle, the Theatre Royal and Eton College, offer specialist access and assistance, but others are on steep hills and are less accessible to wheelchair users because of the old architecture. A full access guide is available on request from the **Royal Windsor Information Centre** (☎ 01753 743900). You can also find information online: ⓦ www.windsor.gov.uk/site/visitor-info/travelling-with-a-disability

Wheelchair-friendly taxis operate from the primary taxi rank on Windsor High Street. You can also call the taxi rank directly (☎ 01753 862020) to pre-book a wheelchair-accessible vehicle.

FURTHER INFORMATION

For information head to the Old Ticket Hall in Windsor & Eton Central Rail, part of the Windsor Royal Shopping arcade.
Royal Windsor Information Centre ☎ 01753 743900
ⓦ www.windsor.gov.uk ⓔ windsor.tic@rbwm.gov.uk
🕒 09.30–17.30 Mon–Sat, 10.00–16.00 Sun (Mar–Oct);
10.00–17.00 Mon–Sat, 10.00–16.00 Sun (Nov–Feb)

ACKNOWLEDGEMENTS

The photographs in this book were taken by Grant Rooney for Thomas Cook Publishing, to whom the copyright belongs.

Project editor: Kate Taylor
Layout: Donna Pedley
Proofreaders: Ting Baker & Emily Anderson
Indexer: Mary Purton

AUTHOR BIOGRAPHY

Robert Savage is a member of the British Guild of Travel Writers. In addition to writing guidebooks he also contributes to *The Guardian*, MSN and several in-flight magazines. In Windsor Robert enjoys nothing more than a pot of coffee in The Crooked House of Windsor and a long stroll through Windsor Great Park.

Send your thoughts to
books@thomascook.com

- **Found a great bar, club, shop or must-see sight that we don't feature?**
- **Like to tip us off about any information that needs a little updating?**
- **Want to tell us what you love about this handy little guidebook and more importantly how we can make it even handier?**

Then here's your chance to tell all! Send us ideas, discoveries and recommendations today and then look out for your valuable input in the next edition of this title.

Email the above address (stating the title) or write to:
pocket guides Series Editor, Thomas Cook Publishing, PO Box 227, Coningsby Road, Peterborough PE3 8SB, UK.

...at did you do." he growled.

Her jaw dropped as words failed her. Sweet Maka, help her. What *had* she done? In his dream, he was so handsome, so giving. The temptation and promise of anonymity were too much to resist, and she had lowered her guard.

"Oh, Great Spirit," she whispered.

"You invaded my dream."

"I never thought that... I mean, I didn't intend..." How could she finish? "Nicholas, please." She needed to recall who he was, no, *what* he was. But her body still trembled from his lovemaking.

"You really had me fooled, all aloof on the exterior, but oh, how you burn underneath..."

Dear Reader,

This is my second paranormal romance in THE
TRACKERS series, featuring Native American
shapeshifters called Skinwalkers. Their world is full of
dark and dangerous creatures with ancient powers and
is loosely based on Lakota myth.

I hope you fall in love with Jessie and Nick. Their
love will be tested and their lives endangered as they
struggle to protect the Seer of Souls from her enemies
and fight the Ruler of Ghosts for control of the living
world.

For more about Nick and Jessie and for a sneak peek at
my third in THE TRACKERS series, please visit me at
my web home, www.jennakernan.com.

Jenna Kernan